By the Author

Bareback

Long Shot

Call Me Softly

CALL ME SOFTLY

by

D. Jackson Leigh

2011

CALL ME SOFTLY

ISBN 13: 978-1-60282-215-3

This Trade Paperback Original Is Published By
Bold Strokes Books, Inc.
P.O. Box 249
Valley Falls, NY 12185

First Edition: April 2011

CREDITS
EDITOR: SHELLEY THRASHER
PRODUCTION DESIGN: STACIA SEAMAN
COVER DESIGN BY SHERI (GRAPHICARTIST2020@HOTMAIL.COM)

Acknowledgments

The Deep South—filled with so many colloquial expressions, unique rituals, and interesting people—is incredibly fertile ground for writers.

I would be remiss if I didn't acknowledge two colorful characters who supplied me with some of my best material: my former coworker, Jim, who turned out to be a hard dog to keep under the porch and moved to Alabama; and my delightful "butter my butt and call me a biscuit" friend Dale. I still chuckle when I think of her pushing the lingering drunks out of her house after a party with a good-natured, "You don't have to go home, but you can't stay here."

My undying thanks go to my editor extraordinaire, Shelley Thrasher. To say that she made this manuscript better would be an understatement. She has uncommon insight and gives me so many opportunities to rewrite and fine-tune.

As always, I have to give a grateful nod to Len Barot and the Bold Strokes family for the opportunity to share my stories.

And last, but not least, I will be forever grateful to my partner, Angie. I never would have taken the first step without her support. I'll always love her.

Dedication

For my grandmother, Alma.
Her bloodline carried the genes
that destined me to spin stories.

CHAPTER ONE

Less than a minute was left in the final chukker, and the score was tied.

The knot of riders and horses jostled around the small white ball of hard plastic, mallets outstretched among the dancing hooves. Some were reaching, while others attempted to hook and restrain the reachers.

With a resounding whack, the ball broke free of the group. It spun downfield toward a blue-shirted rider, who reined his gray steed in position to hit the winning goal.

Suddenly, a green-shirted rider on a dark bay was at his flank, pressing against the gray as they galloped and bumping him off the line of play. The blue rider leaned right, encouraging his gray to push back. But the bay was already a full stride ahead.

In a smooth backhanded stroke, the green rider reversed the course of the ball. The stroke had been soft, giving the bay time to whirl around and pursue. Swinging the mallet this time in a high arc, the green rider smacked the ball hard. Pursuit by the blue riders was useless. Traveling well over one hundred miles per hour, the ball neatly cleaved the space between the goalposts, and the four green-shirted Wetherington Raiders raised their mallets and voices in victory. They galloped from all parts of the field to cluster around and affectionately tap the helmet of their captain and star player.

Swain Butler grinned at her teammates as she unsnapped her chin strap and pulled her helmet off. She wiped off the sweat trickling into her eyes before slapping their high fives with her gloved hand, then cantering out of the group toward the captain of the blue team.

"Good match, Hoyt. You guys nearly had us," Swain said, extending her hand.

Hoyt Whitney, sitting astride his winded gray gelding, accepted her firm handshake. He smiled and shook his head. "You just let us get close so we'd get overconfident. I should have looked over my shoulder and seen you coming."

They walked their horses side by side toward where their trailers were parked.

"It wouldn't have helped." Swain patted the neck of her gelding. "Your gray's good, but Nor'easter here is fast. Did you know his great-granddaddy is Summer Squall?"

"No kidding? No wonder you were on me before I knew it. Abigail must have paid a pretty penny for that piece of horseflesh."

Swain sometimes wondered why her employer kept an active stable since no Wetheringtons were still playing polo. But she paid Swain well to procure, train, ride, and sometimes sell "made" ponies—ones completely broken into the game—under the family colors.

"I picked him up green as a two-year-old. He didn't work out well at the track, so they dumped him right after the trials."

"So why isn't my trainer at the track picking up bargains like this horse?"

Swain smiled and shrugged. "I was just lucky, I guess. Right place at the right time."

Hoyt ran his eyes over the bay. "You seem to get lucky a lot. Think Abigail would sell him?"

"Everything has a price, Hoyt. But he won't be cheap. I've put a lot of training into him. He still needs another season."

"He looked pretty good out there today." He turned his gray toward the Whitney trailers. "When you talk to her, tell her I want to make an offer once she's ready to sell. And tell her to hurry back. We need her here to keep Hitchcock from rewriting the league rules so he can fill his team with ringers."

Her employer's recent silence and her absence during the fall polo season worried Swain. Abigail had traveled to London months ago to bury her son and hadn't returned. At first, she'd called every week to talk with Swain about the ponies and what was going on around town. But her phone calls had become less frequent in recent months and completely stopped three weeks ago. The Wetherington estate without its feisty matriarch was like a three-legged dog. It still ran well enough, but obviously something was missing.

Where was Abigail? When the hell was she coming home?

❖

Lillie Wetherington held her dying grandmother's limp hand gently. The skin felt dry and fragile, like thin parchment. She fought back tears and admonished herself to be brave, but her despair was too deep.

As if sensing Lillie's desolation, Abigail Wetherington opened her eyes briefly. They were clouded with pain and her voice was a feathery whisper. Lillie bent close to hear her words.

"I can feel you trembling."

"I'm just worried about you."

"My beautiful Lillie. So sorry."

A sudden fit of coughing stole her next words, and Lillie grabbed the oxygen mask that Abigail had laid aside earlier and held it to her grandmother's face.

When her coughing finally quieted, Abigail pulled the mask away.

"Too many bad things…happening here. You must go."

Lillie had lived an orphan's dream, adopted by wealthy, loving parents when she was five years old and growing up in London. But that dream had become a nightmare.

The members of her adopted family had met their deaths one by one. Three were gone already, and her grandmother was dying before her now. Individually, each one seemed to be a tragic accident. Together, they painted a terrifying picture.

Someone had a lethal grudge against anyone bearing the Wetherington name. And she was surely next. He had already tried. He would try again.

"Go to South Carolina. You'll be safe…and I need…need you to make things right…" Abigail waved her hand in the direction of her bureau. "I've left letters…in the top drawer."

Lillie went to the bureau and found two sealed envelopes, on which she recognized Abigail's flowing cursive. Her name was written on one. The other was labeled "Swain Butler."

Abigail took a shallow breath. "Promise…to go," she whispered.

Lillie returned to her grandmother's side and sat on the edge of the bed. She covered Abigail's cold hand with hers to warm it. "I'll do whatever you want, Grandmum. You must rest now."

"Trust…Swain."

"Your farm manager?"

Abigail closed her eyes, her words barely more than a sigh. "More than that."

Chapter Two

Swain turned her pony toward the three long Wetherington trailers where her assistant trainer and head groom were preparing to load horses for the trip home. She dismounted and handed the bay off to her assistant, who had already handed his pony off to the groom. He offered her a bottle of water.

"Thanks, Rob," she said, draining it. "Would you ask John to rub him down good tonight? That last turn was pretty abrupt. He may have strained something." She grimaced and rubbed her lower back. "I know I'll be sore tomorrow."

Rob nodded, his gaze flicking over Swain's shoulder at the person standing behind her. She raised her eyebrows at him when unseen hands joined her in the massage of her back, but he just smiled and shook his head. "Sure, boss. I'll take care of it." He chuckled as he led Nor'easter toward the wash area to clean off the salty sweat lathering his coat.

"I can help you with that sore back." The voice purred low and husky.

"Seems to me that last time you 'helped' I had a sore back for a week," Swain purred back.

"I don't remember you complaining." The hands moved lower to caress Swain's muscled butt. "But I'm willing to give it another try. Practice makes perfect."

Swain turned to face Susan Whitney. She and Hoyt were the children of Bonner Whitney, Abigail's close friend and attorney.

Twenty-four years old, Susan had been engaged to Jason Hitchcock for two years, but neither was in a hurry to marry. Jason was still making up his mind between teenaged boys and women. Susan just liked sex, with anybody. They would wed eventually to satisfy their families, but they weren't yet ready to accept the social obligations expected of a married couple.

"Not here, Susan." They were standing between horse trailers, but that didn't mean someone wasn't watching. Swain squeezed Susan's hand. "I have to take care of the ponies right now, but call me later. You can bring some dinner over, and we'll…practice."

Having dismissed Susan, Swain opened the door to the trailer's small living compartment. A late-summer thunderstorm was threatening, and the breeze that had begun to ruffle the broad leaves of the surrounding magnolias had dried her short, dark hair. But the oppressive humidity had kept her polo jersey damp, smelling of sweat and clinging to her body. She wanted to wash and pull on something dry.

The half bath was so small, she grabbed a washcloth and stood before the kitchen sink to strip off her jersey and sports bra. She was bent over the sink, her face coated with soap, when the door opened.

"Dressing," she yelled, expecting that John or Rob forgot to knock.

"More like undressing," Susan said. Swain heard her close the door and engage the lock.

"Susan…" Swain rinsed the soap from her face, then ran the washcloth under her arms and over her torso before turning to her uninvited visitor.

"You're a goddess, you know that?" Susan took the washcloth from her and began to smooth it along the thick muscles of Swain's shoulders and across her bare chest. "You're like a female warrior— an Amazon washing off the blood and gore of her battle." Swain's nipples hardened and her blood throbbed between her legs. Susan tossed the cloth into the sink and began working the buckle loose on Swain's belt. "But soap and water won't wash away your battle lust, will it?"

It was true. The adrenaline rush of her duel and victory on the field still coursed through her. "Susan—"

"We'll be quick, just to take your edge off. Later, at your place, we'll take our time." Susan's hand slipped along Swain's belly and into her pants. Swain sucked in a breath when the long fingers slid against her sensitive clit. "See how wet you are?" Susan grabbed Swain's hand and pulled it under her skirt until Swain's palm was against the damp crotch of her panties. "See how ready I am for you?"

Swain growled and dropped to her knees. She yanked Susan's skirt up and her panties to the floor to plunge her mouth into the dripping curls. She licked and sucked the thick clitoris, then raked her teeth against the swollen tissue.

"Oh, oh. I'm about to come." Susan was panting.

"Not yet," Swain growled. The heady scent of Susan's juices mingled with the musky aroma of sweat and horses. She still wore her knee-high boots and leather knee pads, but she pushed her white riding breeches down as far as she could. She lowered Susan onto one of the bunks and climbed between her legs.

Susan whimpered, bucking her hips against Swain's bare torso.

Swain grabbed Susan's knees and forced them up against her chest, then rubbed her clit, hot and wet, against Susan's sex.

"Yes." Susan opened her folds and bared herself to Swain's thrusts.

Swain was ready.

She hadn't realized it before, but her desire had been building since Nor'easter answered her call for speed. Her blood rose as her backhand swing connected, swelled as she wielded her mallet again to hurl the ball cleanly through the goalposts, and sang through her veins as another opponent fell.

She was more than ready. Her hunger burned hotter with each thrust, then flashed through her like a firestorm.

But her release wasn't enough to sate the hunger of competition, the need to conquer again. She lifted her hips to slide her hand between them and plunge her fingers into Susan's body.

"Oh, yes. Fuck me hard. Fuck me everywhere." Susan moaned, draping her legs over Swain's broad shoulders.

Swain pulled her slick fingers out and rubbed them lower against the puckered muscle before plunging one finger deep inside. Susan moaned again at the intrusion. Swain slid her thumb where her fingers had just been and stroked hard and fast.

Voices sounded just outside the trailer. "Quiet," Swain commanded.

Susan whimpered, but grabbed the first thing she put her hand on—Swain's sweaty jersey—and covered her mouth. It muffled her scream when Swain, still thrusting, took her into her mouth and over the edge with a few broad strokes of her tongue.

❖

Lillie hated flying out of Heathrow in the summer. The airport was teeming with international visitors, vacationing tourists, and students on school-sponsored trips. She huffed as she stood in line at the security checkpoint behind a large group of clowning students.

Bloody Americans.

Truthfully, she welcomed her irritation with the students crowding the airport security gate. At least she could still feel something other than the emptiness, the loneliness of being orphaned again. Something other than the constant fear that she would turn a corner and encounter whoever, whatever was stalking her family.

A chill ran through her. She could feel eyes on her now, had felt them since she entered the airport. She berated herself for being paranoid, but she couldn't help it after all that had happened.

Six years ago, Jim Wetherington, the grandfather Lillie never met, died when his small plane suffered a mechanical failure and crashed.

Lillie's father, Eric, would never speak of the rift that had estranged him from his family in the United States twenty-six years before. But after learning of his father's death, he began to mend his relationship with his mother.

When Abigail finally came to visit, she and Lillie formed an instant bond. Already a young woman, Lillie was either dashing to university classes or keeping appointments vital to her fledgling career as a photographer, but she always made time for Grandmum's visits.

Their small family had a happy few years of reconciliation and renewal. Eric, at last, was planning for all of them to visit the South Carolina estate where he grew up. Then tragedy, almost a year ago, struck again.

Lillie's mother, Camille, died when her car plunged down an embankment and wrapped around a tree. The car was so mangled, it was impossible to determine what might have caused her to swerve off the roadway.

Three months later, Lillie's grieving father, Eric, drowned in the icy river near their home. The inquest recorded an open verdict, and Abigail came to London to help Lillie survive her grief.

Still, the surreal nightmare continued.

In a familiar neighborhood where she and her friends frequented cheery pubs, Lillie narrowly escaped a terrifying assault by a hooded assailant in a dark alley. Even more disturbing, the attack apparently wasn't random. The man had known Lillie's name and, when her friend interrupted his ambush, he escaped into the night.

The city that had always been her home seemed to be conspiring to purge itself of Wetheringtons. Abigail had begged Lillie to return with her to South Carolina and, for the first time, she was ready to consider it.

Then the curse struck once again.

While Abigail was walking down a London sidewalk crowded with a tourist group, someone had tripped her into the path of a car. At first, she seemed to be recovering from her injuries, but her age worked against her. She succumbed to pneumonia and, though Lillie bore the name, the last of the Wetherington bloodline was gone.

At least that's what she'd thought before she read Grandmum's letter.

CHAPTER THREE

Crack. The colt swerved as the mallet connected with the polo ball and crow-hopped several steps. It would have thrown most riders, but Swain anticipated the move and easily kept her seat. She laughed aloud, delighting in the challenge, and turned her steed to gallop toward the next of the balls she had scattered midfield.

Fifteen minutes later, both she and her horse were sweaty and breathing hard. But the colt no longer skittered sideways at the sound and movement of the mallet near his feet.

"You're a madwoman on horseback."

Swain grinned at the man who pulled his golf-cart-sized Gator alongside her as she walked the long-legged Thoroughbred around the perimeter of the field to cool him down.

"Hey, Tim. Just starting to break this guy into the game." She tossed her polo mallet toward the utility vehicle and he caught it neatly in one hand, stowing it beside him without taking his other hand from the steering wheel. She swung her leg over the colt's rump and jumped to the ground. "You mind walking a bit?"

"Naw. It'll help stretch my back muscles." Tim abandoned his vehicle and fell into step beside her as she continued leading the lathered colt around the field. A squat, bear-like man, he had the thick torso, massive arms, and perpetually sore back typical of his blacksmith profession.

A huge wire-haired brown dog loped out from the barn and joined them.

"Hey, Beau. Ya been molesting any poodles lately?"

He greeted Tim with a low woof.

Swain snorted. "Mrs. Hitchcock's poodle is a slut. So, what brings you to speak to the lord of the mansion?"

Tim roared with laughter. He did everything big and loud. "Lord of the mansion? You ain't even lady of the mansion, my friend."

Swain laughed with him at their old joke. "So you came to see to the stable hand, huh?"

"I came to see the best trainer in this state. I was working at the track today and saw a filly you'll want to take a look at."

"I've pretty much got a full string of made ponies, and several others well along in training already," Swain said.

"I'm tellin' ya that you don't want to miss this one. She's another Nor'easter, and I saw Whitney drooling over him Sunday."

"Yeah, he wants to make an offer now, but I may make him wait another season."

"That horse don't need another season and you know it."

"Hoyt's going to know that, too, after you let it drop in front of his trainer that I'm just holding on to him so the Wetherington team can bring home the twelve-goal tournament trophy next month."

The colt jumped at Tim's loud guffaw. "Old Hoyt will be cleaning out his safety-deposit box to get you to sell before then."

"Exactly. There'll be something in it for you, if he does."

The equine world had a well-defined social pecking order. The wealthy owners were at the top. Just below them were the trainers, who influenced how the owners spent their money. At the bottom was the local, common-bred underbelly of the horse business—grooms, farriers, stable hands, feed-store clerks, and the guys who sold and serviced the farm's equipment.

Swain treated them all the same. She always shared the spoils when a helping hand sweetened a deal or a good tip paid off, and that had earned her the underbelly's respect and loyalty. That's why Tim was there to tell her, not Hoyt's trainer, about the filly. That's why they didn't bat an eye at her taste for women rather than men.

They had completed their circuit around the field, and Swain stopped in the outdoor wash area. She pulled her pony's bridle off and replaced it with a halter and lead line.

"I'm headed to Hitchcock's place next week to shoe a few ponies," Tim said. "I reckon I can add some fuel to his fire." Tim pulled a foil pouch from his back pocket and opened it to select a plug of chewing tobacco and tuck it neatly in his cheek.

When Swain unbuckled and pulled the horse's saddle from his back, her assistant trainer, Rob, appeared and took it from her. Beau licked at the salty sweat caked on the leather, but Rob pushed his head away.

Rob nodded to Tim, but addressed Swain. "How's he coming?"

"Good. I'll need you next week to start working with us on ride-offs."

"That soon, huh? Ya got a full string. What's the hurry?"

"I've got a buyer for Nor'easter."

"Damn, Swain. We're a shoo-in for the twelve-goaler if you're still riding him."

Tim laughed and slapped Rob on the back. "This is about making money, boy, not winning trophies."

"So, back to this filly you were telling me about..." Beau's low woof and his sweeping tail stopped Swain mid-sentence.

A stranger was standing on the rear terrace of Abigail's sprawling home, her hand raised in a tentative wave. "Hel-lo there," Swain said under her breath. The woman's height appeared a near match to Swain's five foot eight, and a thick mane of blond curls cascaded across her slender shoulders.

Tim and Rob turned to see what had caught Swain's eye.

"Hoo-rah. Who's the skirt?" Tim muttered.

"No shit," Rob chimed in.

"Mind your manners, boys. Probably someone looking for Abigail," Swain said, her eyes never leaving the beautiful woman. She handed off the colt to Rob and gave Tim a dismissive pat on his shoulder. "Tell Rob when and where, and I'll take a look at the filly." She pointed to Beau, and Tim grabbed his collar to hold him back as Swain headed for the visitor.

❖

Cornflower blue was the only thought in Lillie's head when the woman approached and smiled. Her eyes shone like sapphires contrasted against thick black lashes and tanned skin. Her jeans were tucked into knee-length boots, and the short sleeves of her faded polo jersey exposed tanned, muscled arms. The vision was speaking to her.

"I'm sorry?"

"Can I help you with something?" the woman repeated.

"Oh. Yes! I…I just arrived and I was looking for who might be in charge around here."

"That would be me, I guess. Mrs. Wetherington is out of the country."

"I know, yes, I…I know that." Lillie briefly pressed her fingers against the pain that had begun throbbing in her left temple. "I apologize. I've had a very long trip, and I don't seem to be organizing my thoughts very well right now. I'm looking for Ms. Butler."

The woman pulled off her leather riding glove to offer her bare hand. "Swain Butler."

Lillie blinked at the hand. She expected someone hardened from work and weathered by the sun. She didn't envision the strong, handsome young woman who stood before her.

"I'm Swain Butler," the woman repeated. Her eyes twinkled as she continued to hold out her hand. "At your service, Miss…"

"Wetherington. Lillie Wetherington," she answered, hastily clasping Swain's hand. It was callused and firm, but carefully gentle as it closed around her fingers.

A flurry of emotion rolled through the blue eyes like fast-moving clouds—surprise, curiosity—before they quickly cleared.

"I'm so sorry. The way Grandmum spoke about you, trusted you with her business dealings, I expected someone older."

"No harm done."

Swain was solidly built with wide, muscled shoulders that tapered down to narrow hips and well-developed thighs. Her dark hair was cut short in an attractive but androgynous style. From behind, it would be easy to mistake her for an athletic young man. But when she turned around, the gentle swell of small breasts, the soft angles of her face, and her eyes were much too sensuous to be anything but female. The way those eyes traveled over her now felt like soft, curious touches. The voice was deep and smoky. "So you're Lillie."

"Yes. You know who I am?" What had Grandmum told Swain about her?

"Yes. Abigail spoke—bragged—about you often."

Lillie felt herself flush, and she glanced down at her feet to hide her embarrassment.

"I was very sorry to hear about the loss of your parents," Swain said gently.

"Thank you." Lillie had just met this woman, but the concern radiating from her was comforting.

Swain looked hopefully toward the house. "Abigail is finally home? She should have called. I would've met y'all in Columbia."

During the long flight over the Atlantic, Lillie had rehearsed what she would say. It seemed hardly appropriate, though, to just blurt out the news of Abigail's death while standing on the terrace. It didn't feel like the right time, so she skirted the issue.

"Not exactly, no. She won't arrive for another two days." She held up the keys. "I let myself in the house. I just wanted someone to know I wasn't a burglar bumbling about."

Lillie had felt like she was trespassing. Although Abigail hadn't been there for many months, the house didn't look or smell like it had been closed up. She called out and searched about, but it soon became apparent she was alone in the expansive residence. So she'd found her way out to the wide terrace that overlooked the stables.

"Do you stay there?" she asked tentatively. "I didn't want to go poking about in someone else's rooms."

"No. The upper floor of the barn is an apartment. That's where I live." Swain gestured toward the house. "I'd be happy to show you around and help you get your luggage up to one of the guest rooms."

"Thank you. The driver left my bags in the foyer. I'm sure you have other work to do, but I'd be grateful for the assistance." Lillie was relieved to have an escort. The residence was five times the size of her London flat and a bit daunting.

Swain led her back through a sunroom that opened into a state-of-the-art kitchen.

"The refrigerator is empty except for a few sodas and bottles of water. There's still a supply of soups and other canned goods in the pantry, though. Abigail probably told you that when she left for Europe, her housekeeper decided it was a good time to retire. A janitorial service opens the house one day a week and cleans. But nobody's been living here." She pointed toward one side of the kitchen. "Through those doors are the pantry and laundry room. The door over that leads to a housekeeper's suite." She looked at Lillie. "I've never been to London. That's where you live, right?"

Lillie nodded.

"Well, I don't know how different your appliances may be, but if you need help figuring out how to use something before Abigail arrives, just ask. Number one on the house phones speed-dials my cell phone. Number two dials the barn office."

As they walked through the downstairs, Swain pointed out the formal living room and Abigail's study, which adjoined a cavernous library. They circled back around to the foyer and Swain picked up the two largest of Lillie's bags as though they were weightless. Lillie grabbed two smaller ones and followed her up the curved mahogany staircase. Swain set the bags down at the top of the stairs and indicated for Lillie to do the same with the ones she carried.

"The master suite where Abigail stays is to the right." She led Lillie down a long hallway to the left, opening doors to reveal various bedrooms, most with private baths. "These are all guest rooms. Take your pick."

Two bedrooms on the front side of the house featured rich, masculine colors. The two bedrooms that overlooked the back lawn and terrace felt more feminine. The last door Swain opened was on the right, closest to the stairway. "This is the one you may like best," she suggested.

The room was a calming combination of cool blue and green pastels that accented the dominant crème décor. Swain opened a set of double French doors that led onto a balcony overlooking the terrace. Another door led to an extravagant bathroom.

Lillie nodded her agreement. "Yes. I should be more than comfortable here."

"It's also close to Abigail's rooms." Swain ducked into the hallway to retrieve the luggage. "Would you like to walk down to the stables? Or would you rather settle in here first?"

Lillie rubbed her temple again. "I would like to sit down for a moment." She walked over to the small sitting area in the corner of the room and sank into an overstuffed chair. She gestured toward a divan, indicating that Swain should sit, too. "We need to talk."

CHAPTER FOUR

Swain hesitated, then walked slowly over and sat. Lillie stared down at her hands, her blond mane falling forward around her face. Her long, slender fingers gathered the errant curls and draped them behind her shoulders again. It was a very feminine gesture that Swain found unexpectedly appealing.

When Lillie looked up, her brown eyes were dark and her expression troubled. Swain waited patiently while she nervously smoothed her linen trousers with her hands and crossed, then uncrossed her legs and cleared her throat.

"I'm afraid I have some bad news."

After another handful of seconds ticked by, Swain raised a questioning eyebrow.

"Yes, well. I've rehearsed what to say, but it all seems so inadequate now. I guess there's nothing to do but blurt it out." She took a deep breath. "I'm terribly sorry to have to be the bearer of this news. However, no one but me is left to tell it. Grandmum succumbed to a very bad case of pneumonia. The doctors did everything they could, but…she has passed away."

Swain's breath left her lungs. Her heart stilled for a beat, two beats, three before it fluttered back to life. No. She must have heard wrong. "You said she'd be here in two days."

"She wanted to be buried here in South Carolina. It took me nearly a week to make the arrangements, but her body is being shipped here."

No. It couldn't be true. She sat perfectly still, as if not breathing, not moving would make the words go away. She stared at Lillie in disbelief.

"She died a week ago and nobody thought to tell me until now?" Her voice was even, but her tone bitter and accusing. She felt betrayed, cast aside. Lillie couldn't know what Abigail meant to her, but Bonner sure did. He should have at least shown her the courtesy of a phone call.

The day Abigail hired her had changed Swain's life.

She had been working that year as an assistant trainer and rider for a polo team in Wellington, Florida. The team had traveled to Aiken for a twelve-goal tournament that they won handily. Swain was unsaddling the pony she rode in the last chukker when Abigail appeared and invited her to dinner. She wanted to discuss a job opening.

Abigail was direct, intelligent, and engaging. They talked about horses and the tradition of polo long into the night, and before they parted, Abigail offered her a staggeringly generous long-term contract to be her head trainer at the Wetherington stables and captain of the Raiders.

The offer stunned her, but only a fool would have turned it down. She could stop bouncing from team to team, working under seasonal contracts. She could train and ride horses the way she felt was best. She signed the contract that very night and never regretted it.

Abigail had loved to watch her work the ponies. She was remarkably hale for her seventy-two years and would sometimes saddle a pony and accompany Swain on long rides to build the horses' stamina. They often dined together, talking for hours about everything from sports to philosophy, film to politics, and evolution to reincarnation. She made Swain feel, for the first time in her life, like she had a home. Abigail and the guys who worked under Swain became like family. The only family she'd ever had.

"I'm so very sorry," Lillie said. "I know it seems horrible to have kept it from you, but Grandmum wanted me to tell you in person. She didn't want you to hear it from anyone else, or learn about it in an e-mail or phone call."

Confused now, Swain teetered between anger and despair. "We were friends. Close friends."

Lillie's eyes were sad. She looked tired, very tired. "I miss her terribly," she confessed. They sat in a companionable silence for a moment, sharing their grief, before Lillie spoke again. "She said I could trust you…to help me settle her estate."

Swain frowned. She hadn't had time to digest the fact that she would never see Abigail again. This conversation was moving too fast. "I'm not sure I understand."

Lillie stood and walked over to retrieve an envelope from her purse. She held it out to Swain.

Swain rose and took the letter, turning it over several times and studying her name written on the front.

"Although I imagine it will require several weeks to sort things out, I'll be leaving as soon as her will is read," Lillie said. "I expect that letter contains some instructions for you concerning the horses."

"Surely you're not talking about selling the Wetherington stables?"

"Quite honestly, I doubt that will be up to me. I don't know what is written in Grandmum's will. But I don't plan to stay in America."

If she wasn't planning to stay in America, then why would she keep a polo stable here? Did this woman not understand what the Wetheringtons had built? Did she not understand the tradition and the responsibility that came with her last name? Her fury bubbled up so quickly, she had no time to rein in her caustic words.

"Without so much as a thought, you'd turn your back on a hundred years of breeding, a hundred years spent building an international reputation, five generations of family history? Being adopted by Wetheringtons certainly didn't make you one, did it?"

The pain on Lillie's expressive face didn't cool Swain's flash of anger, but she did regret that the filter between her thoughts and her mouth apparently had failed. She needed to be more careful. Voicing her thoughts would probably only antagonize and further alienate the woman who apparently was her new boss.

"I apologize. It's not my place to question you," she said gruffly. "You were right earlier. I've got work to do, Ms. Wetherington. I'll be at the stables if you need anything."

She turned and left without waiting for a reply.

❖

Lillie was stunned. The sound of Swain's boots pounding down the staircase was fading away before she could form a coherent thought. The personal attack had come out of nowhere. This was the person Abigail told her to trust? This woman, to whom Abigail apparently had confided that Lillie was adopted and who had used that knowledge like a sharp knife?

She couldn't stop the tears that gathered and ran down her cheeks. It had been a very long, very exhausting day. Her weariness was more than physical. Sharing her grief with Swain, someone else who knew Abigail well, had made her feel briefly that she wasn't absolutely alone. Now, she felt even more rudderless in this continuing nightmare.

Lillie jumped at the sound of the door slamming downstairs and went to the French doors of the balcony. Dusk was beginning to settle across the fields, but Swain was striding toward the stables, not looking back at the house. She could almost feel the anger in her stiff posture. She sighed and rubbed her temple again.

Being adopted by Wetheringtons certainly didn't make you one, did it?

Lillie pulled another letter from her purse, one that bore her name. The responsibility of what the letter asked of her settled like a heavy weight on her weary shoulders.

Family secrets are a Southern tradition—a crazy relative, a petty crime, an indiscretion. As you must suspect, the Wetheringtons are no different.

More than thirty years ago, there was a drunken night of bad choices. I'll spare you the details, but tell you that twins were conceived that night.

I loved my husband, Jim, beyond reason, so I found a way to forgive him. Eric never did because he thought he was in love with the girl his father impregnated. He also couldn't forgive me for standing by Jim's side. You know the rest. Eric went to England to study and cut us completely out of his life until Jim died. It was the worst sentence he could have ever imposed. It broke his father's heart.

Jim's penance to me was that he had to pay to abort the only other children he'd conceived, since I could have no more after Eric. He never knew that the girl, instead, had taken the money and fled. She delivered a boy and a girl eight months later and died soon after. Had Jim known he had children born of his blood, he would have immediately taken them into our home. But I feared that looking into the faces of my husband's infidelity every day would destroy our marriage. So, I selfishly kept their existence from him. I let those innocent babies grow up in an orphanage, without parents. It was unforgivable, a much worse sin than my husband's mistake.

No one else knows about this but Bonner Whitney, my friend and attorney. He's helped me keep track of the twins over the years. One, we believe, was killed in a Texas brothel. Swain Butler is the other.

Swain knows nothing of this. I should have told you both the truth before now, but I was too ashamed and always thought I would have more time.

Bonner is to reveal all of this at the reading of my will. Swain will surely be angry, and Bonner is prepared to bear that anger for me.

I need you to do what I've never had the courage to. Speak for me. Explain my shame and regret to Swain. Beg her forgiveness. Most important, don't let her reject her birthright out of pride.

Though you have come into my life by different paths,

I love you equally. And, though blood does not bind the three of us, circumstance and likeness of heart do. I hope that the two of you will learn to trust and hold to each other so I can rest peacefully, knowing neither of you is alone in this world. I implore you to consider making South Carolina your home. I fear you will never be safe in England because the constables don't seem concerned with the evil that stalks your family there.

With this request, I evoke some old Southern advice: Secrets can be like sleeping dogs that bite when startled awake. If they must be roused, call to them softly.

Lillie put the letter away with a sigh. She had no strength to deal with this situation. She needed to settle her business here quickly and leave. She hadn't told Abigail that her stalker was American. She wasn't safe here either.

She had taken photos for an international nonprofit over the past few years and had made friends all over the world. She would change her name and travel. She would never return to the London flat of her idyllic childhood. And she would certainly never live at a polo estate with *Wetherington* on the front gates.

But she had promised. She choked back the tears that threatened to start anew. She missed Mum and Dad. She missed Grandmum. She owed them more than to just disappear.

So she would do as Grandmum asked, even though it obviously would be more difficult than she thought. She had no idea exactly what she was supposed to say other than explain that Grandmum regretted what she did. After tonight, she doubted that she and Swain Butler would become close friends. But Lillie had promised only that she would try.

She wiped away the last tear. She would go down to the barn and apologize. She would make things right with Ms. Butler. Then she would never make promises to anyone again.

❖

Swain's emotions were churning like whitewater. She'd never lost anyone close to her. Hell, she'd never *had* anyone close to her before Abigail. She'd never known her father, and her mother had died when she was just an infant. Even her own twin was a stranger. So Abigail's death was a soul-deep pain that had caught her completely unprepared. And that pain made her want to lash out.

She avoided the barn corridor where she knew Rob and the two grooms were feeding and bedding down the horses. Instead, she stomped up the stairs to her apartment. She slammed the door behind her and stalked through the kitchen to pace the expansive great room.

Swain was angry that Abigail had to go to England and die. In some irrational way, she wanted to blame Lillie. Damn it. This was her home. These were her and Abigail's ponies. Maybe her last name wasn't Wetherington, but Swain Butler was the name behind the Wetherington stables. Swain had hand-picked these horses and trained most of them herself.

And this little London socialite, who'd probably never even been on a horse, intended to just swoop in and sell them without a second thought. Why couldn't the Wetheringtons have adopted her, not a silly girl with no comprehension, no appreciation for what this family held dear?

She would have saddled a pony and headed to the trails to let the cadence of the ride soothe her rattled nerves, but it was already dark, and moonless. As a child, she'd sorted out her emotions at a battered upright piano in the dining hall of the orphanage where she grew up. So tonight, she settled behind the baby grand that took up her dining area and began to play.

The hard, staccato notes of an angry concerto ricocheted off the tall windows and exposed rafters of the open room. *She's going to sell the ponies.* She pounded the keys in an angry rhythm.

She wanted to hate Lillie. She didn't care that Lillie was beautiful...bewitchingly beautiful. She wouldn't fall prey to that soft British accent and those sad brown eyes.

She played song after song, letting the discipline required to play the notes properly help her regain control. The last notes were still hanging in the air when she noticed the letter she'd cast aside.

If the letter instructed her to sell the ponies, she would. Then she'd leave. She'd managed on her own before, and she would again. Swain Butler didn't need anyone, not even the Wetheringtons.

She walked back to the kitchen and found a knife to carefully open the letter. Her hands had been shaking when she sat down at the piano, but they were steady now. She pulled the letter from the envelope and unfolded it. She was not at all prepared for its message.

> *My dear Swain,*
>
> *Not since Eric left to live in England and Jim died have I found anyone who loves the ponies as much as I do. Until I met you.*
>
> *You have been such a joy to me ever since the day I persuaded you to come to the Wetherington stables. Whether it is despite or because of the hardships you weathered as a child, you have grown into a young woman who would make any parent proud. You have a strength and steadiness that the people around you and the ponies you train instinctively trust.*
>
> *While I have been away, you have protected and nurtured the things every Wetherington holds most dear— home and ponies. Now, I ask for your help once more.*
>
> *Take care of my Lillie. She must be so scared and alone right now. She needs a champion. You must teach her to love the ponies as we do. She needs to finally find her real place in the family, and she hasn't yet had the opportunity to do that. Show her what it means to be a Wetherington. I have a feeling you know that better than any who wear the name.*
>
> *She shouldn't live in London alone. You must convince her to make her home in Aiken. I have deliberately left some legal entanglements that will delay the reading of my will to give you time. I promise you will be rewarded.*

I ask this with all of my trust and affection,
Abigail

Swain clutched the letter to her chest and did what she hadn't done since she was a small child. Sinking to the floor, her back against the cabinets, she sobbed. Abigail's death wasn't just words now. It felt real. She'd never again see her, the woman who'd finally made her feel like she belonged. Tears trailed down her cheeks as she screamed at the pain cutting through her. Why did everybody always leave her?

A warm weight settled against her side and she buried her face in Beau's wiry coat until her tears subsided. She still had him. He was the only steady presence in her life.

He'd been a half-starved puppy rooting in the trash at the polo fields when she found him. A fellow mongrel that society had tossed out. She sat back and pushed him away when he began to lick at her tears. She wiped at her mouth when Beau's long tongue swiped across her lips. "Yuck, Beau. You kiss like a guy, and your breath stinks like dog." Her breath hitched between her words and her teasing was forced, but she offered him a small smile. "Wait, you *are* a boy dog, aren't you?"

Beau sat back and woofed in agreement. She stared into his intelligent eyes, finding the strength to steady her emotions. She pulled her shirt up to wipe away the last tears and the sticky dog slobber. "When life kicks you, let it kick you forward, right?" Beau woofed again. "Yeah? Well, you know what? I'm damned tired of getting kicked."

None of this was really Lillie's fault. She had to be hurting, too. Swain had lost one person close to her. Lillie had lost three. Abigail had sent Lillie to her and she'd reacted like a wounded dog. She'd growled and snapped at Lillie, then run under the porch to whimper like the cur that she was. If she wanted to persuade Lillie not to sell the stable, she had to quit licking her wounds and crawl out from under that porch.

Struggling to her feet, she retrieved the letter she'd dropped on the floor and walked over to the tall windows of her living room.

She sighed as she stared out at the stars that pierced the pitch-black sky and settled on the brightest one speaking to her now.

"Okay, Abigail. We'll teach Lillie to love the ponies. But I'm counting on you to help."

CHAPTER FIVE

Exhaustion, a hot bath, and an amazingly comfortable bed were better than a handful of sleeping pills. Lillie was sleeping deeply when the ringing phone pulled her from her dreamless slumber.

She blinked and rolled over to look at the clock. Nine o'clock. "Bloody hell," she muttered. She was usually an early riser. She cleared her throat and fumbled for the phone on the bedside table.

"Hello?"

"Miss Wetherington?" The deep male voice was not familiar.

"This is Lillie Wetherington."

"We haven't met, Miss Wetherington, but I'm Bonner Whitney, Abigail's attorney here in the States. I'm so sorry to hear about Abigail. I've known her for more than fifty years. We'll sorely miss her around here."

"Thank you. A lot of people will miss her, I'm sure."

"Yes, well, I've spoken with the solicitor she employed in the U.K. and wanted to let you know that Abigail's body left London today and should be ready to be picked up early Friday. I've notified the funeral home, but you'll need to go by and make the final arrangements."

"I'll do that, Mr. Whitney. I just have to find some transportation."

Lillie padded to the balcony doors and stared out at the large polo field behind the house. Two riders were jostling over a small ball, their horses pushing against each other, maneuvering to gain an advantage. She easily recognized Swain as one of the riders, her white knit shirt bright against her tanned skin.

"I'm sure Swain can take care of whatever you need. Have you talked with her?"

"We met yesterday. She did offer to assist."

"Fine. Good."

Swain swung her mallet and the ball shot out from under the horses' feet. Both riders pursued it immediately.

"I suppose we will meet after the funeral to discuss my grandmum's estate?"

Swain angled her mount at a full gallop to shoulder the competing horse off course. Another graceful swing of her mallet and the ball spun between the goalposts. Swain threw her head back and laughed with abandon. It was the most beautiful thing Lillie had ever seen. Swain and her mount seemed to react as if the horse could read her every thought. It was a graceful dance, but at the same time so raw and powerful it sent chills down Lillie's arms.

"I'm afraid it may not be as soon as you'd like," Bonner said, drawing Lillie back to the conversation.

"I'm sorry?"

"We have some legal hoops to jump through since Abigail had a will on file here, but drew up a new one recently while she was in England. She stipulated in the new will that we wait at least a month before it is read and probated, but the legal red tape could take as long as two."

"Two months?" It would be weeks before she could disappear. "Why would she do that?"

"I can't say, but I can tell you that Abigail hoped you would stay here in South Carolina during that time."

"I guess we'll make the best of it, then," Lillie said.

"Excellent. Contact me if you need anything. My numbers are in Abigail's address book in her study."

"Thank you, Mr. Whitney."

"Please, call me Bonner."

"Then you must call me Lillie. I'll keep you advised of the arrangements."

"Thank you. Good-bye, Lillie."

She pressed the button to end the call and watched as Swain and the other rider again grappled for a ball midfield. Two months. What would she do here for two months?

The players galloped closer. She hesitated, then retrieved a camera and a telescopic lens from her luggage and shot frame after frame. When she realized she was unconsciously following only one of the riders, she lowered her camera and glanced down at the last frame—Swain wheeling her mount, her mallet raised high like a warrior in the midst of a battlefield. It was an incredible image. Maybe she should add sports photography to her resume. She returned her camera to its case.

Two months, and the one person she needed to depend on was angry with her. She had no way to get around. Did they have taxis out here in the country?

Lillie took a deep breath and exhaled. Okay. She couldn't spend weeks on this farm if she didn't patch things up with Swain. She needed food and transportation, and Swain to help her get those things. She also needed to repair yesterday's damage.

❖

Swain dismounted and handed her reins and mallet to Rob. They'd ridden three sets of ponies and it was time for a break. "That's it for field work today. Go grab some lunch. We'll take Nor'easter and Finesse out to stretch their legs after I do a couple of hours of paperwork."

Rob turned the horses over to John, the head groom, and shuffled his feet. "Uh, I was hoping I could have the afternoon off."

Swain frowned. "I'll ride Nor'Easter, but you need to exercise Finesse. What's so urgent?"

"Today's mine and Annie's anniversary."

"Your third, right?"

Rob nodded. "Yeah. I'm taking her out to dinner tonight, but I haven't gotten her a gift or anything."

"Damn, man. You sure are leaving things to the last minute.

What do you plan to buy her?"

"Hell if I know." He puffed his chest out. "She already got me. What do you get a woman who has everything?"

Swain cocked her head. "I dunno. A sympathy card?"

Rob thumped her on the shoulder. "Yeah, right. Seriously. You're a woman, sort of. What would she like?"

Swain snorted. "Sort of?" Her men friends saw her as one of the guys, but one with inside information on what women were thinking. She was the only reason their wives and girlfriends didn't get kitchen equipment or a fishing rod as gifts.

Rob rolled his eyes. "You know what I mean. Come on. This is important."

She chuckled. If the women of this community only knew just how much they owed her. "Okay. You're right. Annie *is* important. Why she puts up with your ass, I don't know." She paused to think. "Jewelry. A necklace. With small diamonds in it. I saw some nice ones that aren't too expensive at Floyd and Green Jewelers."

"I was thinking of buying her a Wii. She saw their fitness stuff on TV the other day and complained that she needed to take off a few pounds."

"Christ almighty, Rob. A necklace says, 'You're beautiful enough for diamonds.' Do you know what an exercise video game says?"

"That I care about her health?"

"That you think she's fat, but you don't mind because Wii also makes a NASCAR game you've been drooling over."

Rob's face reddened. "Okay. Busted."

"Take the afternoon off and go buy her a necklace."

"You're a great boss."

"Hey, I'm doing this for Annie, not you."

"Yeah, but I'm the one who'll get lucky tonight."

"On second thought, maybe I should go pick out a necklace and take Annie to dinner."

"Not on your life. I'm not letting you within fifty feet of my wife."

Swain grabbed Nor'easter's bridle from where it hung on the

wall and inspected the bit. "Go on, I can ride both horses and save my paperwork for tonight."

"Thanks. I owe you." Rob turned abruptly toward the barn entrance and almost crashed into Lillie.

"Oh, hey. Sorry. I didn't see you." He stuck out his hand, looking Lillie over and giving her a wide smile. "Rob Garris. You were here yesterday, right?"

Lillie clasped his hand in brief greeting. "Yes. Lillie Wetherington."

Rob's smile faltered. "Miss Wetherington." He was suddenly more formal. This was the new boss lady. Swain had gathered the men together that morning to tell them of Abigail's death and the new boss in residence. She hadn't said it was the beautiful blonde who'd showed up on the patio yesterday. "I'm so sorry to hear about Mrs. Wetherington. She was a great lady. She sure knew the ponies." That was a high compliment among the polo crowd.

"Thank you, Rob."

He glanced at Swain and looked relieved when she dismissed him with a nod toward his truck.

"Right. On my way."

Swain studied Lillie warily. After her outburst last night, she wouldn't be surprised if Lillie had come to fire her.

But Lillie didn't look angry. She looked great. Her cascading curls were pulled back loosely and tied with a black ribbon. She was dressed more casually today, in jeans and a black tank top under an unbuttoned khaki camp shirt with the sleeves rolled up on her forearms. On her it looked like high fashion.

She was exactly the kind of young woman any prominent family would be proud to have as their daughter, their granddaughter. Not at all like a boyish lesbian with manure on her boots and sweat running down her back. Swain tamped down her peeve, her tone polite. "What can I do for you, Miss Wetherington?"

"Please, call me Lillie. I…I've come to apologize for yesterday. I rather made a mess out of breaking the news of Grandmum's passing. I can't excuse my callous behavior, except to say I'm still a bit dazed over everything that has happened. I'm truly sorry."

The sincerity in Lillie's soft brown eyes caught Swain off guard. Maybe she'd been too quick to judge this woman. She averted her gaze to the bridle in her hands and fidgeted with a buckle. "I need to be the one to apologize." Swain took a deep breath and looked up. "I was as shocked as you were that those words came out of my mouth. I should be the last person on earth to say such a thing."

Lillie cocked her head. "Why is that?"

She rarely told anyone about her childhood, but she suddenly needed Lillie to know that she understood how much her words must have hurt. "Because I was orphaned as a child, too."

Lillie's eyes swirled with hurt, then resentment. Swain's message had hit home. The insult she hurled last night was inexcusable. She had knowingly gone for the jugular, used the knife she knew would cut a fellow orphan the deepest. But the shock of Abigail's death had left her raw and triggered her deepest defenses.

"I'm deeply sorry," Swain said gently. "And I have no excuse for *my* callous behavior." She mimicked Lillie's words, but offered her most sincere smile.

Lillie's gaze softened. "It seems neither of us was at our best. Perhaps we can begin again."

"I'd like that." Swain was surprised to find she really meant what she said. Not because it served her seduction of Lillie into the family's passion for polo, but because…well, she wasn't sure why. Maybe because Lillie was one of the most beautiful women she'd ever seen. Maybe she just wanted to hear more of that soft, lyrical British accent.

"Who d'you want saddled next?" John stepped out of the tack room halfway down the long corridor. "Sorry. Didn't know you had company."

The spell between them was broken, and Swain was suddenly aware that she and Lillie had moved closer during their conversation, close enough to give the impression of something intimate between them. She stepped back and glanced toward the man. "Nor'easter, John. I'll take him on the trails to stretch his legs." She held out the bridle in her hands. "But I need a new bit on this."

John nodded and took the bridle from her before disappearing back into the tack room.

Swain turned to Lillie. "Will it happen soon?" *How long before I'm homeless?*

"What?"

"The reading of Abigail's will."

"Oh, the will. No. Mr. Whitney called this morning and said that a bit of legal work to sort out would cause a delay. In fact, he said it may take several months." Lillie shifted uneasily on her feet. "That leads to the other reason I'm here. There's no food in the house and I'm afraid I'm without transportation. Are there any taxis about?"

"Abigail's BMW is in the garage. I've driven it regularly to keep it maintained. The keys are hanging in the kitchen next to the door that leads out to the garage."

"Um, well."

"Just stay on the opposite side of the road than you're used to."

Lillie shoved her hands in her pockets. She blushed and averted her eyes. "Yes. Well, you see…I was hoping you might have time… I'm not familiar with the area, and I'm afraid I don't have much experience driving at all. I do have a license, but parking was such a bear in London, it was always easier to take the underground or hail a cab."

An idea began to form in Swain's mind. "Do you ride, Ms. Wetherington?"

"Lillie, please. Ride? I'm not sure I understand."

Swain waved toward where John had cross-tied Nor'easter in the hallway and was preparing to saddle him. "Horses. Do you know how to ride?"

Lillie hesitated. "I haven't since I was a child." She straightened her shoulders and raised her chin. "But I can. I remember being quite good at it, actually."

She smiled at Lillie's bravado. "I'll make a deal with you."

Lillie's eyes narrowed. "A deal?"

"Yes. You see, I still have two horses to exercise and I just gave Rob the afternoon off. It's lunchtime and, since you have no food in the house, I'm guessing that you're getting pretty hungry. I'll take you to get some lunch and groceries if you'll help me exercise the ponies later."

Lillie's confidence deflated. "I don't know that I'm up to dashing headlong up and down a polo field."

"I'm talking about a leisurely ride on the trails just to stretch their legs and build their stamina. The other horse I need to exercise is Abigail's old mare. She's really gentle."

Lillie nodded enthusiastically. "I could do that."

Swain raised her voice to carry down the barn corridor. "Hold up on that, John. I'm heading into town for a bit. I'll ride him when I get back."

Lillie's smile was so brilliant, her unguarded beauty so stunning, Swain's stomach did a small flip. She suddenly couldn't remember why she'd ever been angry at Lillie, why she needed to be cautious. But she wanted to be the cause of that smile again and again.

CHAPTER SIX

Swain had barely finished her side salad and picked up the first half of her French-dip hoagie when Lillie polished off her thick corned-beef sandwich and stared at Swain's plate. Swain pushed the second half of her sandwich toward her.

"No, I couldn't," Lillie protested, but unconsciously licked her lips.

"Go ahead. I don't usually eat lunch."

Lillie only hesitated a moment before transferring the food to her own plate. "I'm sorry to be so ravenous. I've had nothing but airplane food for nearly two days."

Swain found Lillie's unladylike appetite amusing. It was the first crack she'd seen in her guest's proper British manners. "I'm just shocked that someone as thin as you can hold that much."

Lillie wrinkled her nose in an expression Swain found incredibly cute. "High metabolism," she said, dipping the sandwich in the cup of beef broth on Swain's plate.

"I'll be sure to keep my fingers out of the way." Swain picked up a French fry from her plate and chewed it thoughtfully. "I have a favor to ask."

"A favor?"

"Yes." Swain carefully composed her request. "We're in the middle of the fall polo season, when the professional teams are preparing for Florida's winter season. It's the best time to sell several of the ponies I've been training."

"Not to bring up yesterday's unpleasantness, but I thought you were opposed to selling the horses."

Swain pushed her plate away and sat back in her chair "I'm talking about our usual business of training and selling ponies. Not about breaking up the stable."

Lillie looked surprised. "I'm sorry. I always thought polo was a hobby, not a business."

"Polo is a tradition, a passion." Swain corrected her gently. "It's not a highly profitable business, but we make enough to cover expenses."

"I see. Then how can I help? As you can tell, I know very little about the sport."

"I told the rest of the staff this morning about Abigail's death. I also informed them you came here to run the farm in Abigail's place."

"Why did you do that, since I don't plan to stay?"

Swain spoke in a low voice so no one else lunching in the deli could overhear. "I guarantee you the news that Abigail has passed will be all over town before we make arrangements for her burial. Nor'easter will likely bring in the highest price we've ever gotten for a pony. Whitney's absolutely salivating to buy him. But if even a hint slips out that you're closing the stable, everyone'll think we're desperate to sell and the amount of Whitney's offer will drop faster than a whore's panties."

Lillie stared at Swain for a moment, then burst out laughing.

Swain scowled. "I'm serious, Lillie."

Lillie covered her mouth with her hand but her shoulders still shook with laughter. "I know, I know." She struggled to compose herself, dabbing her napkin at the tears leaking from the corners of her eyes. "I just can't believe you said that. Whore's panties? It'll be bloody hard to get that image out of my head."

Swain blushed, then chuckled, too. "I guess I've been hanging out with the guys too much lately. It's not often I have lunch with such polite company."

"Perhaps we should do something about that," Lillie said.

"Perhaps we should."

They smiled at each other.

"Colorful expressions aside, I do understand your point. As you wish, mum's the word."

❖

In the grocery store, Swain patiently pushed the cart while Lillie frowned and scanned the shelves. They'd covered two-thirds of the store and their basket remained empty.

"I guess a lot of our brands aren't familiar," Swain finally said. "If you tell me what you want to cook, I'll try to point you toward the right things."

Lillie did the nose-wrinkling thing again. "I'm afraid I have a confession to make."

"A confession?"

"I've never shopped for groceries before."

"Never? Your mother never took you to the grocery store?"

"Our cook did the shopping. She made marvelous meals, but wouldn't let anyone in her kitchen. I always wanted to, but never learned to cook...or shop for food."

Swain tried to wrap her mind around that concept. "I see. Wow. You've never been in a grocery store?"

"Don't look so gobsmacked. I'm sure you know other women who don't cook."

Swain made a show of scratching her chin and staring at the floor, as if in deep thought. "I've met people who never learned to swim." She raised her eyes to Lillie's. "I know a man who never learned to read."

Lillie playfully pushed Swain on the shoulder. "Now you're just making fun of me."

Swain laughed. "Okay. You tell me what you want to eat and I'll help you find the ingredients and show you how to make it."

"Really? *You* know how? You don't mind teaching me? Are you sure you have time? I don't want to be a burden."

The sudden light in Lillie's eyes, the excitement in her expression warmed Swain in unusual places. Sort of like that smile back at the barn.

"Sure. I can do that. What's your favorite dinner? We'll buy the stuff and cook it tonight."

"Oh, yummy. Steak-and-kidney pie."

"Yuck. Kidneys? Pick something else."

Lillie looked disappointed. "Pork pie?"

Swain shook her head.

Lillie's eyes began to twinkle. "Bangers and mash."

Swain scowled. "I don't even want to know what that is."

"Yorkshire pudding."

"I don't cook desserts."

"That's not a dessert."

"I don't know how to make Yorkshire pudding."

"I thought you knew how to cook."

"I do. I'm just not up on British cuisine." Swain stopped. "Do you like Cajun food?"

"I'm not sure."

"Do you like shrimp?"

"I love all fish and seafood."

Swain grinned. It was time for Lillie to learn to eat like a Southerner. "Then you're in for a treat. Before I ended up in Florida where I learned to ride polo ponies, I spent a year in New Orleans. I started out washing dishes in a restaurant, but ended up working as the chef's assistant." She wheeled their cart with purpose toward the seafood section in the corner. "Tonight, Miss Lillie, I'll prepare the best shrimp and grits you've ever put in your mouth."

"Grits?"

"You'll love 'em."

❖

"It's all a bit overwhelming after being raised in a flat," Lillie said when the hulking Wetherington mansion came into view again.

"The property totals five hundred acres," Swain said. She steered the BMW down the shaded drive. "The main house and grounds take up only three acres. The stable, polo field, and paddocks sit on about a hundred acres. Another hundred is dedicated to hay fields and about three hundred to woods." Swain couldn't picture Abigail's only child living in a London walk-up, considering Eric grew up on the South Carolina estate. "Why did you live in an apartment instead of a house?"

"Well, it wasn't just an apartment. It had three bedrooms and baths, not counting the cook's quarters. It took up the entire top floor of our building. Mum and Dad always enjoyed the city, and it was close to where Dad taught music at the university."

"Sounds fancy." Not like the single bed and footlocker she had in the children's home.

"I suppose."

Swain pulled the car into the garage next to a vintage Mercedes 450 SL convertible from the 1970s.

"Whose car is that? It's lovely," Lillie asked as she got out of the BMW. She ran her hand down the gleaming white fender and along the soft tan leather of the interior.

"Abigail said it belonged to your father. They gave it to him on his eighteenth birthday, but he drove it for only a few months before he left for England and never returned to the States." She studied Lillie. She'd only known her for a day and Lillie had no reason to confide in her, but curiosity won out. "Whatever happened must have been horrible for a son to stop speaking to his parents for more than twenty years."

"Does it still run?"

Okay. That subject was obviously off-limits. "I'll say. Abigail said her husband drove it religiously a couple of times a month to keep it up. After he died, she continued the ritual until I came to work here and she asked me to do it for her. We can take it tomorrow to get your temporary license if you like. Do you know how to drive a stick shift?"

"Yes, but not very well. Perhaps I should stick to Grandmum's car." She looked up nervously. "Do you think they'll make me drive?"

Swain shrugged. "I doubt it. You'll probably just have to take a written test that's mostly identifying signs. If you're worried, though, they have a study booklet available online to give you some practice before we go to the licensing bureau. Abigail refused to use computers, but we have several in the barn office."

"I have a laptop."

"Even better. You should be able to log into the barn's wireless Internet from the house."

They took the groceries inside and put them away quickly. Swain eyed Lillie's attire.

"Your jeans will do fine for riding," she said, "but you'll need to wear something other than those shoes."

"Grandmum and I wore the same size. I'm sure she has some riding boots upstairs."

"You go look and meet me in the barn," Swain suggested, turning toward the back door. She didn't want to go into Abigail's private quarters and rifle through her things. It would be the ultimate admission that she was never coming back, a reminder that Swain's home at the Wetherington estate would soon be history.

❖

Swain was talking to a groom, her back to Lillie and her shoulder propped against the wall. Lillie slowed her pace, letting her eyes move from the wide span of Swain's shoulders to the knee-high pair of scuffed riding boots. She imagined the tight muscles of that delicious rump moving under soft skin…flexing as she pulled Swain tighter between her legs—*Bloody hell!* She shook her head to clear it, then smiled at her salacious thought. Everything that had happened in the past year had numbed her feelings and her interest in life. She was relieved that her pulse was racing again.

Swain turned at the sound of her footsteps, her smile fading as she looked at Lillie. "You feel okay? You look a little flushed."

"No, really. I'm fine. A little nervous, but excited about riding again."

Swain studied her, then nodded. "Okay, but it'll be a few minutes. The mare I want you to exercise is in one of the outer pastures, and John's bringing her in. Would you like that tour I offered yesterday while we wait?"

"That would be wonderful," Lillie said, a little too brightly.

Swain turned out to be an apt tour guide. Most of the barn's large office was a museum of the nearly one hundred years of Wetherington polo. Long glass cases on both sides of the room held shelves of trophies, awards, and framed photographs dating back to the early 1900s. "There's a lot of history here," Lillie commented.

"The Wetheringtons got out of the breeding business about thirty years ago, but a fireproof vault in the basement of the main house has stud and breeding records dating back to 1930, kept in vacuum-sealed cases."

"Amazing," Lillie muttered, studying the photographs and trophies.

Swain pointed to a framed black-and-white photograph. "That was the original stable. It burned to the ground in 1940 when a visitor violated the cardinal rule against smoking in the barn and left his cigar butt smoldering in the feed room. Twelve top polo ponies died that night. Rumor has it that, after the fire, the rest of the wealthy community shunned the man so thoroughly that he finally moved his family to Canada."

"I'll be sure to confine my cigar smoking to the house," Lillie deadpanned.

Swain grinned and pointed to another photograph. "This building replaced the burned stable. But sixty years later, the plumbing was shot and the wiring dangerous. So Abigail had it torn down and replaced it with this more modern structure. I think it was mostly a project to keep her occupied after her husband died."

"Did you know Granddad?"

"No, I didn't. He died a few months before Abigail offered me this job."

Swain led Lillie out into the corridor. The post-and-beam construction of the main part of the barn was reminiscent of a mountain lodge.

Lillie closed her eyes as she stepped into the feed room and inhaled the smell of fresh hay and molasses-coated oats. Equipment rooms in both wings held rows of polished saddles, bridles, polo equipment, and assorted shovels, rakes, and brooms needed to keep the barn tidy. Everything was impeccably clean, right down to the high-tech rubber flooring of the hallway where the gray-haired groom she'd seen earlier had Nor'easter and Finesse cross-tied for saddling.

"I can't believe how tidy everything is," Lillie observed.

"She fired a damn good farrier once because he left a hoof file in the hallway," the groom said.

"Lillie, this old goat is John, the head groom. Don't worry about his grumpiness. He's always that way." There was affection rather than irritation in her voice. "If he'd forget an expensive file, he'd likely forget a nail that could end up in the bottom of a horse's foot."

"I suppose your living quarters are just as neat," Lillie said. "Didn't you say your apartment is here in the stables?"

Swain gestured toward the ceiling with her chin. "Upstairs."

"Would it be too much of an imposition to see that part, too?"

Swain hesitated. "I need to saddle the horses so we can finish our ride before it starts getting dark."

"You go on ahead. I'll saddle the ponies," John said.

"Thank you, John," Lillie said, smiling at Swain.

John ignored Swain's glare, so she pointed to a door across from the office. "That way."

The door opened to a narrow staircase that led to a second door. As they started up the stairs, Lillie put her hand on Swain's arm to stop her.

"You don't have to show me. I don't want to invade your privacy. I just love the architecture of this building and was curious to see what the living area looks like."

Swain shrugged, but smiled. "It's beautiful. Maybe I'm afraid you'll like it so much you'll decide to send me to the main house so you can live here."

Lillie smiled back. "I make no promises."

The stairway was a back door of sorts, leading into a laundry room, then to the small but well-equipped kitchen. Separated from the kitchen by a tall counter, the huge living area had the same warm oak siding on the walls and ceiling as the stables below. Though the room was beautiful, Lillie immediately noticed the baby grand piano that sat where a dining table should have been. She walked over and pushed the cover back to caress the keys.

"Abigail intended to put that in storage when she redecorated some rooms in the main house, but I talked her into storing it out here. Do you play?" Swain asked.

"Poorly, but I love to listen." Lillie murmured. She looked up. "What do you play?"

"I can play most anything after I hear it a few times. But I prefer classical."

"Dad did, too. He played beautifully. He said all the Wetheringtons were musically inclined." *All who were true Wetheringtons.*

Swain's cell phone rang and she checked the phone's display. "Ah. This is about a horse I may want to look at, so I have to take it. Make yourself at home and continue to look around if you like." Swain walked into a room that appeared to be a small personal office, leaving Lillie standing by the piano.

A fireplace with gas logs was cut into the wall on the right of the living area. Straight ahead, eight-foot-tall windows flanked French doors leading to a deck that overlooked the paddocks.

A doorway on the same wall as the fireplace was open and Lillie peeked in at a large bedroom decorated in soothing shades of blue. It was beautiful, except for the ratty faux-fur rug thrown on the otherwise pristine queen-sized bed.

❖

Swain was tucking her phone back into her pocket when a shriek sent her running for the bedroom. Lillie slammed into her, nearly climbing up Swain's body in her attempt to escape.

"It moved. Oh, my God. It moved!"

"What? What moved?" Swain pushed Lillie behind her and scanned the floor for a mouse that probably had found its way up from the feed room.

Lillie pressed against her back, clutching Swain's shirt. She reached around Swain to point at the bed while still hiding her face between Swain's shoulder blades. "There. On the bed. Something's in that rug. It moved."

Beau sat up and yawned.

Swain chuckled. "That isn't a rug. At least not yet."

"What is it is?"

"A dog. My dog."

Lillie peeked over Swain's shoulder as Beau stood and jumped down from the bed. He paused to stretch—his chest touching the floor with long legs in front of him and his butt in the air—and yawn again, exposing huge white teeth.

"Are you absolutely sure that's a dog?"

Swain was suddenly aware of Lillie's breath on her neck. "Uh, I'm not totally sure, but he barks and licks himself like a dog. He may be a cross between an Irish wolfhound and a golden retriever."

"He's huge."

"Don't say that so loud. He's very sensitive about his size. He thinks he's a poodle."

"A poodle?"

Beau's long hairy tail swept back and forth. Swain grasped Lillie's hand to pull her alongside. "Beau. Come introduce yourself to Miss Wetherington."

Beau sat in front of Lillie. He woofed softly and politely raised his front paw. Lillie looked uncertainly at Swain, then took the large paw in her hand. "I'm very pleased to meet you, Mr. Beau."

Beau's tail thumped against the floor.

Lillie straightened and stared at the bed. "He's very nice, but you keep the barn and your flat so neat, I can't believe you let him shed all over that beautiful quilt."

Swain shrugged. "He gets a bath weekly. More often if he gets into mud or something nasty. I've had dates who left more hair in my bed than him."

"Perhaps you should go out with men who aren't so hairy."

Swain was caught off guard by Lillie's apparent assumption

that she was heterosexual. Was she that naïve? People often mistook Swain for a man on the phone or from a distance, and she was accustomed to people assuming she was gay. Not that it bothered her. She never hid her sexuality. Life had already cheated her of too many things. She'd decided at a young age that she wouldn't let it cheat her of being who she was, too. She didn't plan to change that now. Still, something other than her ego was at stake here. If Lillie found her desire for women offensive, she'd never get a chance to persuade her to stay in South Carolina. Then again, if Swain didn't tell her, someone else surely would.

"I don't date men," Swain said.

Lillie raised an eyebrow, but she didn't act as though she was offended. Swain wasn't sure what to make of it.

"I date women."

Lillie nodded and pursed her lips. "That would be the logical alternative to men, wouldn't it?" she said absently.

"If that makes you uncomfortable, I'd rather talk about it now and clear the air."

"No. That's not what I'm thinking at all."

Swain waited for more of a reaction. God, this woman was frustrating. "Then what are you thinking? It can't be any worse than I've heard before."

"If your girlfriends shed that much hair on your sheets, perhaps you should recommend a better shampoo or encourage them to use a razor for that unwanted body hair."

Swain's laughter rose so fast that she nearly choked on it. "I need to keep an eye on you, Miss Wetherington. I'm not sure our little Southern town is ready for a British invasion."

CHAPTER SEVEN

The ribbon that had held Lillie's hair had long been lost, and her curls flew around her head like a golden halo as she cantered her mare across the meadow to where Swain and Nor'easter waited.

"That's no fair. Your horse is much faster than mine."

Despite her admonishment, her cheeks were flushed and her eyes alight with pleasure. Swain imagined her as a Celtic queen galloping across the moors.

"Nor'easter's the fastest in the stable. The fastest I've ever trained," Swain said, smiling. "I didn't mean to leave you behind, but I needed to stretch his legs."

"He's beautiful."

"You're beautiful." The words were out of her mouth before Swain could censor them. That seemed to happen a lot around Lillie.

Lillie ducked her head, her flushed cheeks turning an even brighter red.

"I'm sorry. It seems whatever runs through my head comes out of my mouth around you. It's just…riding across there, your hair flying…but you must hear that a lot."

"Thank you, but, no, I don't."

Swain cocked her head. "Then your countrymen are blind, undeserving heathens."

Lillie laughed. "I never knew Americans were such charmers."

Swain dipped her chin in an abbreviated bow, acknowledging the compliment. She squared her shoulders and sat straighter in the saddle. The breeze carried the faint scent of freshly mown pastures, and if she closed her eyes, she could imagine herself a knight escorting her lady across a field of heather.

They walked their horses side by side down a broad, shaded path. The silence was comfortable, but didn't last long. Lillie was full of questions.

"Was Nor'easter bred here in South Carolina?"

"No. In New York. This little town is somewhat of a secret to all but the equine community. We have world-class polo and steeplechase, as well as Thoroughbred racing. Some really famous horses ran their first race as two-year-olds right here in Aiken."

"Really? I'm no expert, but I do watch the Triple Crown on the telly every year. Any names I would recognize?"

"Summer Squall, Nor'easter's great-granddaddy, is one. Conquistador Cielo, the 1982 Eclipse Horse of the Year, and Swale, who won the Kentucky Derby and the Belmont Stakes in 1984, were both trained here."

"Amazing." Lillie was quiet for a moment. "Ah. Summer Squall, Nor'easter. I get it. Clever. So, do all your ponies come from famous racehorses?"

"Not all, but most. Bloodlines are important. The best sires are the ones with genes strong enough to pass their best traits to their offspring."

Bloodlines. Although Swain's coloring was different from that of Eric and Abigail, she looked very much like the photograph of Jim Wetherington in Abigail's bedroom. She had the same dark hair and blue eyes, the same strong chin and intelligent brow. Lillie tried to imagine how Abigail must have felt when she looked at Swain and saw the features of her late husband. Did Swain even suspect she was a Wetherington? Her grandmum had feared how Swain would react if she learned Abigail had been the one to decide Jim's bastards would be left to grow up in an orphanage. She had already missed out on years of her son's life. She apparently had been afraid Swain would disappear, too.

"So, how does a horse bred for the track end up on the polo field?"

"A trainer may bring a half dozen yearlings to train here, knowing probably only a few will actually go on to race. Those first months of training weed out the ones who don't show the potential their pedigrees promised. The trainers sell them here cheap before they pack up their hopefuls and head to the tracks in Florida or New York. Even though they didn't work out on the flat track, most are excellent hunter-jumpers. Some make very good polo ponies."

Lillie pondered what Swain had said. "If Nor'easter is so fast, why didn't he make a good racehorse?"

Swain rubbed the horse's neck. "Too aggressive. Nor'easter liked to lean into and bump any horse racing next to him. That'll get you disqualified and fined on the flat track, but it's exactly the quality I'm looking for in a pony."

Lillie eyed the horse's long legs. "He's not exactly a pony."

Swain chuckled. "He's nearly sixteen hands. The horses originally used for polo were pony-sized, closer to fourteen hands. But as the sport developed, the players began to use taller, faster horses to get downfield quickly."

"That doesn't explain why they still call them ponies."

"Polo horse? It doesn't have the same ring to it."

Lillie laughed and shook her head. "Simple as that?"

"Some things are simple, Lillie."

❖

Lillie remembered how to sit a horse, but her leg and back muscles apparently had forgotten. She gritted her teeth and tried to hide her stiffness, but was unable to stifle a low groan when she dismounted.

While Swain unsaddled Nor'easter and carried the equipment to the tack room, John hooked Finesse into the cross ties. "Don't use the liniment she's gonna give you for that soreness," he said. "It'll burn your backside off. Take a long, hot bath, do some stretching, and pop a few ibuprofen."

He pulled the saddle from Finesse and pointed to a bucket of water and a large sponge. "Use that to wipe down her sweaty areas, especially where the saddle was. The salt will irritate her skin if you don't. I'll clean up your tack." Swain returned and John disappeared into the tack room.

They worked in silence for a while, then Swain led Nor'easter into a stall and returned. When she unhooked Finesse from the cross ties and squatted to massage her front legs, the mare relaxed and rested her chin on Swain's back while she worked.

"Is she all right?" Lillie asked.

"She's fine. She's well into her twenties, and she gets a little stiff. So she enjoys a good rubdown after her exercise." That was clear. The mare's eyes were nearly closed. When Swain stood, Finesse blinked as though just awakened and heaved a big horsey sigh. "Go on with yourself," Swain said. She slapped the mare affectionately on the rump, and Finesse walked down to an open stall door and went inside.

"Well, she's certainly well trained."

"Abigail raised that mare from a baby," Swain said, picking up their buckets and sponges. Lillie followed her to the wash stall and watched her rinse them and put them away.

"Are you always so neat?" Lillie asked.

Swain shrugged. "It comes from growing up in the orphanage. Our keepers were very strict."

"Your keepers?"

"Yeah. The turnover in the staff was pretty high, so we didn't have a chance to get to know them very well. So we called them the keepers. Not to their faces, of course."

Swain pulled several brushes down from a shelf and handed a stiff dandy brush and a soft finish brush to Lillie. She slid a stall door open and the black gelding inside nickered to them. He stepped toward Swain and rubbed his forehead against her chest affectionately. "This is Black Astor. After Nor'easter, he's the best in our string."

"He's very handsome." Lillie held out her hand and Astor sniffed at it before turning back to Swain.

"You familiar with the brushes?"

"Yes. I know how to use them." Lillie began to move them over Astor's already gleaming coat.

"Okay, then. You give him a good brushing while I comb him out," Swain said, moving to the horse's long tail.

They worked in silence for a few moments. Lillie wondered briefly why Swain was grooming horses when she had Rob, John, and two other full-time employees to do the work. But she was enjoying spending time with someone other than just herself, and she had to admit Swain was attractive and interesting company.

"How old were you when you left the orphanage?"

"Eighteen. That's when they show you the door."

"How awful. Eighteen is so young. How did you know what to do, where to go?"

Swain shrugged. "Most of us already had minimum-wage jobs in the area. A trailer park nearby rented single-wides, so a lot of the kids went there because they could hang out with the same people they knew in the orphanage and maybe share a trailer with someone to split the cheap rent."

"I had a friend whose family kept a second home in a caravan park on the shore. It was fairly nice."

Swain snorted. "These weren't nice. They were rusted and roach-infested. That's why they were cheap."

Lillie squatted to brush Astor's legs. She didn't like to think of Swain living in such a place. "Is that where you went when you left the orphanage?"

"No. The kids there just got into trouble. They partied too much, drank too much, and did too many drugs. Some ended up in jail. The orphanage had a pretty good library and I had read about lots of places that I wanted to see, so I hit the road."

Swain patted Astor on the butt and led Lillie to the next stall where a handsome bay gelding with smart black leggings and a blaze of white from forehead to nose greeted them by searching their hands for treats. "This is Domino. He's half-Arabian, half-Thoroughbred. He's not the fastest, but he's the most agile and has the stamina of a diesel engine. If I have to, I can ride him in the first chukker, rest him, and ride him again in the final period." When Swain began to comb Domino's tail, Lillie went to work with her brushes.

Domino tried to swipe the riding gloves sticking out of Swain's back pocket, but she caught his nose and playfully pushed his searching mouth away. "He's also a prankster. He can open most gate latches. We didn't know that when we first got him. John turned him out in a paddock that first day, but Domino opened the gate and came back in the barn where he discovered the door to the tack room wasn't completely closed. John was in the office and heard the ruckus. In the few minutes it took him to get off the phone and investigate, Domino had pulled almost every saddle off the racks and into a pile on the floor."

Lillie laughed. "Really?"

Swain smiled. "Yeah. John was furious. Now we tie the gate latch down with a piece of baling twine when he's in the paddock."

"You are such a handsome boy," Lillie crooned to Domino. "I can't believe you would be so mischievous."

Domino bobbed his head as if in agreement and Swain chuckled. "Oh, he's guilty all right. Just watch what you put down around him. He'll have it in his mouth in a minute and carry it off like a dog."

They continued like that until Lillie had been introduced to and brushed three more horses. "Well, including Nor'easter, you've met the primary string I ride in the matches."

Swain slid open the door to another stall and a fine-boned filly stepped toward them. Lillie's breath caught in her throat. The filly's chestnut coat gleamed like polished copper in the sun streaming from the skylight overhead. Delicate ears pricked forward at the sound of Lillie's gasp, and huge, soft brown eyes blinked at her. Lillie offered her hand, and fine whiskers tickled her palm when the filly sniffed her fingers.

"This is Sunne, short for Sonnengöttin. That's German for sun goddess," Swain said.

"She's beautiful," Lillie whispered reverently. The filly stepped closer to sniff Lillie's boots. She lifted her head and brushed her velvet nose against Lillie's cheek, making her smile.

"She likes you," Swain said.

"I'd love to ride her next time." Had she said next time? She probably wouldn't be able to walk tomorrow.

"Let's wait until you've had a little more practice. We just got her from the track, where all they learn is to jump out of the gate and run for dear life. It usually takes us a few weeks to teach the racers there's a trot and easy canter between walk and gallop."

Swain gave Sunne a pat and stepped out of the stall. Lillie reluctantly followed.

"Don't we have to brush her?" She followed Swain back to the wash stall.

"They were all groomed earlier today," Swain said, taking the brushes from Lillie and putting them in the cabinet. "I just wanted you to have a chance to meet them."

Lillie was surprised that Swain was so honest. Obviously she planned to engage Lillie in her equine pursuits. But she couldn't stay here. The Wetherington name on the gates was a bull's-eye on her chest. She started to tell Swain her plans hadn't changed, but was reluctant to ruin their tentative truce.

"How many horses do you have here?"

"It's a thirty-stall barn, but we currently have only twenty-five stalls occupied."

"That's a lot of horses."

"The three of us who ride on the Wetherington team each have six mounts. Our fourth team member is a woman who keeps her string of ponies on her own farm. The other seven horses include Finesse, who's retired from competition, and six in various stages of training."

"You said three of you ride?"

"Me, Rob—the guy you bumped into earlier—and one of the assistant grooms, Javier. He has good instincts, so I decided to give him a shot." She shrugged. "I wouldn't be where I am today if somebody hadn't done that for me when I was mucking stalls. I'd planned to talk to Abigail about promoting him to apprentice trainer, but—"

But she was gone. Swain didn't have to finish her sentence. Lillie understood what she couldn't say aloud yet.

Swain paused at the door to her apartment. "If you give me a chance to shower off the horse sweat, I'll come up to the house and cook dinner for you."

Lillie was tired and her backside ached. Their shopping trip, ride through the woods, and grooming tour was more physical activity than she'd had in months. And she had enjoyed every minute of Swain's company. She gazed into those clear blue eyes, gauging Swain's intentions. What had the afternoon been for her? Pleasure or duty? "Thank you for the lovely offer to cook, but could we save that recipe for tomorrow night? Right now, a sandwich and a bath sound really good."

Swain smiled back. "No problem. Let me get some liniment from the wash stall. You should rub it on those sore spots and you'll be good as new by morning."

Lillie caught Swain's hand. "Thank you, but John already warned me about your liniment. I'll just tough it out with a few aspirin."

"John's a weenie."

"So am I." Lillie laughed softly and realized she was still holding Swain's hand. It was warm in hers. "I had a really good day today. The best I've had for a very long time."

Swain nodded, her expression softening. "I had fun, too."

"I hate to monopolize your time, but would you accompany me to the funeral home and help decide on the arrangements tomorrow?"

Swain's hand tightened around hers. "Sure. I don't mind. You shouldn't have to do that by yourself. Would around ten be okay? That'll give me some time to get a training session in first."

"Thank you. Ten is fine."

"Okay."

Lillie reluctantly pulled her hand from Swain's grasp. Their playful banter, the exhilarating ride, and the unspoken physical attraction between them were a welcome respite from the worries that had been her only company over the past year. But she couldn't let herself get caught up in it, no matter how wonderful the day had been. She was leaving as soon as the estate was settled. "See you in the morning."

CHAPTER EIGHT

This is just so wrong. Why do Americans have to be different from everybody else? The rest of the world drives on the left side of the road."

"Actually, most of the world drives on the right side. I looked it up."

Lillie careened around a sharp curve, and Swain held on tight even though her seat belt was securely fastened. She hadn't had a ride like this since she got on the roller coaster at the state fair.

"Okay. I meant the civilized world. Obviously, you Americans aren't civilized because you drive on the wrong side of the road."

Lillie braked hard at the stop sign, then stomped the gas to pull in front of an approaching car. The driver of the other car honked angrily at being cut off and Lillie honked back, pressing harder on the accelerator.

"The speed limit is thirty-five because we're in the city limits now," Swain warned her.

Lillie let up on the accelerator a bit. "How fast was I going?"

"Sixty-five. That's miles per hour, not kilometers. I don't know how much that is in kilometers, but in miles per hour, it's too fast through this neighborhood."

Lillie rolled her eyes and looked over at Swain. "We're not all metric. We measure speed in miles per hour, too."

"Watch out!"

Lillie looked back at the road and slammed on the brakes just in time to avoid a family of geese waddling across. Christ, she was about to give Swain whiplash.

"Lillie, pull over. Turn into that parking lot."

"What's wrong?" Lillie drove into the parking lot of a small shopping center and stopped the car.

"How much experience do you actually have?" Swain's heart beat wildly, but it'd been doing that since she'd climbed into the compact BMW with Lillie only inches away.

Lillie blushed and shrugged. "Dad took me to the country a few times to practice."

"And you drove like this?"

"No. I was just learning." Lillie sighed and looked down at the seat. "I've felt so bloody helpless since I got here. I didn't want you to think I was completely incapable."

It pleased Swain that Lillie cared what she thought of her, but she couldn't help teasing her. "You thought careening around the streets like a maniac would impress me?"

"That's how cabbies do it, and they have lots of experience."

"Ah. Well, now that we know you can drive a taxi in London, how about if we treat this like a drive in the country?"

Lillie shrugged nonchalantly. "If you insist. I didn't know you were so squeamish. Now that I know, I'll slow down. For you."

"Thank you." God, this woman was fun.

❖

"I'm so very sorry to hear about Mrs. Wetherington's passing." The funeral-home director was a tall man with a deep, gentle voice. He held Lillie's hand and patted it in sympathy. "I served on the local school board with her a few years back. She was a very loved, genteel pillar of our community and will be sorely missed."

"Thank you." Lillie thought she'd gotten past the crying, but tears began to well in her eyes. Swain wrapped a supportive arm around her shoulders as they followed the director to his office.

"I'm not sure I can do this," Lillie whispered.

"It's okay. I'll take care of it. If you don't like something about the arrangements, just speak up, okay?" Swain snatched a tissue from a box strategically placed on a table in the hallway and handed it to Lillie.

Lillie dabbed at her eyes and relaxed into Swain's side. "This is the third time in the past year I've buried someone close to me. You'd think I'd get better at it." Swain's arm tightened around her shoulders, holding her securely.

"That's exactly why this is so hard for you."

They sat in padded mahogany chairs pulled close together while the director shuffled through some papers on his desk and gathered the proper forms.

Lillie held tight to Swain's hand, steadied by her calm.

As it turned out, they had little to decide.

"Mrs. Wetherington was a person of foresight," the director informed them. "And, in keeping with that, she made her own arrangements right after her husband's untimely death. All that's left is for you to decide when. Recognizing her social position, she has consented to a visitation here and a memorial service at the church she attended, followed by a private graveside service in the church cemetery. She also recently wrote a short obit for the paper and mailed it from London. She must have guessed how serious her illness was." He offered a copy to Lillie. "It's very short, but I'm sure the newspaper will do a longer article on her, recounting all her contributions to the community."

Lillie held it out so Swain could also read the four short paragraphs.

Abigail Beatrice Wetherington has joyfully passed on to a place where the polo fields are endless and her beloved ponies never tire.

She gratefully joins her husband Jim and her son Eric, who preceded her in death, confident that those who loved her will protect and nurture her earthly legacy.

She leaves behind two very special people she will always hold close in her heart, Lillian Marie Wetherington and Rebecca Swain Butler.

In lieu of flowers, please send donations to Equine Rescue of Aiken.

"That's it?" Lillie asked.

"We'll add a paragraph, of course, that gives the times of the visitation and memorial service. And we can get it printed in the newspaper."

Swain was strangely quiet, but Lillie suddenly found her bearings. "That won't be necessary. I need to place an advertisement, so we can take care of the obituary notice at the same time."

"Very well. I'll add the service times and print it for you."

"What exactly is a visitation?"

Swain shook herself from her silence. "It's sort of like a wake the day before the funeral, but lasts only a few hours, not all night, and it's held at the funeral home. People come to your house after the burial and bring food and stay a while."

Lillie nodded and gratefully squeezed Swain's hand, which she still held. "Very well. We'll hold the visitation tomorrow night and the service at three Saturday afternoon, with the burial immediately afterward." She turned to Swain. "Does that sound appropriate?"

"Yes. That sounds fine."

Lillie finally released Swain's hand and stood. "Thank you, sir. We'll see you Friday evening."

"Do you have a number where I can contact you if anything else comes up with the arrangements? I don't expect any complications, but you never know when it comes to airlines."

Lillie turned to Swain. She didn't have a clue.

Swain quickly scribbled her cell-phone number on a notepad. "You can call me if you have any problems," she told him.

When they returned to the parking lot, Lillie indicated that Swain should drive. They climbed in the car, but Swain didn't start it right away. Lillie could feel the weight of her thoughts. "That wasn't so bad with you there to help," she said softly. "Are you all right, love?"

Swain's throat worked, and when she spoke, her voice was tight. "She listed me in her obituary right along with you. I'm just her farm manager. I'm sorry. I had no idea she'd do that."

When Swain looked up, Lillie was surprised at the vulnerability, the turmoil she saw there.

"She told me that you were more than that," Lillie said. She ached to say more, to tell Swain what had been cruelly kept from her since childhood. But as much as she wanted to heal her new friend's soul-deep pain now, the time for speaking of certain things had not yet come.

Call softly.

❖

A visit to the local Department of Motor Vehicles office determined that Lillie's international driving permit would be sufficient unless she decided to settle in South Carolina. Next stop was the newspaper.

They placed the obituary quickly, but Lillie also wanted to advertise for a temporary housekeeper so she wouldn't starve during the coming months. The newspaper clerk gave them a form to fill out, and they moved over to a high table where people could stand and write their advertisements.

"I said I'd cook for you," Swain said, frowning. She had only a few months to seduce Lillie into loving the Wetherington stables as much as she and Abigail, and she needed Lillie's dependence on her culinary skills as an excuse to spend a lot of time together.

"You're busy enough with the horses. You don't have time to babysit me, too."

"It's not a problem, really."

"I've already taken far too much of your time yesterday and today."

"I don't mind." She gave Lillie her most hopeful smile. "I like having dinner company for a change."

"What should I offer for a salary?" Lillie asked, ignoring Swain's repeated offer.

"You wouldn't have to pay me."

Lillie tapped her pencil impatiently on the table. "I would like to know that when someone is having dinner with me, it's because they enjoy my company, not because they're afraid I'll starve. Now, what should I offer for a salary?"

This would be harder than Swain thought. Lillie had been here only two days and was quickly finding her independence. Swain shrugged. "I know the going rate for a good groom or a stable hand."

Lillie shook her head, but smiled. "I'm sure there's no comparison. What about Abigail's previous housekeeper? The one who retired. Can we get in touch with her?"

"I guess. She was planning to move to Florida. I don't know if she's still around." Swain opened the Internet browser of her cell phone to look up the number, punched it in, and handed the phone to Lillie. "Mrs. Riley," she told her as the phone rang.

"Hello, is this Mrs. Riley? This is Lillie Wetherington, Abigail's granddaughter. Yes, her illness was unexpected. Thank you. Mrs. Riley, I could use a little help—"

Swain's attention shifted to the saucy redhead who entered the newspaper office and bounced over to the counter.

"Hey, Wanda. I need to run that ad again for a shampoo girl."

"Well, hey, Gloria! I've got it right here in the files. The last one didn't work out either?"

"Washing hair should be a simple job, don't you think? That's the third one I've fired that can't seem to do it without drowning my customers. Those little old ladies with their perms and weekly appointments are my bread and butter, you know. And they're fragile. You have to be gentle." Gloria dug around in a very large purse and pulled out a book of business checks. "Same as always?" she asked, clicking her ballpoint pen.

"Hasn't changed."

Gloria wrote the check quickly. When she turned to leave, she spotted Swain smiling from across the room. "My, my. Looks like this day just got a lot more interesting." Gloria's grin grew as she sashayed across the room. She skipped the usual social pleasantries and went right for a quick kiss on the lips, then ran her fingers through Swain's dark hair. "Looks like you're past due for a haircut, hon. My last appointment's at seven. How about you drop by around seven thirty?"

Swain glanced over at Lillie, who was ending her phone call. She stuffed her hands in the pockets of her jeans and shied away from the distraction of Gloria's combing fingers. "Can't tonight, G. I'll call and make an appointment for next week. I've got too much going on right now."

Gloria stepped back, but rested her hand possessively on Swain's forearm. "Oh, honey, I heard about Abigail. I am so sorry. When's the visitation and the funeral?"

"Friday night, Saturday afternoon. You coming?"

"Of course I am."

Swain glanced again at Lillie, whose attention was focused on Gloria's hand on her arm. "Uh, Gloria, this is Lillie Wetherington, Abigail's granddaughter. Lillie, this is Gloria."

"How do you do?" Lillie said politely.

Gloria didn't move her hand from Swain's arm, but smiled broadly at Lillie. "I'm just fine, sugar. You came all the way from England? Abigail never stopped talking about you once your daddy finally let her come for a visit. You have beautiful hair. So did Abigail. Now, you don't worry about a thing, hon. I'll call the funeral home right away and let them know I'll be over before the visitation to make sure her hair and makeup are perfect. It's the least I can do after all the years she came to my shop every week."

"Thank you." Lillie looked at Swain uncertainly.

"Gloria is…was Abigail's hairdresser," Swain said.

"For the past fifteen years," Gloria said. "We'll talk more at the visitation. I just love your accent." She squeezed Swain's arm and gave her a quick kiss on the cheek. "See ya later, stud. Gotta go. Time's money. See y'all Friday."

They stared after the chattering whirlwind that was Gloria. "Stud?"

Swain blushed at Lillie's amused expression. "Gloria's known for her colorful exaggerations."

"I see. Let's post this advertisement. I'm getting hungry. How about some lunch?"

"Only if you promise to help me exercise ponies this afternoon. That is, if you aren't too sore." Swain had noticed Lillie's stiff movements as she got in and out of the car.

"I'm fine. Perfectly fine," Lillie said lightly. "Of course I'll help."

"The old British stiff upper lip, eh?" Swain mimicked Lillie's accent.

Lillie raised an eyebrow at the tease and snatched the car keys from Swain's hand. "Let's see just how stiff your lip is, shall we? I'm driving, sugar," she said, parroting Gloria, but failing to duplicate the accent.

Swain made the sign of a cross and raised her eyes to the sky. "Bless me, Father, for I have sinned—"

Lillie's laughter drowned out the rest of her confession.

CHAPTER NINE

"But I want to help."

After their ride that afternoon, they had retreated to their respective residences for quick showers. Swain was already in the kitchen of the main house, pulling out the ingredients to begin preparing their meal when Lillie padded barefoot into the room.

Swain nearly choked. Lillie's cropped T-shirt and low-slung designer sweat shorts exposed long tanned legs and an expanse of soft, flat belly from which an emerald navel stud twinkled. Swain opened the refrigerator and pretended to be looking for a missing ingredient. She needed a moment to rein in her hormones and prayed the cold air would help cool the burn surging through her veins and settling in her groin. "Have you ever even boiled an egg?"

"Are we going to boil eggs?" Lillie stepped closer to peer into the fridge over Swain's shoulder, oblivious to her discomfort.

"No, but boiling eggs is the most elementary level of cooking." The jasmine scent of Lillie's shampoo filled Swain's nostrils and made the blood pound in her ears. She momentarily contemplated sticking her head, and other parts, in the freezer compartment.

"How can I learn if you won't let me help? You're no different from Mum's old cook, mean Mrs. McDonald."

Swain took a deep breath and closed the refrigerator, then laughed at Lillie's adorable pout. "You really do want to help, don't you?"

"Please. I've always wanted to learn to cook."

"Okay. Come stand next to me here at the sink. Your first lesson is how to clean shrimp."

Swain pretended not to notice the expression of revulsion on Lillie's face when she slapped a large, cold shrimp in her hand before grabbing one for herself. "You hold it in your left hand like this, then use your right hand to pull the head off."

Lillie turned a little green, but followed Swain's movements.

"Now peel off the shell except for the very end of the tail. Look for the dark vein that runs down the spine of the shrimp and use your knife to slice alongside and extract it." Swain demonstrated.

Lillie clumsily mimicked her and beamed when she held up her completed shrimp. Swain had already cleaned ten in the time it took Lillie to clean one.

"Excellent!" Swain popped the head off the final shrimp and handed it to Lillie to extract the vein. She smiled at Lillie's concentration. Swain let her eyes drift downward, slowing over Lillie's hips before gliding down those long, silky legs. This was fun. Her mind was already jumping ahead to other recipes she could teach her new student. Especially if she wore those sexy shorts every time she came in the kitchen.

❖

Even Lillie's silk nightshirt seemed to chafe her heated skin as she crawled into the big soft bed. Too big for one person, she thought. The house still seemed to echo with her and Swain's laughter as they cooked and dined together. Lillie couldn't remember when she'd had such a totally relaxing time.

The meal was scrumptious, but Swain's company was even better.

Lillie saw no sign of the temper that had flared the first day they met, no inkling of the insecurity she'd glimpsed in the funeral-home parking lot. She was treated, instead, to four hours of unadulterated Deep South charm, all wrapped up in one tall, dark-haired, blue-eyed, sexy package. Lillie sighed, then giggled. God, she felt like a horny teenager.

She smiled to herself, remembering the surprise on Swain's

face when Lillie had discovered Beau waiting patiently by the back door for his mistress and insisted that he join them in the house. She chuckled at the hint of jealousy in Swain's eyes when Beau adoringly attached himself to Lillie's side throughout the evening. She was sure she heard a muttered "traitor" when she stepped away to retrieve napkins from the pantry.

Lillie's face, and other parts, heated as she relived teetering on a stool to pluck a bowl from the top shelf of the cupboard, then falling into Swain's strong arms to be lowered carefully to the floor. When she closed her eyes, she could almost smell the raspberry-vanilla scent of Swain's skin and could still feel the strong heart thumping against her shoulder.

Swain's steadiness, the calm that radiated from her, was a magnet. Swain didn't seem to notice, but Lillie had seen the stable workers and horses gravitate to her, relax in the shelter of her confidence, and defer to her leadership. She'd also had a glimpse inside, albeit briefly, of the hurt and lonely orphan when Swain learned she was listed in Abigail's obituary. What did it cost her handsome new friend to be the post everyone else leaned on? She had seen only a flash of it that first night, but what would it be like if the tempest, the passion lurking under that composed demeanor was ever really unleashed? Lillie shuddered from both trepidation and anticipation.

She punched her pillows and turned on her side, away from the seductive light of the waxing moon and from her ruminations. She wasn't a swooning maiden. She was a grown woman, here to bury the family matriarch, take care of unfinished business, then disappear. No matter how tempting the sexy Ms. Butler was, she needed to stay focused.

❖

Swain tightened her arms around the pillow bunched under her cheek and stared out the tall windows at the tree branches dancing under the autumn moon.

Sharing a dark, barracks-like dorm with twenty-three other girls when she was growing up made her relish this spacious bedroom flooded with natural light. Lying on her stomach, she savored the soft cotton sheets against her breasts. Normally, she reveled in the privacy, the solitude that allowed her to sleep nude.

But not tonight.

She closed her eyes and imagined the press of smooth flesh and hard nipples against her back. Her nostrils flared as if to call up an elusive fragrance. Her skin tingled as her thoughts conjured the sensation of silky curls brushing along her bare backside.

She opened her eyes again to the moonlight and stared blankly at the stars. Because her mind wouldn't shut down, she decided to let it work. She ticked off the list of horses that needed to be ridden the next day. Maybe she'd head over to the track and look at that filly Tim had mentioned. If Lillie did close the stables, she would go back to Florida with a string of her own ponies. Maybe she'd buy that filly for herself. That's what she'd do tomorrow. But now, she needed to sleep.

There were no bedtime stories at the orphanage, so Swain had learned that if she would meditate on certain things, they'd sometimes fill her dreams the rest of the night. She closed her eyes, willed her body to relax, and concentrated on random images. Soon, she began drifting into that woozy place between consciousness and dreamscape.

She's pounding down the polo field on horseback with her mallet raised high, riding an opponent off course, leaning over her steed's shoulder and feeling the solid thwack as she connects with the ball. It flies between the goalposts and she lifts her mallet in celebration. Her teammates thunder toward her, guiding their ponies close enough to touch the heads of their upraised mallets to hers. Someone yells, "Who's our captain?" They begin to chant her name. "Swain, Swain, Swain!" The chorus of male voices swells and fills the air around her until its tenor changes. Now it is a single feminine voice, a siren calling her.

She's suddenly in a different field. Swain wheels her horse around and sees her. She's riding effortlessly, her thick mane of curls flying, her white steed cutting a path through the flower-filled meadow. Swain's heart lifts and she canters forward to meet her. When she reaches the center of the field, she jumps from her horse and holds her arms up, beckoning and catching her queen. They laugh as they fall onto the ground to roll in their bed of wildflowers. When they stop their tumble, smiling brown eyes blink up at her. She feels the length, the heat of the body resting under hers and lowers her head to capture the full lips that have summoned her.

Swain jerked awake. She rolled onto her back and brushed her hand down her belly. Her fingers slid between her legs and she groaned. She was wet. She was ready. Lillie had done this to her. It was Lillie in her dream.

Swain often enjoyed the company of women. Strong and athletic, or soft and feminine. It made no difference. She loved all types. She admired their strength and stamina. Their grace and intelligence charmed her. She enjoyed their beautiful bodies.

But when she was with Lillie she felt more than appreciation, something new—exhilarating, yet comforting.

She circled the hard prominence under her fingers and it swelled further. She needed release…release from the ache between her legs, from the pounding in her veins, from the primal need to take and be taken. Most of all, she needed to escape the spell Lillie was weaving over her.

CHAPTER TEN

A fter a restless night, Swain's internal clock that woke her every morning at six failed. Beau was still snoring, too, when she woke with a start and turned to look at the clock. *Shit.* It was a quarter to seven, and Tim was due any minute to trim hooves and reset shoes on five horses.

She rolled out of bed, took a three-minute shower, and dressed quickly. She was shoving the last bite of a hastily toasted bagel in her mouth when Beau began to paw at the door leading downstairs to the barn. He barked sharply and his long tail began to whip.

"Hold on," Swain grumbled, pulling on her boots. "You've never been that happy to see Tim before."

As she followed Beau down the stairway, she could hear Tim's unmistakable low rumble. But a softer, feminine voice made her pause on the steps.

"Maybe I should go check on Swain. She usually has the first horse in the cross ties waiting for me when I get here. She must be sick. That's it. She must be under the weather."

"She seemed fine when I saw her last. Perhaps I better go. She may not be dressed."

"No! I mean, what if she's contagious? I'll go. I'm immune to everything, never catch anything."

Swain shook her head at Tim's efforts to protect her from Lillie. He was most likely worried that she was upstairs lingering over some overnight company. It wouldn't be the first time. Fending off the deadly lash of Beau's tail, she opened the door at the bottom of the stairs and stepped out into the hallway.

"Beau!" Lillie called in a delighted voice. She knelt to give his ears a good scratch.

"There you are." Tim sounded tremendously relieved.

"We were just coming to check on you two." Lillie smiled up at Swain.

Swain smiled back. "Must have been the rich food. We overslept a little."

"Dinner was wonderful. I'm ready to sign up for the next class." Lillie's smile dimmed. "I guess we won't have time for that tonight."

Swain had to stop herself from smoothing the worried wrinkle in Lillie's brow. "Probably not. The visitation starts at seven, so you'll need to be there before that."

"You'll go with me, won't you?" Lillie's eyes were pleading. "I'm a bit nervous, not knowing anybody."

Tim jumped in to answer. "Of course she will. And I'll be there, too. You know me. And Rob will be there. You know him." He was babbling. Lillie seemed to have that effect on men, so Swain decided to rescue him.

"We'll all be there and promise not to leave you to brave it on your own." Swain squeezed Lillie's hand gently. She hated the worry on Lillie's face, so she changed the subject to something lighter. "Now, what can we do for you so early this morning? Did you really want to see us, or were you just hoping for breakfast?"

Lillie playfully bumped her shoulder into Swain's. "I've had breakfast, thank you very much. I do know how to pour cereal. I thought if I came down here and you put me to work, I wouldn't sit around all day fretting about tonight. If Tim is about to shoe horses, I'd like to watch and learn what I can."

Swain nodded. The more time Lillie spent around the ponies, the better. She clapped Tim on the shoulder. "Tim's the best farrier in the state. I'm sure he'd be happy to have an assistant."

"Sure, sure. I can always use the help," Tim said, beaming. He hitched up his sagging pants and motioned for Lillie to follow him. "You can help me get the equipment from the truck."

❖

"Okay. You have to hold the mallet firmly, but at the same time relax your wrist and shoulder so you can properly rotate them when you swing."

It had surprised but delighted Swain when Lillie asked to learn the basics of polo after she finished helping Tim shoe the horses.

"Like this?" Lillie's face was a study in concentration, making her practice swing stiff and forced.

"Not bad, but you need to relax more." Swain took the mallet from her and demonstrated again. When she handed the stick back, she moved around to stand behind Lillie. "You also need to get used to bending at the waist at the same time, like you would in the saddle, to reach all the way on the ground. Some riders hang over their pony's shoulder as they approach, then swing their arm. But that can throw your pony off balance as he runs. You should bend as you swing. It's all one smooth movement. Here, let me show you."

Swain wrapped an arm around Lillie's waist to pull her close. She was only about an inch taller, so it was a perfect fit as she molded her body against Lillie's back and wrapped her hand over Lillie's on the mallet. Together, they raised it. Swain's chest pressed against Lillie's shoulder blades as she guided her down through the sweeping movement. But Lillie remained stiff and the first attempt was jerky.

"Relax." Swain wasn't surprised at the huskiness of her voice. Lillie's clean scent was making her head buzz. The graceful curve of her neck was inches away from Swain's lips, and her hips pressing into Swain's groin was making it hard to think. Lillie trembled, then relaxed against her. They swung the mallet together again, this time in a smooth arc. "See? Exactly like that."

"Again?" Lillie's request was little more than a whisper.

"Close your eyes this time, bend your knees like you're in

the saddle, and visualize yourself galloping down the field." Lillie closed her eyes. "You see the ball midfield and turn your pony toward it. It's coming closer, closer. You're a long way from the goal, so you want to hit it as hard as you can. Don't bend yet. Wait. You're five strides away." Swain guided her arm to raise the mallet. "Now." As they swung the stick downward together, Swain prayed Lillie couldn't feel her nipples harden as they brushed against her shoulders. "Very good."

"I might have taken my eyes off the ball at the last minute and missed. Maybe we should do it one more time."

Was Lillie flirting with her? Swain smiled and was about to comply when Rob approached on the pony he'd been saddling in the barn. Suddenly, she was acutely aware of how their position—Lillie bent over with Swain pressed against her hips and back—probably looked. She abruptly straightened and stepped back as her neck and ears grew hot. "Um, I think you get the idea. Let's get you mounted, uh, in the saddle so you can try it on horseback."

At that moment, John led two ponies out of the barn, saddled and ready to go. He held Swain's mount while she gave Lillie a leg up on a seasoned bay gelding and handed her a mallet.

"Should I get Miss Wetherington a helmet?" John asked.

Swain considered his question, then shook her head. "We won't be mixing it up today, just practicing some swings. Unless she hits herself in the head with her own mallet, she should be okay."

"Perhaps you should watch *your* head," Lillie said, lifting her mallet in a mock challenge. She turned her pony and trotted off to join Rob, who was loosening up his horse by jogging in large figure eights.

John chuckled. "I'd keep an eye on that one."

"Doing my best." Swain grinned. "Toss us some balls out around midfield, will you, John?"

They took turns galloping toward the balls and smacking them toward the goalposts. Lillie missed the first few, but she was soon nailing them dead-on as her confidence grew. Swain watched her wheel her mount around to return after a particularly good hit. Lillie couldn't drive worth a damn, but she was a natural horsewoman. Her cheeks were flushed and her smile dazzling. *Beautiful.*

"That's probably enough for today," Swain said as Lillie drew near. "We need to walk these guys a bit to cool them down, then we can grab some lunch." She usually worked through lunch, but she didn't want to miss an opportunity to spend more time with Lillie.

"One more," Lillie begged. "I want to hit one more."

Swain laughed. "Okay. One more." She signaled for Rob to send a ball back toward midfield so Lillie could line up for one more shot. But Lillie didn't wait for the ball to come to a stop. She spurred her pony forward to intercept and raised her stick. In her eagerness, she leaned over her pony's shoulder too soon. When the experienced gelding shifted to adjust his course to accurately intercept, Lillie was thrown off-balance, tumbling over his shoulder and under his feet.

Swain watched in horror as the horse galloped on downfield and Lillie lay in the grass, not moving. She kicked her pony forward and, before he came to a full stop, jumped from his back.

"Oh, my God. Lillie!"

"Don't move her." Rob's face was pale as he looked down from his horse. "I'll go call the EMTs."

"Bloody hell," Lillie mumbled into the grass. She rolled over and stared up at them. "Don't do that. I'm okay, I think. Ow." She had started to push herself into a sitting position, but sank back and clutched her left arm.

"Go call them, Rob," Swain ordered.

Rob galloped away and Swain ran her hands down each of Lillie's legs, checking for injuries.

"My legs are fine," Lillie grumbled.

Swain cupped Lillie's face, looking into her eyes. Her pupils looked okay. She felt along Lillie's neck and gently along her skull. Damn it. She should have made her wear a helmet.

Lillie caught Swain's frantic hands as they slid along her collarbone, feeling for a break, and held them. "My head is fine, too. The only thing that hurts is my shoulder."

Rob galloped back. "John's calling for help."

"Help me up. I'm bloody fine."

When Lillie was standing, Swain wrapped a protective arm around her waist. "You should let the medical people decide that. Your arm could be broken or your shoulder dislocated. We need to take you to the hospital for X-rays."

"It doesn't hurt that badly." Lillie was feeling stronger now and a bit foolish for tumbling off her pony. "Stop making such a fuss. Haven't you fallen off a horse and gone arse over teakettle before?" She flexed her arm, then rotated her shoulder. "See. I couldn't do this if it was broken or dislocated."

Swain hadn't missed the wince when Lillie moved the shoulder. She began to brush some of the grass out of Lillie's hair and stopped. "Damn. You're bleeding." Swain stared at the small rip in Lillie's T-shirt and the red stain around it.

Lillie frowned. "Where?"

"Right here on the back of your shoulder." She turned Lillie and started walking her toward the main house. "Rob, take care of the ponies, will you? And send the medics up to the house when they get here."

Lillie sat on a tall stool in the kitchen and batted Swain's hands away. "Stop it. If you want to be useful, help me get this shirt off and clean up whatever's bleeding on my shoulder." She tugged at the T-shirt.

"Hold on just a minute." Swain pulled the bloody shirt away from the injury site and carefully helped Lillie strip it off over her head.

Lillie stared at the bloody tear in her shirt. "Oh, no."

Startled by the distress in Lillie's voice, Swain peered at the cut. The bleeding appeared to have stopped. Was something else wrong? Did Lillie have some health condition that made a small cut more dangerous than usual? "It doesn't look that bad."

"Yes, it does. This was my very favorite shirt and it's ruined."

Swain looked over Lillie's shoulder at the white shirt. "Celine" was written in a faint, pink script across the chest. "Celine?" Swain frowned. What woman goes around writing her name in pink on other women's clothes?

"Yes. I was twelve when Dad played a show with her and got her to sign it for me. That's not a stamp. That's her actual handwriting. See up here at the top in the small letters? 'For Lillie.' It was a teenage crush, but the shirt still means a lot to me because Dad was my hero that night."

Lillie held the shirt up for a clearer view, but Swain had her gaze fixed farther down, on the two creamy breasts nestled inside a skimpy, white lace bra. She jerked her eyes up as Lillie turned around. "Uh, right. The singer."

A knock sounded at the back door and Swain frowned. "Could you…" She grabbed the shirt in Lillie's hands and pressed it to her chest. "…uh, cover up a bit until I see who it is."

She went to the back door and stepped outside to greet the two paramedics—a stocky woman and a muscular, bearded man.

"What's up, girl? You don't look too hurt," the woman said.

Swain smiled. She knew the female paramedic well. She was heterosexual…and happily married. "Hey, Mandy. It's not me. It's Lillie, Abigail's granddaughter. She's inside. I don't think she's hurt bad, but she took a spill off a horse and has a cut on her shoulder. I'd appreciate it if you'd check her out."

"Okay. Let's take a look."

Swain held the door open for Mandy, but stopped her friend's burly partner with a hand in his chest. "We had to take her shirt off." She wasn't about to let some guy come in and ogle Lillie's breasts like…well, like she had.

"I'm a trained health professional."

"I don't care. You wait outside."

Mandy shook her head, but smiled. "I'll yell if I need you."

The man shrugged. "I'll wait in the truck."

Swain hovered while Mandy checked Lillie's pupils, palpated

ribs, and probed the sore shoulder. She cleaned the cut and closed it with two small adhesive strips. Then she and Lillie commiserated over the torn shirt.

"What about her shoulder?" The discomfort in Lillie's face when she tried to raise her arm concerned Swain.

Mandy took the hint to get back on subject and began to gather her medical supplies. "Take some ibuprofen for the pain and put an ice pack on it, twenty-minute intervals for the rest of the afternoon. Nothing appears broken, but if you have any excessive pain or swelling, you should get it X-rayed."

Still sitting in just her bra, Lillie had chill bumps along her arms because of the air-conditioning.

"Let's get you upstairs." Swain gently held Lillie's uninjured arm as she slid off the stool.

"Y'all go ahead. I'll let myself out. Oh, and when you shower, be sure to wash out those scrapes on your face and arm, then put some antibiotic cream on them."

"Thank you for your help," Lillie said. "It was nice to meet you."

"No problem. Y'all take care now."

Lillie didn't protest as Swain led her upstairs.

"Could you get me another T-shirt from the second drawer over there?"

Swain fixed her eyes on Lillie's boots, pulling them off for her, while Lillie carefully removed her bra and slipped the clean shirt over her head. Swain looked up only when she was sure Lillie had covered herself. "Why don't you get comfortable while I go find some ibuprofen and an ice pack? I'll be right back."

When Swain returned, Lillie lay with her eyes closed. Her thick blond eyelashes fluttered against pale cheeks, full lips parted slightly. She was loath to disturb her. But the fine arch of her brow was drawn with pain.

"Lillie," she said softly.

Dark eyes blinked open. "Oh, I almost fell asleep."

Swain cupped an arm around Lillie's shoulders to help her sit up. "Take these," she said, offering her two pain pills and a glass of water. The medicine taken, Swain cupped Lillie's chin and tilted her face toward her. With a damp washcloth, she carefully cleaned the scrape that marred her smooth cheek.

Lillie's gaze was warm, her voice feathery. "You have very gentle hands."

Swain frowned. "I feel responsible."

Lillie smiled slightly. "Oh. I was hoping I was getting the extra attention because you've decided that you like me."

Swain blushed and tried unsuccessfully to suppress a small smile. "I do like you, Lillie Wetherington, even when you try to be a show-off and fall off your pony."

Lillie sighed. "So much for impressing you with my polo skills."

Swain spread some antibiotic cream on the scrape and dropped her hands to her lap, but her gaze locked with Lillie's. "In the past year, you've lost both your parents and your grandmother. Now you've flown halfway around the world where you know no one, to figure out what to do with a bunch of ponies and property you've never seen before. I'm incredibly impressed with how brave you are."

Lillie's eyes shifted away. "I don't feel brave. I'm actually terrified about the thing at the funeral parlor tonight and the service tomorrow. I don't know any of the customs here. I'm afraid I'll do something socially awful."

"Don't worry. I'll be there."

Lillie looked up again, her gaze imploring. "Will you? I don't mean just drop in. Will you go with me? Help represent the family?"

"Lillie, I don't—"

"Please, Swain. Grandmum would want you there, I know it."

Could anyone say no to that beautiful face, those full lips? Swain shook her head, but smiled. "Okay. It starts at seven. I'll come back about five and fix us a sandwich before we leave."

Lillie kissed her lightly on the cheek. "Thank you. You are every bit the gentlewoman Grandmum said you were."

Swain stood and gathered the debris of her medical

ministrations. She stared down at Lillie, her eyes sad. "No, I'm not, Lillie. I'm a stray mutt Abigail hired to ride her ponies. Nothing more."

Lillie lay back against the ice pack Swain had prepared and closed her eyes as she listened to her retreat down the stairway. "Oh, Swain. Soon you will learn who you really are," she whispered. "I just pray you don't hate all of us when you do."

CHAPTER ELEVEN

True to her word, Swain stayed by Lillie's side for the two-hour visitation at the funeral home. She refused, however, to walk over to the casket where Abigail's body lay.

She wanted to remember Abigail tall and proud in the saddle. Abigail taking her turn sitting up with a sick horse. Abigail sitting in the summer twilight on the terrace and talking for hours about the ponies.

Swain knew what it felt like to have people absent from her life. The absence of nurturing parents was a numb, empty hole. The absence of the twin brother she hadn't tried to contact since the day they left the orphanage was a nagging guilt.

But the loss of Abigail in her life was something new. It caused a sharp, heart-deep pain.

Swain had friends. They were good people she genuinely enjoyed. They had her back when she needed a favor.

But her relationship with Abigail had gone beyond casual friendship. They had shared pieces of themselves. Abigail wanted to know what it was like for Swain to grow up in an orphanage. Swain wanted to understand what it felt like to find the love of your life, like Abigail had in her late husband. Abigail was the first person with whom Swain felt she could confide the bleakness of her childhood and her longing to belong somewhere, to someone.

She was still chewing on her thoughts as she and Lillie stood by the graveside and threw the first handfuls of red soil onto Abigail's coffin. The few who were invited to the interment dispersed, but

Swain stayed to watch the workmen. They sealed the vault, then shoveled dirt into the yawning hole until it covered Abigail and buried Swain's hope that the Wetherington estate would be the place she could forever call home.

Even under the September sun, she was cold inside and out. So cold it surprised her when she felt the warmth of Lillie's body against her side and the comfort of Lillie's fingers curling around her icy hand.

"We should go, Swain," Lillie said gently. "Mrs. Riley has gone ahead to open the house for guests, but they'll be expecting to see us."

Swain pulled her eyes from the workmen and stared at the fine bones of Lillie's long, manicured fingers grasping her larger, callused hand. They were an unlikely pair, the wealthy mistress of the house and the hired help. Still, it felt right. She felt better with Lillie at her side.

❖

Lillie surveyed the crowd drifting between the living room and the formal dining room. Where had Swain gone? The long process of making the transportation and funeral arrangements had given Lillie time to adjust to her loss. She had said her good-bye long before they stood at the graveside. But Swain's pain was still fresh and her absence worried Lillie.

She forced her attention to the man who had been rattling on without the least concern that she hadn't joined the conversation.

"I've been to England many times. They have wonderful polo there. I had the rare opportunity to see the princes play on the same team as their father. What amazing young men. The British have wonderful traditions. You must be anxious to settle things here and return."

Edward Hitchcock reminded Lillie of the politicians who carried their snobbish family crest on their chests, but would stoop as low as necessary to get what they wanted. He had been flattering her for the past twenty minutes, working up to his real purpose.

"I still need to decide about quite a few things, Mr. Hitchcock. I expect to be here a while longer."

"Yes. Well, maybe I can expedite matters for you. I don't want to be presumptuous, but the Wetherington stable has been a stalwart in this polo community for as long as anyone can remember. My son is to be married soon, and I am proposing to buy the estate in its entirety and keep the stable intact...as a wedding present for the new couple. I'd be happy to speak to Bonner about a price."

Lillie narrowed her eyes. She was losing her patience with these people. American men could be so arrogant. Yes, she was young. And, no doubt, they thought because of her hair color that she was less than intelligent. That rankled even more. She took a deep breath. When she spoke, her voice was tight and controlled.

"You, and the three people who approached me before you, *are* being very presumptuous. The fact is—"

"The fact is that the estate won't be settled for several weeks. Abigail had extensive holdings, some overseas." Bonner Whitney had appeared at Lillie's elbow and interrupted without apology. He gave Edward a stern look. "You will certainly have a more appropriate time to talk about this."

But Lillie wasn't backing down. "The fact is, Mr. Hitchcock, *if* the estate falls to me, I haven't decided what to do with it. If and when I do decide, you will have to deal with me and Swain Butler, not Grandmum's attorney."

"My mistake, Miss Lillie. But Abigail would have wanted to keep the stable intact. I simply was eager to put my offer to you before you accepted a lesser deal. Please forgive my indiscretion and accept my sincere condolences on your loss."

Edward wisely withdrew to collect his wife and say their good-byes now that he had accomplished his mission. His proposal was on the table.

Lillie took the tumbler of cognac Bonner had poured for himself and downed it in one long gulp. Perversely pleased that it burned as hot as her anger, she coughed and cleared her throat. "Thank you, Mr. Whitney, but I didn't need rescuing."

"Indeed. I was attempting to rescue Edward."

The twinkle in his eyes forestalled any biting remark she might have thought to utter. Bonner wasn't the enemy.

She shook her head and smiled. "I'm afraid I need a break. I'll check on things in the kitchen."

Mrs. Riley was busily washing dishes that the never-ending stream of guests had dirtied. Lillie settled on a stool and absently rubbed her sore shoulder. "Mrs. Riley, you must let me pay you for today. I know you postponed your plans to be here. I couldn't have done without you."

Mrs. Riley set the casserole dish she was rinsing in the drain and dried her hands on a dish towel. "Oh, no, dear. Your grandmother wasn't just my employer. She was my friend. I'm happy to do this for her."

"Then you should be out there with the other guests, not working in the kitchen."

Mrs. Riley squeezed Lillie's hand. "I'd much rather be in here doing something than out there mingling with that crowd. Don't get me wrong. Some are very nice people. Others—"

"Others can't even let the dirt settle on Grandmum's grave before they're going after her assets like hungry dogs," Lillie said bitterly. "And where is Swain?"

Lillie had awakened that morning sore and bruised in spots she didn't know existed. The ache in her shoulder was making her testy.

Mrs. Riley smiled and plunked down a bottle of water and two ibuprofen on the counter. "Swain said you'd need these."

Lillie narrowed her eyes. "Did she, now? Did she think that would make up for leaving me alone with that room full of sharks?"

Mrs. Riley patted Lillie's leg. "No, dear. She's down at the barn nursing a sick horse."

Lillie's irritation vanished. "Did she say which one? Is it serious?"

Mrs. Riley pointed purposefully to the pills, and she downed them when it became evident she wouldn't get an answer until she took her medicine.

"Just like Abigail, God bless her soul. Nothing's more important than those horses." She pulled off her apron and surveyed the remaining food. "Mary's here. I'll ask her to help me start clearing the table out there. That'll let everybody know it's time to leave. You just go stand by the front door to say good-bye when they shuffle that way. We'll have everyone cleared out in thirty minutes. Then you can go to the barn and see for yourself."

Mrs. Riley was as good as her word. Twenty-five minutes later, the last guest clasped Lillie's hand and offered his condolences on his way out the door. Lillie hurried up the stairs and changed her black dress for a comfortable pair of baggy jeans. She slowed only when she pushed through the kitchen door and found Mrs. Riley and her friend, Mary, meticulously labeling containers of food that covered the kitchen's table and most of the counters, then storing them in the huge refrigerator-freezer.

"You go ahead, dear," Mrs. Riley said. "We'll put all this away. I'll make a list with heating instructions for you. There's enough food here to keep you fed until you can hire someone to help around here."

Lillie impulsively hugged Mrs. Riley. "Thank you so much. You're a treasure. Please drop me a postcard when you get settled in Florida."

"Don't you worry. I'll keep in touch. Now go check on your horse."

With one last, quick hug, Lille was out the door and trotting toward the barn.

❖

The scent of fresh hay and oiled leather welcomed Lillie into the semidarkness of the barn where the night lighting cast sporadic soft pools of illumination down the long main corridor. The low murmur of Swain's rich alto and a brighter light halfway down the hall told Lillie exactly where to find her. As she neared the stall, she realized Swain was talking to her patient, not the veterinarian. Lillie slowed to a stop and listened.

"Come on, girl. You've got to get better. I sure don't want to have to ship you off to the vet school for surgery. We've still got trails to ride. You've got pastures to run. And there's Lillie. I think she likes you. Abigail would want you to stick around for Lillie."

Lillie crept forward to peek into the stall, her breath caught in her throat. Finesse, Abigail's mare, was the one ill. Swain was stroking the mare's back as she checked the drip of the IV suspended overhead. The mare's head hung low, but her ears twitched as though she was listening to Swain's every word.

Swain ran her fingers through her hair and her shoulders slumped. "Christ. I don't need you to leave me, too. Too much is changing too fast."

Lillie's throat tightened at the desolation in Swain's voice. Was this beautiful, gentle animal about to die? She crept silently back toward the entrance and slumped against the frame of the wide doorway.

What was she doing here anyway? She didn't want to care about these horses. She didn't want the attraction she felt to this woman. She didn't want to be burdened with the Wetherington name any longer.

A sudden thought ran through her like a cold chill. If word got out that Swain was a Wetherington, would she be in danger, too? Swain wouldn't run like Lillie planned to. She would never leave the ponies. That is, if she wasn't so angry that she told them all to go to hell.

Please, Lillie, you have to make Swain understand.

The night air was heavy with the scent of flowers. She closed her eyes and inhaled deeply. It smelled like Grandmum. She began to hum a lullaby, a tune Abigail said she had sung to Eric when he was a boy. She sang it for Lillie as they grieved for Eric and Camille. Her humming gave way to words, and she sang it softly to herself. When she finished, she felt another's presence and slowly opened her eyes.

"That's beautiful," Swain said.

"It's a very old lullaby. There are a lot of different versions of it, but Grandmum called it 'All the Pretty Little Ponies.'"

"Are you okay? I'm sorry I had to leave you on your own."

"I was standing here, feeling sorry for myself. Then the smell from the blossoms on that tree over there reminded me of Grandmum and, when I closed my eyes, it sort of felt like she was here, making everything all right."

"Magnolias."

"Sorry?"

"Those are magnolia trees. The blooms can smell pretty strong. It reminds you of Abigail because she wore a designer cologne that was a softer, lighter version of their scent."

Lillie raised her chin and squared her shoulders. "That explains it." She took Swain's hand and tugged her back into the barn. "Now tell me what's wrong with my grandmum's horse and what we can do to sort her out," she said as they walked toward the mare's stall.

"Colic. The vet was here earlier. He gave her a shot to relax her, filled her stomach with mineral oil, and started an IV. But he had to leave for another emergency."

"Will she be all right?"

"I won't lie to you, Lillie. She's not a young horse and her intestine could twist."

"Oh, no! Could she die?"

"If her pain gets worse or she doesn't pass some manure by morning, I'll have to decide if we should transport her to the veterinary school for surgery."

"If?"

Swain stopped. "Lillie, surgery can be very expensive. Finesse is well past her usefulness on the polo field. She's also too old to breed. And…and Abigail isn't even here anymore to ride her." Her face was serious as she studied Lillie. "We don't even know if the Wetherington stables will be here in a few months. If the horses are sold off, nobody will want an old mare with a history of colic. She could easily colic again and cost them a ton of money in vet bills."

But Lillie had already lost too much. She was determined not to lose anything else without a fight. "None of that matters. As long as the sign out there still says Wetherington, we will do everything possible to get our mare well again. Do you hear me? Everything."

Swain nodded, her eyes shining with new respect, and Lillie knew she'd said the right thing. At this moment, that felt very important.

"Then I'll do everything in my power to get her well."

Lillie persisted. "How can I help?"

"You pay John and me to take care of the horses. I'm going to the office now to call him."

"I want to help. Don't call John. Show me what to do."

Swain hesitated. "It means probably staying up all night, taking turns walking her every time she finishes a bag of IV fluid."

"I want to help," Lillie repeated stubbornly.

"Lillie, we could do all this and she could still die."

"We have to at least try."

❖

Sunlight was streaming in the office window when Swain woke with a start and rolled over, hitting the floor with a thump.

"I was just fixin' to roll you off that couch myself and send you upstairs. It's hard to concentrate on this feed order with you over there snoring." John frowned at her from his desk on the other side of the room.

Swain bolted up. "Finesse. Where's Lillie?"

"Easy." John went to the coffeepot and poured Swain a cup. "The mare's just fine. I cleaned a wheelbarrow-load of manure from her stall when I got here two hours ago. Ms. Wetherington went back up to the house to get some sleep. She did a fine job. She must have walked that horse most of the night while you snored in here." The coffee he handed her was black and strong, exactly what she needed.

Swain sipped it and glanced at the wall clock. Seven thirty. "We both haven't had much sleep in the past thirty-six hours. Finesse came down with colic Saturday. She'd pass a little manure, then stop up again. I didn't think she'd make it. Last night, we were so tired we started switching off every two hours. I walked her last at two this morning. Lillie was supposed to wake me at four to take over."

"Seems the dam burst about three o'clock. Ms. Wetherington said she watched her another hour and cleaned up the stall. When I got here at five thirty, the stall needed cleaning again and that old mare was rattling her bucket for her morning feed."

Swain groaned and rubbed her face.

John gave her a hard stare. Swain was his boss, but he was her senior by nearly thirty years and occasionally treated her like a daughter. "When I got here, the two of you were curled up on that old couch together like a couple of kittens. You sure nursing a sick horse was all you were doing?"

Swain choked in mid-swallow and sloshed hot coffee into her lap as she tried to cough up liquid that went down the wrong pipe. "Damn it." She glared back at him. "She's the boss lady. I don't fool around where my bread is buttered."

"I'm just saying there's a bed upstairs. You didn't both have to crowd up on that old couch."

She made a show of brushing the hot liquid from her pants rather than answer John's observation. "I'm going upstairs to shower," she grumbled. "When Rob gets in, tell him to saddle Domino and Astor. We'll work them first."

❖

Swain stepped into the shower before the water had time to heat. She needed it cold to wake her up and sharpen her focus. She shivered, but it wasn't from the water. It was from the memories that were beginning to surface.

She dimly remembered Lillie curling against her side to share the narrow space and murmuring that everything was okay now. She wrapped her arms around Lillie…just to make sure she didn't fall off onto the floor. Lillie snuggled her face against Swain's neck, her breath a whisper on Swain's skin as she instantly fell asleep.

Swain, on the other hand, was fully awake. Her hands were resting on the bare flesh of Lillie's back where her shirt had ridden up. Lillie shifted again and Swain bit back a whimper when her leg fit snugly against Swain's crotch.

Then Lillie was still, and after a long while, Swain was able to relax and slip back into an exhausted slumber.

She wasn't sleeping now. She was naked and aroused. She moved her soapy hand across her breasts and groaned. She slid her hand down between her legs. It only took half a dozen strokes to trigger her orgasm. But it wasn't enough. She wanted Lillie's fingers stroking between her legs, caressing her breasts, and tweaking her nipples. And she wanted her hands on Lillie's body.

Gasping for breath, Swain shut off the water and rested against the hard tile of the shower. What she remembered next troubled her more than her desire.

She recalled the cold when Lillie left her. Then a blanket was tucked snugly around her and soft lips briefly touched hers. She remembered fingers combing through her hair, gentling her back to sleep.

She stepped out of the shower and ran a towel roughly over her skin as though she could rub away the unfamiliar longing Lillie's touch had ignited. This was a very bad idea. It was stupid to think that, in a few short months, she could persuade Lillie to leave her life and friends in London and stay here with a bunch of smelly horses. It was a sure bet she'd be taking her bewitching beauty and that mesmerizing soft British accent right back to England.

Swain had never felt this unsure, this disoriented. Not even when she was eighteen and had stood outside the children's home with uncharted waters ahead and nothing to anchor her.

CHAPTER TWELVE

S wain slid her feet from the stirrups and dropped to the ground, groaning at the stiffness in her lower back. The colt she'd just exercised was green and his movements on the polo field jerky. Add to that, a short night sleeping on the too-lumpy sofa.

"You need to use some of that liniment you keep trying to push on everybody else," John commented, slipping off the colt's bridle and exchanging it for a halter.

Swain glanced wistfully toward the house while John unsaddled the colt. "I'd like to go up to the house and have a good soak in that hot tub by the pool, but I'm not sure I could stay awake that long."

John handed the saddle and bridle to an assistant groom. "Well, I think you're just going to have to manage. Miss Lillie called about an hour ago. She wants you to come up there when you're finished here for the day."

Swain didn't miss John's use of Lillie's first name and followed as he walked the colt to the wash stall and hooked him into the cross ties.

Rob joined them, slouching against the wall. "Did she say what she wants?" All of the stable's employees were nervous waiting for Abigail's will to be read.

John's face was thoughtful as he sponged the sweat off the colt's dark hide. "Nope, she didn't say. We had a good little chat, though. She's a really nice young woman. Smart, too."

When Susan or some other local woman stumbled down from Swain's quarters in the early morning hours, she appreciated the fact that John wasn't one to talk about another person's business. But she was tired, so his tendency to be tight-lipped about his conversation with Lillie was irritating her now. "She's probably been sleeping all day while I worked. I'll head up there after I shower and grab something to eat."

"She said send you up right away. Maybe you need to go see what she wants before you go bad-mouthing her."

Chuckling at John's reprimand, Rob chimed in. "I heard *you* were the one sleeping most of the night while she took care of the sick horse."

Swain scowled but didn't answer. Men. Just show them a pretty face and loyalty went flying out the window.

❖

That pretty face nearly took her breath away when she opened the back door. Lillie had pinned her hair up in a loose twist, accentuating her delicate features, and was lost in concentration as she studied the written instructions in her hand and compared them to the timer on the microwave.

"You really don't have to watch it cook. The microwave shuts off when the time's up."

Lillie wheeled, a broad smile illuminating her face. "Hello. I hope you aren't too tired to be hungry. I'm cooking dinner for us."

Swain had nursed her grumpy mood all the way to the house, intending to let Lillie know she didn't appreciate being summoned at the end of a long, exhausting day. Instead, she could feel her traitor face stretching into a smile that matched Lillie's. "Should I be worried?"

Lillie put her hand on her hip and gave Swain a mock glare. "Of course not. I have expert instructions." She hesitated and glanced at the microwave. "I'm just not sure how to tell when something is done. The instructions say, 'between six and eight minutes.' How do you know if six is enough or eight is too many?"

Swain laughed. "Well, you won't be able to tell by staring at it. You cook it until the middle's hot enough."

Lillie dropped her chin and shook her head. "Everything is so simple for you."

Swain noticed for the first time the faint lines and shadows of fatigue on Lillie's lovely face and wondered if they were still talking about cooking. "Few things are as simple as they seem."

Lillie looked up and her eyes were so full of longing and sadness that they tore at Swain's heart. She took Lillie's hands in hers and stepped closer. She was inches away from pulling Lillie into her arms, a breath away from tasting her full lips when the buzzer on the microwave sounded.

The moment between them gone, Lillie stepped back to retrieve the casserole. She didn't say anything, but dug a forkful out of the center of the dish and held it out for Swain to taste.

Swain closed her eyes and hummed her approval. "God, that tastes just like Mary Chandler's turkey-supreme casserole. I don't know anybody who can duplicate this, even with the recipe."

Lillie gave a chagrined shrug. "Okay. I confess. It *is* Mrs. Chandler's casserole. It was left over from Saturday, and I just reheated it according to the instructions Mrs. Riley left."

"Wow! I'm starved." Swain looked at the table for the first time. It was neatly set for two with fresh salads, linen napkins, and polished silverware next to both plates. The only thing missing was candlelight. "Everything looks great."

Swain politely pulled out a chair to seat Lillie. Lillie smiled at Swain's compliment, but put her hand out to stop her from also sitting.

"Would you please let my other dinner guest in?"

Swain was confused. She saw only two plates. "I didn't hear the doorbell."

Lillie pointed toward the back door and called out. "Beau?" A low woof and rattle of the doorknob confirmed the big dog was waiting patiently by the door. When Swain opened it, Beau gave her a haughty glance and trotted immediately to lie next to Lillie's chair. Swain rolled her eyes, but took her seat and they hungrily dug into the food.

They chatted as they ate, about Finesse and the other horses.

When the conversation moved to the people who came to the house after the funeral, Lillie aggressively stabbed at her salad.

"Some of them made me so angry, looking over Grandmum's paintings and furniture like they were at an estate sale. Several actually approached me with offers for—" She stopped.

Swain waved her fork dismissively, realizing that Lillie was afraid talking about selling the horses would invite another bout of Butler temper. "I got my first inquiry about the ponies an hour after we got home from submitting Abigail's obituary to the newspaper. They're like buzzards circling."

Lillie stopped stabbing her salad. "Yes, well, Bonner Whitney helped me fend off the most persistent bidder. He wanted to buy the entire estate, stable and livestock included."

"Really? Who was that?"

"Edward Hitchcock. He wants to give it to his son as a wedding present."

Swain frowned at her plate, her fingers worrying her napkin. If Susan and Jason married and lived in Abigail's house, she could kiss her privacy good-bye. Susan would be knocking on her door every other night.

"You don't like Hitchcock?"

"No, Edward's fine."

"You don't like his son?"

"Jason's a great guy."

"Then what is it?"

"Nothing. It's a good offer. You should consider it. I'm sure Jason would keep all the ponies, including letting Finesse enjoy her retirement years here."

She'd have to go back to the Florida polo fields for sure. Susan was fine for an occasional tumble, but hell would freeze over before Swain would be Susan's employee. She began to clear the dishes from the table.

Lillie put the casserole dish on the floor for Beau to finish. "I know you must be extremely tired, but could I ask one more small favor? It shouldn't take long."

"What can I help you with?" She was relieved at the subject change.

"I must have received thirty applications already for the housekeeper's job, and the advertisement will be in the paper for several more days. I was hoping you could look through this first lot for any names you recognize. I don't intend to interview more than ten, so I'd welcome any input to help me narrow the pool."

"Sure. I can do that."

Swain finished the dishes while Lillie spread the stack of applications across the table. Swain glanced through them as Lillie booted up her laptop and prepared to make notes.

"Not this one. She was dismissed from her last job for stealing."

"Oh. Was she arrested?"

"No. Her father's a minister in town, so they didn't press charges."

"She goes in the reject pile then."

"Don't know this one, or this one." Swain glanced at the next and automatically put it in the reject pile.

"What's wrong with her?"

"She'd want to do more than change your bedsheets."

Lillie found it amusing that Swain was being protective. "Is she attractive? Maybe I wouldn't mind."

Swain narrowed her eyes. "This girl's looking for a Sugar Mama."

"Sugar Mama?"

"Some rich woman to spend money on her. You'd get very little actual work out of her."

"I see. Perhaps I'll give that one a pass then."

Swain nodded curtly and resumed leafing through the applicants. She stopped. "Hey, this one's a guy!"

"A man? I don't think so." Lillie pursed her lips as Swain read the resume.

"It would be like having a butler. That could be kind of cool. Maybe he's gay. Not too many straight guys would apply to be a housekeeper. You could go shopping together, watch soap operas on television, lunch together." She held out the resume for Lillie to peruse.

Lillie pointed to the reject pile. "I don't watch 'soap operas,' as you call them, and I'm sure I wouldn't be comfortable alone with a man in the house," she said tightly.

Swain shrugged and let the matter drop. She picked up a single sheet that was more of a letter than a resume. "Remember the woman who was helping Mrs. Riley? That was Mary Chandler." She handed the paper over to Lillie.

"That was her delicious casserole we just ate?"

"Yes."

"She doesn't list any job experience."

"She's had lots of experience she didn't put in that letter. She organizes the fund-raiser each year to buy school supplies for needy children. And, if anybody's sick in the community, you can bet Mary will take over a ham or some soup—something to make them feel better. She has a great reading voice and records books for people whose eyesight is failing. It's nothing professional, just her in her living room with a digital recorder. They keep them at the local library where people can check them out."

"She sounds like she's already busy enough."

"Yeah, well. Her husband got laid off from his job last year at the nuclear plant where everybody around here works. That's probably why she's looking for a job that pays. But I'm sure you have a lot of applicants with real experience."

"I'll put her in the 'consider' pile." If Swain respected this woman so much, maybe she'd keep her on after Lillie left and Swain took her rightful place as the Wetherington heir.

Swain held up the last resume Lillie had printed. "Is this it? Do you have more?"

"I can check my e-mail."

Swain moved to look over her shoulder. "Hey, that's me." Lillie's screensaver was a slide show of her and the guys practicing on the field out back. "Where did you get these?"

"I took them from the balcony the first morning I was here."

Swain looked at her with new respect. "Wow. These are really good."

Lillie blushed and tapped the keys for her e-mail to download. While they waited, Swain took a closer look at the "consider" pile to see if any had references she recognized.

It was Beau's whine that alerted her something was wrong. He had been lying next to Lillie's chair, but was now sitting up with his head resting on Lillie's thigh. Lillie had her hands frozen, suspended over the keyboard. Her face was pale.

"Lillie, are you okay?" When she didn't answer, Swain grasped one of her hands. It was ice-cold. "Hey, are you okay?"

Lillie shuddered and dropped her hands but held tight to Swain's. She closed her eyes and leaned back. Beau licked at their joined hands and whined softly. "I guess I'm more tired than I thought. If I offer you dinner tomorrow night, do you think we could continue this then?"

Swain rubbed Lillie's hand with hers. "Are you sure? Maybe you hit your head when you fell the other day. Do you have a headache?"

Lillie gave her a weak smile and withdrew her hand. "I'm fine. Just tired. Thank you for being concerned."

But Swain could feel her nervousness. Lillie's other hand was clutching the wiry ruff of Beau's neck. "Okay. I'll go and let you get some rest." Swain stood. "You know, don't you, that hitting 'one' on any phone in the house speed-dials my cell?"

"Yes, you told me earlier, and I saw the list by the phone in the office. One for you, two for the barn office."

When Lillie stood and walked Swain to the door, Beau pushed past them and acted as a sentry outside, eyes and ears alert as he scanned the yard.

"I'll see you in the morning, then."

Lillie's hand on her arm stopped her. "I was wondering about the alarm." She pointed toward the set of buttons on the wall next to the door. "Does it work? I haven't noticed it being on since I got here."

Swain was surprised. Until now, Lillie had seemed perfectly at ease in the house. "It works fine. I just never activate it unless I plan to be gone overnight. Somebody's around most of the time. It'd be pretty hard for burglars to carry off much without someone noticing. So, I leave it off for the cleaning people."

"I'm just not used to such a large house. It gets a little scary being here alone at night. I'd feel better if the alarm was on."

Something in Lillie's demeanor triggered Swain's protective instincts. What wasn't Lillie telling her? "That's not a problem. The cleaning people have the code. I'll let them know it'll be on if nobody's at home." She showed Lillie how to activate and deactivate the system.

Lillie crossed her arms over her chest and stared at her feet. "I don't mean to be such a scared ninny."

Swain stepped close, ducking her head to capture Lillie's gaze and hold it. "You should have told me before now that you were uneasy in the house alone."

Lillie's palm was soft against Swain's face. "It's fine. It didn't bother me at first because I was too tired and too stressed to think about it." She gently kissed Swain's cheek. "You're very sweet to worry about me." Her thumb caressed Swain's lips before she dropped her hand. "Thank you."

Swain blinked slowly, forcing down the desire that tore at her. She wanted to pull Lillie against her, to fill her arms with Lillie's warmth, fill her head with Lillie's scent. Instead, she stepped through the open door and out into the night. "Sweet dreams, Lillie."

CHAPTER THIRTEEN

L illie watched Swain walk down the long drive to the barn. Beau hesitated, looking back at the house, then finally followed his mistress. She set the alarm and turned to stare at her laptop, hugging herself for a long moment before she returned to her chair and clicked her e-mail open.

She stared at the e-mail header, and the terror of what might be stalking the Wetheringtons flooded back.

Lillie had called her off-again, on-again girlfriend, Rayne, for a night out. After sharing a bottle of wine over dinner, they were starting to feel on again, so they left the restaurant for a nearby women's bar, where they danced and imbibed liberally.

"Come home with me, love," Rayne purred as they stumbled out of the bar. *"I'll drive you back to get your car in the morning."*

Rayne ran a fitness center and was always a good tumble. It was exactly what Lillie needed to forget her troubles.

"Just let me get my mobile from the car so I can let Grandmum know I won't be home."

"I'll walk with you."

"No need. I'm just around the corner."

Rayne lit a cigarette and propped herself against her car to wait.

Lillie didn't see him. The side street wasn't as well-lit as the main street, so the alley near her car was completely dark. Also, the alcohol she'd consumed had dulled her watchfulness.

He jerked her into the alley and used his weight to crush her against the rough brick wall. She tried to scream, but his sweaty hand covered her mouth. He reeked of cigarettes and whiskey.

"What would Daddy say if he knew his little girl was a muff-diver? Do you lick her pussy or does she lick yours? Maybe you lick each other at the same time." He pressed his hips forward and she could feel his erection through their clothes as he rubbed against her belly. She struggled to free herself. "I guess this means you'll never give Granny another little Wetherington, huh?"

He wedged his thigh between her legs and ran his hand inside her shirt to roughly squeeze her breast. "Well, you know what? I can help you with that." He began to fumble with his pants.

Lillie bit hard on the hand that covered her mouth and he jerked it away from her teeth. She filled her lungs and screamed as loud as she could.

"Lillie?" Rayne's boots hit the pavement loudly as she ran toward them.

"Bitch!" he growled, before drawing back his fist and hitting her so hard her teeth cut into her cheek.

He fled down the long alley, disappearing into the darkness. Rayne skidded around the corner and immediately ran to Lillie, letting the assailant escape.

The police took a report, but because she wasn't seriously hurt, they did little to investigate. Then, shortly after she received the first e-mail from him, Abigail's accident happened. In his next e-mail, he bragged that he had pushed her into the path of the car.

Lillie went to the police again, but her stalker was very Internet-savvy and they were unable to trace the origin of his messages.

She paused over the keyboard. Perhaps the stalker thought she was still in London. She opened his e-mail and her hope dimmed.

I watched you board at Heathrow. Did you think I didn't know about the estate in South Carolina? I am coming to you soon.

Could she have been more foolish? She could give the police little description of him other than he was a white man, who wore dark clothing and a black ski mask. But she'd never forget that voice. And he had easily tracked her here.

Her panic rose like bile in her throat. She needed to leave now. She could talk with Mr. Whitney about liquidating and depositing whatever Abigail had left her into an account she could access from anywhere in the world she happened to end up.

What about Swain? Damn it. She shouldn't care, but she did. Lillie closed her eyes. She wasn't sure how much more she could deal with, but she had to calm down and think this through. Wetherington blood might not flow in her veins, but they had been her family since she was four. She loved them. She owed them. And now there was Swain, the lost Wetherington, to worry about.

Secrets are like sleeping dogs that bite when startled awake. If they must be roused, then call them forth softly.

Damn the bastard who was stalking her. He wouldn't chase her off before she did what had been asked of her. She would stay until the will was read, then tell Swain everything. It would be up to her to protect herself after Lillie was gone.

CHAPTER FOURTEEN

They settled into a comfortable routine over the next week. Lillie would start the day reviewing resumes and checking references. About midmorning, when Swain and Rob finished working the first group of ponies, Lillie would take a break and walk down to the barn. They would saddle whatever pair of horses needed exercising and work them on the trails for a couple of hours. Lunch would be something light in Swain's apartment, then they went about their separate tasks until Swain came up to the house to prepare dinner and review Lillie's progress in hiring a housekeeper.

On Friday, Lillie was running a bit late, conducting her last interview from her list of ten finalists.

In her late twenties, Catherine Strom was poised and attractive. Her resume was impeccable and she was a licensed chef. Lillie had included her in the finalists to be interviewed because she listed Swain as a reference.

"How do you know Swain?" she asked.

Catherine blushed and tucked a stray strand of auburn hair behind her ear. "We're friends."

"Have you known each other long?"

"About three years. We met in Columbia, where I was a cooking student. She's sampled my cooking, so I thought she could vouch for me."

Is that all she sampled? Lillie was annoyed at her jealousy.

"With your qualifications, I have to wonder why you're applying for this job. It's only temporary, a few months, most likely."

"That's why I'm interested. I was hired to take over the sous-chef position at a local restaurant. But, after I accepted the job and moved here, the man who has held that job for years discovered he'd have to delay his retirement until December to receive full benefits. I'm financially secure enough to sit around until December, but I prefer to work. I love cooking."

Catherine held up a grocery bag she had brought with her. "I realize I would have other duties, but your ad said the primary task would be to cook. I took the liberty of preparing an assortment of samples for you to taste and included several traditional English dishes."

Lillie was impressed. "Thank you. You're the only applicant to do that."

"I hope it may increase my chances, and they advised us to do it in cooking school," she confessed with a smile. "Would you like to sample some now? They're still warm."

Lillie studied Catherine. She wanted more than a housekeeper. She wanted someone willing to teach her to cook. She could easily see them shoulder to shoulder in the kitchen, giggling like girls as Catherine taught her how to prepare a new dish.

The sound of Swain's boots thumping against the hardwood flooring made both of them turn toward the open door.

"Lillie? Oh, sorry. I didn't realize you were still interviewing." Swain smiled at Catherine. "Hey. It's good to see you again. How are you?"

Catherine smiled back. "I'm fine. Thanks for letting me know about this opening."

Swain stepped into the room. "What smells so good?"

Catherine indicated the bag at her side. "I brought some samples to influence Ms. Wetherington in my favor."

Swain grinned as she peeked into the bag. "Yeah? That's not very fair to the other applicants."

Lillie was piqued at their familiarity. She was trying to conduct a professional interview. "Perhaps you could take the food to the kitchen while we finish up here," she pointedly suggested.

Catherine looked uncomfortable and Swain surprised at Lillie's brusque dismissal, so she softened her tone. "Please, if you don't mind. We won't be long."

"Sure thing." Swain smiled again and held up the bag. "Thanks, Catherine. This means we won't have to cook tonight." She disappeared through the doorway.

"It didn't start out that way, but Swain and I really are just friends," Catherine said. She apparently hadn't missed that Swain's "we" meant her and Lillie.

Lillie was embarrassed that she was so transparent. "I'm afraid Swain has been burdened with making sure I don't starve before I can hire someone to cook for me."

"She's quite a chef herself."

"Yes, she is." She gathered the pages of Catherine's application and stood. "I see that all your contact information is on your resume. I expect to make a decision over the weekend and notify everyone early next week."

Catherine stood and extended her hand. "It's been very nice to meet you. I didn't know your grandmother, but please accept my condolences."

"Thank you. Everybody here has been very kind."

She walked Catherine out and rested against the door after she closed it. Why hadn't she told Catherine that she and Swain also were just friends? Lillie shook her head and headed for the kitchen. She didn't want to think about why.

❖

Swain had unpacked the food and was taking some glasses from the cabinet when she realized Lillie was watching her from the doorway.

"What would you like to drink with your dinner?" she asked.

"Water would be fine."

Swain retrieved two bottles from the refrigerator and set them on the table, but Lillie didn't move to take her seat.

"I didn't mean to interrupt. I'm sorry. Every evening when I've come up for dinner, you were always waiting for me to get things started. When I came in and didn't see you or any food set out to prepare, I guess I worried that something was wrong."

"No, I should have rung you and let you know I was running late. I apologize for snapping at you. It's just been a long day."

Swain waved toward the table. "We shouldn't let this food go to waste. Catherine's a very good chef."

Lillie took the seat Swain pulled out for her and spooned up portions of steak-and-kidney pie for both of them. She took a bite and closed her eyes. "Mmm. This is incredible."

They ate in silence for several minutes before Lillie spoke again. "She's very pretty."

Swain chewed slowly, trying to decipher her tone. *Is Lillie interested?* Swain tamped down a sudden surge of possessiveness. Lillie didn't belong to her. And she liked Catherine. But not for Lillie. Swain stopped in mid-chew. Wait. Maybe that wasn't what Lillie was asking. "Catherine? Yes, she is. She told you that we once dated?"

Lillie nodded. "She insinuated that, yes." She put her fork down. "This is truly delicious, but I'm afraid I won't hire her."

Ah. Swain felt unreasonably happy that Lillie apparently wasn't interested in Catherine, but worried about Swain's interest in Catherine. She sat back in her chair. "Lillie, you can hire anyone you want. But don't pass her over because—"

"The reason—"

"Wait. Let me finish, please." Swain wrapped her fingers around Lillie's. "Catherine and I dated for a short time several years ago and have remained friends. Catherine's bisexual and has moved here to be close to a guy she's been dating pretty seriously."

"I see."

When Lillie squeezed Swain's hand and released it to pick up her fork again, Swain immediately felt the loss. "I just thought you should know that if you hired her, she wouldn't be hanging around the barn all the time with me."

Lillie waved her fork dismissively. "That hadn't crossed my mind."

Swain frowned. Maybe her first thought had been correct. "Or…in case, you were interested."

"Interested?"

Swain worried her napkin, folding and unfolding it in her lap. They hadn't acted on their attraction, but undeniably something more than friendship was simmering between them. Did Lillie feel the same attraction for Catherine? "Interested in asking her out."

"Oh." Lillie's smile started with just a curl of her lip. "She seems nice. And very attractive." Then it grew into an all-out grin. "But, actually, I hadn't thought of that either."

Swain was relieved, but wagged her fork at Lillie to let her know she realized she was being played. "Okay. So if neither of us wants to date her, why won't you hire her? We could eat like this every night. That is, if I'm still invited when you don't need me to cook."

Lillie looked up from her plate. "I hope you will continue to come up to share dinner. I enjoy your company. Very much."

"I enjoy your company, too."

They gazed into each other's eyes, letting the unspoken words hang between them. Swain finally broke the silence. "If not Catherine, who do you want to hire?"

"Mary Chandler."

"Really? Mary's an excellent choice. But what made you pick her over the others?"

Lillie shrugged. "She needs the job more. Her turkey casserole that we ate the other night was fantastic. And I felt instantly at ease around her. She reminds me of the mum of a friend I had in primary school. I loved going to my friend's house because her mum always had fresh biscuits baked and let us help in the kitchen sometimes."

Swain shoveled a forkful of apple crumble into her mouth and hummed as she chewed and swallowed. "Maybe we can get Catherine to share some of her recipes with Mary."

Lillie laughed at Swain's antics. "I like Catherine very much.

Maybe if we ask her over as a friend, we could wheedle a few recipes out of her."

Swain nodded. But she really didn't want anyone else sharing her time with Lillie. Not even her very good friend Catherine.

CHAPTER FIFTEEN

S wain looked in the mirror and grimaced at her reflection. What in God's name was she doing?

Lillie had accepted her invitation to go to the track and check out the filly Tim had urged her to consider. So Swain thought she'd take a little extra time and show her around the quaint, historic town. It was just part of her plan to fulfill Abigail's request that she teach Lillie what was important to the Wetherington family. Wasn't it?

Standing in front of that mirror, she realized she'd changed shirts for the second time, searching for the right one to bring out the blue in her eyes. Swain sighed. While she'd been seducing Lillie with ponies and polo lessons, *she* had unwittingly fallen prey to her big brown eyes and her sweetness laced with a dry British sense of humor.

The very thought of Lillie made her skin flush and her heart beat faster. When she awoke that morning, she'd lain in bed, wondering. Was Lillie still sleeping, curled around a pillow, the sunlight dancing across her soft features? What would it be like to kiss Lillie awake?

She stared in the mirror at the same reflection that always looked back when she combed her hair and brushed her teeth. She was also looking at a stranger. She'd never felt this inexplicable anticipation, this overwhelming need to be near one particular person. But anything more shouldn't, couldn't happen between them. "We're just friends," she muttered to her reflection. Maybe if she said it often enough, she'd believe it.

❖

The racers were ghostly shadows as they galloped around the training track in the damp fog of the early morning. The rhythmic pounding of hooves would grow louder and the shadows would materialize into horse and jockey as they approached the backstretch where Swain and Lillie leaned against the track's railing.

The sun was barely up and the October breeze carried a chill. Lillie wrapped both hands around the travel mug and took a long sip.

Her alarm had gone off while it was still dark, and she had dressed with her eyes barely open before stumbling downstairs to climb into Swain's truck at five thirty. Neither horse nor human should be up exercising at this ungodly hour, she'd complained. Swain only smiled and pressed the travel mug into her hands. She had been surprised to find it thoughtfully filled with Earl Grey tea rather than coffee.

A chestnut filly began to emerge from the dense fog, her jockey balanced in the characteristic half crouch. Lillie raised her camera and held down the shutter to shoot continuous frames. The young horse wore a headstall that held rubber half-cups over her eyes to limit her vision to the track directly ahead. She breezed by at a relaxed canter.

"That's the horse," Swain said, her eyes glued to the pair as they began another loop around the track.

"How do you know?" Dozens of horses were exercising on the long dirt oval.

"Tim said it was a chestnut and that Alex Steiner's the trainer, and that jockey is one of Alex's exercise riders."

"You're right. That's one of mine."

Swain turned to greet a tall woman who'd walked up behind them unseen. "Hey, Alex. How's it going?"

"Can't complain. I've got one or two that look promising this year. How about you?" Her face weathered by long hours in the sun, Alex was still a handsome woman with dark eyes and brown, shoulder-length hair. Her face, lined with character, begged to be photographed. Alex glanced over when Lillie squeezed off a few shots in her direction, then turned her attention to Swain. "I hear your team's the one to beat for the cup this year. But I also hear you may not have a team come tournament time."

Swain shrugged nonchalantly. "Idle gossip by wishful thinkers."

Alex nodded thoughtfully. "Maybe. But the scavengers are circling and, given the circumstances, I'm surprised to see you out here. I wouldn't think you'd be looking at horses when the ponies you have might be sold out from under you."

Lillie frowned. "I think that's a bit premature," she said sharply. "The Wetherington stable is not on the auction block."

Swain quickly interceded. "Alex, this is Lillie Wetherington, Abigail's granddaughter."

When Alex looked back at Lillie, her eyes held a new respect. "My apologies, Ms. Wetherington. I'm only repeating the local gossip. The horse community is small, and more than a few here would love to get their hands on Swain's ponies before word gets outside South Carolina and they have to compete against Florida money. She's got quite a reputation as a trainer."

"So I'm learning," Lillie said, stiffly. "You'd do me a favor if you'd circulate word that it will be another four to six weeks before my grandmum's will is read. We have no idea what her wishes are for the stables, so our stock is currently not for sale." Lillie leveled a hard stare at Alex. "Neither is my head trainer available for hire."

Alex glanced at Swain and grinned. "I'll pass that along."

At the sound of approaching hooves, they all turned back to the track. Alex stepped up to the railing and signaled her jockey. "Ease her into a gallop when you turn into the homestretch. Let her loose when you come round the turn into the backstretch," she told him. The jockey nodded and moved the filly into the flow of horses.

Swain spoke as the filly disappeared around the first turn. "Actually, I'm looking at this one for myself."

Alex clicked her stopwatch as her horse passed the halfway mark on the homestretch. "What makes you think I'll let this one go? She's fast. Very fast."

As the filly rounded the turn leading into the backstretch, she galloped alongside a long-legged colt. The colt's jockey glanced over at his challenger, then gave his horse full rein. The filly began to edge ahead, but the colt dug deep and regained the lost ground. Her ear flicked back in the colt's direction. Her jockey was working the bit and tugging to the outside, but the filly ignored him and drifted inward, bumping shoulders with the colt. When he faltered, she surged ahead, cutting him off.

"Yeah, I can see that she's going far as a flat racer."

Alex swore under her breath. "Make me an offer."

"I'll take her off your hands for twelve hundred."

Alex snorted. "She's every bit as fast at Nor'easter. Once she's made, she'll be worth twenty times that much."

"Takes at least three years to finish out a polo pony, plus I've got to feed her for at least another year before I even start. Her bones are too young for polo. How much longer do you want to feed and board a horse that's likely to be disqualified every race?"

"Three thousand."

"Do I need to mention the fines you'll pay every time she bumps somebody? Eighteen hundred."

"Two thousand and not a penny less." Alex glanced at Lillie, than back to Swain. "And I'm going that low only because you're using your own money."

"Sold." Swain and Alex shook hands. "I'll have someone pick her up tomorrow."

"Good enough." Alex extended her hand to Lillie. "Pleasure to meet you, Ms. Wetherington."

"Lillie, please."

Alex nodded. "Lillie, then. My condolences on your grandmother. Abigail was a well-respected horsewoman."

"Thank you. Grandmum loved her ponies. Whatever happens, I hope to do the best possible thing for Wetherington Stables."

Alex nodded thoughtfully, then slapped Swain on the shoulder. "You owe me a beer when you win the Cup this year."

Swain shrugged. "Might not win. The Whitneys may make an

offer too sweet to pass up on Nor'easter before we ever get that far."

Alex waved as she walked away. "My bet's still on you."

They turned back to the track and watched as the filly slowed, then the jockey walked her to cool down. When the pair exited the track, Swain turned to Lillie. "I need to catch that jock to have a few words with him," she said.

"I'll wait here and take a few more pictures."

Swain jogged after the horse and rider, and Lillie turned her gaze back to the track.

A tall, dappled gray colt shook his head, nearly pulling his jockey out of the saddle in his eagerness to stretch his legs. She smiled at the colt's antics as the jockey gave the young horse more rein. The colt's ears pricked forward and his nostrils flared as he stretched into a graceful gallop. These horses truly were bred to run and they did so with enthusiasm.

She continued to follow the gray as he galloped past a man standing next to the railing. Something odd, something uncomfortable jerked Lillie's attention back to him. The early morning fog had burned off, but the distance was too far to see his face clearly. She lifted the camera to peer through its telescopic lens. Fear gripped her, a tight vise around her heart. The ball cap pulled low on his forehead and a pair of aviator-style sunglasses concealed his hair and eyes. Even so, something too familiar about his shoulders, his stance sent chills down her spine.

He brought a set of small binoculars up to his eyes. Lots of people were watching through binoculars, but this man wasn't following the horses. He appeared to be looking straight back at her. He lowered the binoculars, but didn't move. He didn't need to remove his sunglasses for her to know he was still staring at her. She could feel his gaze raking her skin and she shuddered, her panic rising.

"Ready?" Swain was back at her elbow. "Are you in a hurry to get home or could I interest you in having breakfast somewhere?"

With her heart pounding and near panic twisting her stomach, eating was the last thing on Lillie's mind. Her panic began to recede, however, with the security of Swain's steady presence. She drew a trembling breath and tried to sound casual. "You have plans for us?"

"Indeed, I do," Swain replied, gallantly tucking Lillie's hand in the crook of her arm. She flashed a charming smile and exaggerated her Southern accent. "I would be pleased, Miss Lillie, if you would let me be your escort today," she said, guiding them toward her truck.

She glanced back to where the man stood. He was gone. She'd probably imagined him. She tightened her hold on Swain's arm. "I'm at your disposal."

❖

Their first stop was the General Elliott Inn, a bed-and-breakfast. The wide wraparound porch was dotted with chairs that invited you to rock and watch the horses in the pastures across the road at the New Bridge Polo Club. Swain took Lillie's hand and led her straight to the kitchen where Kate, one of the inn's two owners, was preparing breakfast. Lillie recognized her as one of the visitors who came to the house following Abigail's funeral. She was surprised to see several of the inn's guests also seated in the kitchen, watching the preparations.

"Hey, stranger. This is a surprise." Her hands busy with the food preparation, Kate presented her cheek to Swain for a kiss.

Swain obliged and pulled up a stool for Lillie to sit and watch. "Where's Ward?"

"On the golf course. I'd rather him be there than underfoot."

Kate smiled at Lillie. "Ms. Wetherington, welcome to my humble kitchen. Your grandmother would drop in from time to time and mooch breakfast. I hope you're here to continue the tradition. Can I set an extra table for you two?"

Lillie looked to Swain, uncertain of their plans. When Swain nodded, Lillie smiled back at Kate. "That would be delightful. Thank you."

"Swain, dear, do you mind? You know where everything is."

"Okay to set up on the veranda?"

"Yes. It's nice out and that's where everyone wants to eat today."

"Can I help?" Even though Lillie was surely safe in Kate's kitchen, she felt anxious without Swain at her side.

"I've got it. You should stay here and watch Kate make crepes. It's an art that she's perfected."

Kate chuckled. "Compliments won't get you extra servings, Swain Butler."

Swain grinned. "Worth a try." She peered at Lillie and hesitated. "Are you all right? You look a little pale."

"I'm fine," Lillie said, offering a weak smile. "A bit of breakfast will be welcome, though."

"You do look a little peaked, dear," Kate said. "Sit. Let Swain set up and we'll get you fed right away." She handed two plates of food to the couple who had been watching, and they followed Swain outside.

"Those two are regular customers and the only guests here this morning, so we're being a little informal." Kate plunked a glass of orange juice in front of Lillie and began another set of crepes. "Drink that before you fall out of that chair." She nodded in approval as Lillie obeyed. "Now, what brings you two to the neighborhood?"

"We were at the track early this morning to look at a horse, and Swain offered to show me around town. You're our first stop. The house, what I saw of it coming in, is lovely."

"Thanks. Though it's a bed-and-breakfast, the downstairs mainly revolves around the restaurant. I do some catering and we host special events like private parties, wedding receptions, and the like. The dining room is only open to the public on Friday and Saturday nights."

"So breakfast isn't open dining? I'm so sorry. I didn't mean to impose." She stood, intending to collect Swain and leave.

"Not at all. Abigail was always welcome, and you are, too. Any time at all. I'm not usually on my own, but my assistant got married and ran off to New York." Kate frowned. "This is a bad time, too.

I've got several big catering jobs coming up. It's so hard to find good help."

Lillie began to relax in the cheerful ambience of Kate's kitchen as the conversation edged out thoughts of her watcher. For that, she was more than grateful.

"Well, perhaps I can repay you for your hospitality by referring an excellent young chef who has just relocated here and is looking for work." She filled Kate in on Catherine's qualifications.

"She sounds perfect," Kate said. "You sure know a lot about her to only have been here a few weeks yourself."

"She was an applicant for the cook position I advertised, but way overqualified just for me. Swain has known her several years and referred her."

"Ah, I see. Just about everybody in town knows Swain."

Lillie was surprised at the surge of jealousy that washed over her.

Apparently reading her expression, Kate quickly explained. "Everybody knew Abigail and she often had Swain in tow." Kate paused and studied Lillie. "Please don't take this wrong, but I think Swain was the daughter Abigail never had. I could just choke that son of hers for cutting them off like he did. You were practically grown before she ever got to meet you."

Lillie stared at her juice and shrugged. "I'm sure Dad had his reasons, but I felt a bit cheated, too."

Kate resumed her cooking. "Anyway, those two are cut from the same cloth."

"I'm not sure I understand."

"Abigail was probably one of the wealthiest women in town, but would be the first to pitch in to help. Swain's the same way. She's not wealthy, but she'll ride horses all day and still show up to lend a hand to whoever needs help."

"She's been very obliging since I arrived."

Kate gave Lillie an odd look and chuckled. "I'm sure she has." She turned to extract a tray of tea biscuits from the oven. "Anyway, about a year after Swain landed in town, I got really sick with bronchitis one week and was completely booked with reservations for the weekend. My assistant was starting to panic at the thought of cooking alone for all those people. Swain heard about it and came right over. She's a chef, too, you know."

"Yes. I've had the pleasure of dining on her shrimp and grits."

Kate smiled broadly. "Fantastic, isn't it? She helped me the next weekend, too. She wouldn't take a penny for all she did while I was laid up." She handed Lillie two finished plates. "Swain should have a table ready. I'll join you after I check on my two guests."

Lillie found Swain on the veranda where she had set up their table a discreet distance away to allow both parties some privacy. The white linen tablecloth moved lazily in the slight breeze that ruffled a trellis of purple morning glories opening their petals to the sunshine.

She closed her eyes at the first mouthful. "These crepes are divine."

"Aiken is small, but has plenty of hotels and fine dining that meet the standards of people who've traveled all over the world," Swain said.

"Have you?"

"Have I what?"

"Traveled much?"

Swain snorted. "When you turned eighteen at the children's home, you were on your own with two hundred dollars and your clothes. I figured that, at best, I could get a bus ticket to Charlotte or Atlanta, where I hoped to find some way to support myself. But when they turned my brother and me out, we each got twenty-five hundred. I'd read about lots of places I wanted to see, so I figured I'd hit the road and work here and there until I found a place I wanted to settle." She laughed. "New Orleans was my first stop, then Florida. But I never got past Wellington once I saw them playing polo there."

"Did they tell you why they gave you more than the usual?"

"Yeah. They said it was restitution paid by the driver who killed our mother."

"Your mum was killed in an accident?"

"Yeah, sort of. She was in labor and driving herself to the

hospital. Another driver turned in front of her and she hit his car. She actually died of a blood clot several days after she delivered me and my brother, but the doctors said it resulted from her injuries in the car accident, not from giving birth."

Was Swain aware of how clearly her emotions showed on her face? Her expression went from hurt to angry to sad in a matter of seconds.

"The other driver was charged with involuntary manslaughter. I guess some judge decided that growing up without a mother was worth only five thousand dollars." Swain frowned. "I'll never understand people who think money can wash away their sins."

THIRTY-TWO YEARS EARLIER

Bonner Whitney placed a thick briefcase on the desk and opened it. "One hundred and fifty thousand dollars, Mr. Johnston."

Tyrell Johnston stared at the piles of money. It was more than five times what he made in a year fixing cars.

Bonner closed the briefcase and laid a paper on top, placing a pen next to it. "This is a legal document saying you will not bring any lawsuit or financial claim against my client in the future."

Tyrell put down the pocket knife he was using to clean his fingernails and grunted as he picked up the pen. He signed quickly and handed the paper to Bonner.

"Tomorrow, Mr. Johnston. Don't let your daughter miss that appointment." Bonner pulled a business card from the inside pocket of his suit coat. "This is the doctor who will take care of the problem. It's not a clinic. It's a private practice. Very discreet. All the medical expenses have been paid. It is imperative that this is taken care of immediately."

"Not soon enough for me," Tyrell muttered as he went back to cleaning the car grease from under his fingernails. "If I catch that boy sniffing around my daughter again, I'll shoot him."

"The family is eager to put this unfortunate incident behind them. Eric is on his way to attend a university overseas—to get a clean start."

He looked up with contempt. "Clean start? Mr. Whitney, I kin sit here all day and scrape at the grease from under my nails. But, like them filthy-rich Wetheringtons, ain't nothing ever going to get all the dirt off 'em."

CHAPTER SIXTEEN

S wain had insisted they take the Mercedes convertible that morning, and Lillie understood why when they drove slowly along the Avenue of Oaks on South Boundary. Huge trees lined the street on both sides, their branches creating a canopy over the roadway.

"This is so beautiful," Lillie said. "It must be spectacular when the leaves change color."

"They won't turn," Swain said. "These are Southern live oaks. They're evergreen so don't lose their leaves in the winter like other oaks. These trees were planted more than a hundred years ago when people were still driving through here in carriages."

She detoured a few blocks from the downtown specialty shops to show Lillie the historic Wilcox Inn, its huge white columns and second-floor veranda reminiscent of Civil War–era Charleston. A few blocks from the inn, they parked next to an old carriage house.

"This is Hopelands Gardens," Swain explained. "Fourteen acres of beautiful gardens right in the heart of downtown. Mrs. Hope Iselin donated it to the city. They called her the 'grand lady of racing' because she was a big supporter of the sport both here and in England. That's why the Aiken Thoroughbred Racing Hall of Fame and the Carriage Museum are also located on the property."

"Fourteen acres? That's a bit of exercise, isn't it?"

"Don't worry. We won't walk all the trails today. We'll tour the racing museum, then find a shady spot to take a break before I show you a real treat this afternoon."

The racing museum was filled with old photographs, trophies, and artwork, but Lillie's brain was beginning to overload with the seemingly endless history lessons Swain provided with each piece. Her version of a quick tour involved several hours.

"That was lovely," she said weakly, relieved when they stepped back into the sunlight of the gardens.

Swain blushed and looked at her feet. It was an adorable look for the usually suave trainer. "I bored you silly, didn't I? I'm sorry. Abigail and I used to spend hours in there. I forget that not everyone's that interested in horses and history."

Lillie smiled. The more she learned about Swain, the more she wanted to keep peeling back the layers of this complicated, enticing woman. "Kate was right. You are the daughter Abigail must have wished she had."

Swain didn't answer, turning away from Lillie to gather a blanket and picnic basket from the car. She waved toward a brick walkway. "Shall we?"

With her attention absorbed in the pictures she was constantly shooting of the squirrels and lingering fall flowers, Lillie was soon completely lost as the pathways wound around like an English maze. But Swain seemed certain of their direction and finally stopped next to a shaded pond filled with lily pads.

They spread their blanket on the grass and sat with the basket between them.

"I'm having a wonderful time," Lillie said, taking the glass of wine Swain offered. "Thank you for making the time to do this for me."

She sipped her wine, closed her eyes, and turned her face to the sun. They had risen early and she was a bit sleepy.

"I sometimes wished I was her daughter." Swain's voice was little more than a whisper, but it startled Lillie from her lethargy.

Swain's admission tore at Lillie's heart. She wished Abigail had found the courage to be honest with her. "You remind me of her, you know."

"I do? How do you mean?"

"Your love for the ponies and polo. Your air of confidence. You walk into a room and instantly command it."

"I don't know about that." Swain plucked at the grass under her hand, her expression guarded.

"You do. I envy you that confidence. You seem to know exactly who you are." As soon as the words were out of her mouth, Lillie realized her near slip. Swain was so innately Wetherington, Lillie had to constantly remind herself that she didn't know about her dad. Swain, of course, heard the words in an entirely different light.

"Swain Butler is nobody. Just a name my unwed, teenaged mother made up."

With all her talk of bloodlines, how could Swain look in the mirror and not see her own? Lillie ached to tell her.

Swain looked up at Lillie, her words bitter. "When you're introduced as Lillie Wetherington, people know who you are and treat you like you're somebody."

"I'm just the child of an unwed mother, like you, Swain," Lillie said gently. "All they really know is that the Wetherington family was kind enough to adopt me." But not Swain. That would be her first thought if Lillie told her now.

The conversation had suddenly headed down the wrong track. It was best to turn back to more solid ground. *Call softly.* She gave Swain her most impish grin. "Besides, I've seen people respond, too, when you're introduced."

"Yeah, right."

"They absolutely do. When they hear Swain Butler is around, they immediately hide their best ponies and lock up their daughters." Lillie wiggled her eyebrows suggestively, and Swain barked a laugh at her antics.

Her grateful gaze acknowledged Lillie's ploy to lighten the mood. "Let's pack this stuff and go have some fun."

❖

"Sailing?"

"No, but a lake near here has a marina that rents sailboats. We can do that another day if you like. That is, if you know how to sail, because I don't."

"Skeet shooting."

"Not today." Swain glanced over at Lillie. "You know how to handle a gun?"

"No, but I'd like to learn. I'll teach you to sail if you'll teach me how to shoot."

"Deal." Swain smiled at the opportunity to spend more time together. Lillie's playful guessing game had put all serious conversation behind them, and Swain was buzzing with the anticipation of how Lillie would react to the surprise she'd arranged. She ignored the nagging little voice that kept repeating, *She's leaving, she's leaving.*

She pulled the Mercedes slowly into a dirt parking lot with a large truck and long trailer parked next to a two-horse carriage. A matched pair of bay geldings turned their heads to watch them. "Come meet my buddy and help me talk him into a giving us a ride."

She chuckled at Lillie's eager scramble to get out while Swain raised the top and locked the car. She walked over to the wiry, white-haired man propped against the truck and shook his hand.

"These guys look great, Howard. How are they working out for you?"

"They're a pleasure to drive. But you'll find that out."

Lillie stood at the front of the rig, murmuring to the horses as she petted their long faces.

"Howard, this is Lillie Wetherington."

Howard walked over and extended his hand. "Pleased to meet you, Ms. Wetherington. Sorry to hear about Mrs. Wetherington. She had a lot of friends around here."

Lillie shook his hand. "Thank you." She stroked the nearest gelding's neck. "Your horses are very beautiful."

Howard nodded. "You've got a natural eye for good horseflesh."

"So are we all set?" Swain asked.

"All set," Howard replied. "I'll meet you back here in three hours."

"I owe you one, Howard."

"Nope. Just repaying one of the many favors you've done me. Y'all have a good time."

Lillie's expression was one of childlike joy. "We're going for a ride in the buggy?"

"This isn't just a buggy, Lillie. This is a lightweight competition carriage."

"You mean like a racing buggy?"

"Sort of. Instead of a flat track, the drivers have to take their team through an obstacle course, and they get points for their time as well as other things. One person sits up front to drive, and a second person stands on this platform in the back and uses his weight to help the carriage make tight turns by leaning in the right direction."

Lillie's smile disappeared. "I have to stand in the back?"

Swain laughed. "Not today. We'll go to a competition some time so you can see how it's done. But today, you can ride up front with me."

Lillie's smile was instantly back.

Swain helped her into the seat and climbed up beside her. She pulled on a pair of thin leather gloves and picked up the reins, then made a kissing noise and the horses moved slowly down a wide dirt path.

"This is Hitchcock Woods," she explained. "More than two thousand acres. A foundation solicits donations for operating and upkeep expenses to maintain it. Even though Abigail didn't ride here much, she was a regular donor. She supported anything equestrian."

"So it's not just for carriage driving?"

"Nope. Hikers, runners, dog walkers, horseback riders, carriage drivers are all welcome. No bicycles or motorized vehicles. Those would scare the horses." Swain flicked the long reins to softly slap them against the horses' backs, and their walk picked up to a trot. When they took a quick turn, Lillie wrapped one hand around Swain's arm and held on to the seat's rail with the other. Swain chuckled at her delighted expression. A road of hard-packed clay stretched before them. "Ready to go faster?"

"Yes!"

Lillie's fingers tightened around her arm when she flicked the reins again and gave a firm "hup." The pair of geldings picked up their pace to a blazing-fast trot, their bodies moving in perfect sync.

The carriage swayed as it bumped over small ruts. Lillie laughed wildly, the sound a melodic accompaniment to the rhythmic hum of the wheels and the steady beat of the horses' hooves. Swain's chest swelled because she was responsible for Lillie's pleasure.

She slowed the horses as they neared the end of the straightaway, then turned them onto a winding trail before gently pulling on the reins.

"Why are we stopping?"

"You want to learn to drive, don't you?" She began to peel the leather gloves from her hands.

"Really?"

"Sure. But you have to wear gloves. These reins will rub blisters on your hands before you know it." Instead of handing the gloves to Lillie, Swain took her left hand and fitted the supple leather over Lillie's slender fingers.

"I know how to put gloves on," Lillie said quietly in Swain's ear. Swain felt her cheeks flush, but she didn't look up from her job of adjusting the glove over Lillie's hand. She couldn't stop herself from finding excuses to touch Lillie, and she'd been caught. Chastised, she offered the other glove, but Lillie held out her right hand and made no move to take it. Swain looked up to see her smiling.

"You did such a good job with the left, I thought you should put this one on as well."

She carefully fitted the second one to Lillie's hand, taking more time than necessary. "Soft on the bit," she coached when she handed over the reins.

Lillie felt tentative at first, but the team was very responsive. They took the curves slowly, her confidence growing with each one. "Shall we go faster?"

"As soon as you feel comfortable."

Lillie lightly slapped the reins against the broad backs and the horses quickened their pace. She directed them around a wide turn to find another long straightaway stretching before them. As if anticipating her thoughts, the horses flicked their ears back and forth, awaiting her command.

She lifted the reins again and uttered a soft "hup" as she'd heard Swain do. The horses smoothly shifted from a fast walk to a jog. Another flick of the reins and they moved to a fast trot. She bent forward, this time her "hup" bold and firm. They responded, stretching their legs in the ground-eating pace of their Standardbred bloodlines.

Lillie's blood sang and laughter bubbled up from deep inside, only to be carried away by the wind that cooled her cheeks and whipped her hair.

Swain's arm was firm against her back, holding on to the seat. When they hit a shallow rut and the carriage swayed, Swain's hand moved to her rib cage, steadying her since her hands were occupied with the reins.

Swain touched Lillie's shoulder and pointed to where the road disappeared into a curve just ahead, so Lillie reluctantly slowed the team to take the turn. The horses had obediently shortened their stride, but tossed their heads impatiently.

"They want to go again and so do I," Lillie said emphatically.

Swain laughed. "There's more to driving than going fast. Bear off to the right when you come to the next fork."

Lillie learned how to settle the team into an easy trot and, after a long series of practice turns, they were back on the straightaway and Swain nodded permission to open them up again. At the road's end, she signaled for Lillie to slow them to a walk. The sleek bays resisted at first, pulling at their bits to be off again, but finally settled. Like the horses, Lillie wasn't ready to stop.

"Your friend said he wouldn't be back for three hours."

Swain indicated her watch. "It's already been two and a half. We need to take the last thirty minutes to cool them down. If we walk them back from here, we should hit the parking lot about the same time as Howard."

Lillie relaxed back against the seat, suddenly aware that Swain hadn't moved her arm even though she didn't need to hold on. Only the clop-clop of the horses' hooves against the hard-packed dirt filled the comfortable silence. A whisper of melancholy curled around her and she could feel Swain watching her.

"Why the sad look? Aren't you having fun?"

"I'm having a fantastic time. I'm sorry now that I waited until Grandmum died before I visited here. I missed so many opportunities to share this with her." If only Lillie had come sooner, Grandmum might still be alive. She looked up at Swain, whose blue eyes were dark with understanding. "But I'm glad I got to share it with you."

"We all have regrets, Lillie, but you shouldn't dwell on them," Swain said, stroking Lillie's back in a comforting gesture. "People make mistakes. You just have to take what you can learn from them and let them go. I'd never win a polo match if I didn't."

Lillie hoped Swain remembered that when Abigail's secret was finally revealed.

CHAPTER SEVENTEEN

"This is probably a stupid question, but are you hungry? We can just go home if you aren't."

"Starving." Lillie eyed the odd house where Swain stopped the car. "Quaint."

It featured a traditional Southern wraparound porch enclosed on one side with large windows. Reminiscent of French provincial architecture, the building's second story was a square roof embedded with windows trimmed in hot pink. Lillie found it rather gaudy.

"Does it remind you of anything?" Swain pointed to a hand-painted sign by the entrance to the parking lot. *Riley's Whitby Bull* was printed next to a lighthouse sporting pink stripes.

"Whitby? As in the seaside town of Whitby in North Yorkshire?"

"Yeah."

"I went on holiday there several times with friends to see the regatta."

"We have a rowing regatta near here a couple times a year."

Lillie grinned. "My friends and I enjoyed the women rowers. They were notorious for the parties they threw after the boats were put away."

Swain's expression darkened. "Women rowers." She growled the word like it was a bad taste in her mouth. "I'd have thought you'd be above that sort of thing."

Her reaction amused Lillie. It sounded like she had some experience with the rowdy rowers, too. "We were first-year university students celebrating the end of the term. I can't say that sort of thing still appeals to me."

"I'd hope not," Swain muttered, guiding them inside the restaurant.

An attractive young hostess greeted them. "Swain! I didn't see you on the reservation list." Ignoring Lillie, the hostess wrapped her arms around Swain in a tight hug. "I haven't seen you all summer, hot stuff. I know you're busy with polo and junk right now, but that's no excuse for missing the June regatta."

Swain looked embarrassed by the young woman's enthusiastic greeting, but gave her a quick squeeze before stepping back and edging closer to Lillie. "I didn't know you were working here. This is Lillie Wetherington. Lillie, this is Kendall Stevensen."

Kendall's smile dimmed a few kilowatts to a level more in keeping with her job. Her gaze moved over Lillie and settled on Swain's hand discreetly resting against the small of Lillie's back. "Pleased to meet you," she said, her enthusiasm gone.

"Pleasure, I'm sure," Lillie replied, with cool politeness. She offered her hand, but Kendall's handshake was limp and brief. Her eyes narrowed at the sound of Lillie's British accent. Lillie pressed ever so slightly against Swain's side and met Kendall's look with a challenging glare of her own. When she raised an eyebrow at Kendall's boldness, the girl broke off her gaze and stepped over to her hostess podium.

"Our reservation is under Wetherington," Swain said. "If I'd put it in my name, Lorraine might have seated us by the kitchen door."

"I could still do that," she said under her breath. She picked up a couple of menus and turned a businesslike smile their way. "Follow me, please."

Despite her muttered threat, Kendall led them to a very lovely table beside a window. She watched Swain seat Lillie before settling in her own chair, then handed them the menus and offered the standard, "Enjoy your meal, ladies."

Swain glanced up at her retreating figure.

"Rower?" Lillie scanned the menu as though she wasn't really interested in the answer, but made sure her tone let Swain know she'd been caught with her hand in the same cookie jar.

Swain chuckled. "Yeah. Been there, done that. Like you, I found they party a little too hard for my tastes."

Lillie laughed, too. She had resented Kendall's intrusion into her outing with Swain, but was reassured by the fact that, when presented with another option, Swain had clearly chosen her.

She scanned the menu again, this time really reading the selection. "What? No fish-and-chips? Whitby is known for its fish-and-chips."

Swain rolled her eyes. "I could have saved a lot of money if I knew you preferred some greasy fast food."

Lillie lowered her menu. "This menu is rather pricey. After the wonderful time you've shown me today, you should let me pay for dinner to reciprocate."

Swain bent forward, her voice low and playfully indignant. "And let Kendall spread the word that I'm a kept woman? No way!"

Lillie laughed. "No, I guess we couldn't do that."

They ordered the butterflied quail with cucumber sauce and the Minnesota elk steak with mushroom brandy sauce and ate slowly, sharing bites of food from each other's plates while they talked. There had been enough earlier talk about wishes and regrets, so Lillie chose the only subject that could make Swain forget everything else.

"So, when's the next polo match?"

"A tournament starts at New Bridge tomorrow and runs through Sunday. The Wetherington Raiders, our team, plays a match first thing. The semifinal match is on Saturday morning and the championship match on Sunday."

"Will the horses be rested enough to play their best on Sunday?"

"Yeah. That's why I ride every one of them at least every other day."

"You're not riding today. I hope I haven't kept you from something you should be doing."

"No, I always rest them the day before a tournament starts. So, I don't have much to do but check the equipment after John and Rob pack it in the trailers. We'll be up and gone very early tomorrow morning to give the horses time to settle at the field and us time to scope out our competition. It's a long day, but you're welcome to come along."

Lillie frowned. "I'm afraid tomorrow is Mary's first day. I'm sure I'll need to spend time with her. Mr. Whitney is coming by in the afternoon to fill out the proper paperwork and tax forms for her employment." She would much rather spend another day with Swain.

"It's not a problem, Lillie. Like I said, it's a really long day with four back-to-back matches. Sunday is the day you really want to go. It's like a big social, not just horses running up and down the field."

"I could go with you Saturday."

"That would be okay, too. We have only two matches with a two-hour break in between, so the day isn't so long."

"What do people wear to polo matches?"

"Anything from shorts or jeans to linen suits, sundresses, and big hats. Sunday is the day people tend to dress up, though a lot of people don't at all."

"Ah. That explains all the hat boxes in Grandmum's wardrobe."

Swain laughed. "Yes. Abigail always wanted to look her best to accept the trophy."

Lillie smiled. "You're awfully smug. Are you that sure you'll win?"

"No, not this tournament. With some teams up from Florida and down from the northern states, the competition will be tough, but I'm sure we'll be in the final. We've got good riders and great ponies. Nor'easter has hit his stride this season. He's better than any pony I've ever ridden. When I saddle him for the last chukker of the championship game, the other team better watch out."

"It sounds exciting."

Swain nodded emphatically, her blue eyes luminous. "Abigail loved all of it, the ponies and the pageantry. She hated the winter break between our fall and spring seasons here. So, she'd get restless and we'd load up the ponies and head to Florida for a tournament or two. That's one reason I'm confident. We've played those teams and stacked up well against them."

"Then I suppose I'd better start planning what to wear to accept the trophy."

Swain pushed the remains of her dessert around the plate. "I'm glad you're here. It's better when you have someone to share it with. When Abigail was gone most of the past year, it wasn't as much fun."

Lillie took Swain's hand. "I'm very glad I'm here, too."

❖

Beau was sitting by the front door of the main house and followed when Swain pulled the Mercedes into the garage. He greeted her briefly when she climbed out of the sports car, then ran to the other side to lavish his attention on Lillie.

Swain shook her head, but smiled. "Great. You've stolen my dog,"

"And a very handsome dog he is," Lillie cooed, bending to hold Beau's big head in her hands and look him in the eyes. His tail thumped against the car.

"He gets all the girls."

"You're very handsome, too," Lillie said as she breezed past on her way into the house.

Swain had to grin at the compliment, no matter how lightly given.

Something seemed odd when they entered the house, but she brushed it away. Everything felt different when she was around Lillie.

Lillie went to the refrigerator and pulled out a bottle of water. "Would you like something? I could open a bottle of wine."

Swain was tempted. Her pulse quickened at the thought of sharing a glass of wine on the terrace in the gathering dusk. Being with Lillie made her feel alive. But putting herself in such a romantic setting would be quite a test. They had already done way too much hand-holding, food-sharing, and soul-baring over the past twelve hours. It was seriously threatening her resolve to keep their relationship on a friendship level. She was relieved that she had work to do.

"That sounds tempting, but I'm sure John's still at the barn, waiting for me to check our preparations for tomorrow. I need to do that so he can go home."

Swain usually loved the last-minute equipment checks because they fed her excitement, her anticipation of the coming match. But the disappointment on Lillie's face made her regret her pressing responsibilities tonight.

She sighed and headed for the back door, slapping her hand against her thigh to summon Beau. She turned when he didn't respond.

"Beau, let's go," she said sharply. But Beau had his nose to the floor, sniffing something they couldn't detect. He whimpered and ran from the kitchen.

"Damn dog." Swain threw up her hands and followed with Lillie close behind as Beau raced to the front of the house. He was sniffing the floor of the foyer furiously and bolted up the staircase just as she grabbed for his collar.

"Beau," she shouted.

She started to follow him up the stairs, but a tug on her arm stopped her. Lillie's face was pale and her hand on Swain's arm was shaking.

"Don't go. Call the police. Someone could be hiding up there."

Swain suddenly realized what was amiss earlier. "The alarm wasn't activated when we came in. Did you turn it on before we left?"

"Yes, I did." Lillie's voice trembled.

"I'm sure it's nothing," Swain said. "The cleaning crew came today. Maybe they forgot to engage it when they left. Beau loves the crew manager. He probably smells her scent from earlier today and thinks she's still in the house somewhere."

She didn't want to add to Lillie's fear, but this didn't feel right to her either. She knew all the women on the crew. They had check lists so that they never forgot anything.

"If anybody besides us is in the house, Beau will find them first. Trust me. He can sound really fierce. No burglar would mess with him. We'll go up there and probably find him sprawled in the middle of your bed, shedding hair on your sheets."

"You need a weapon," Lillie insisted. "Wait here." She disappeared into the living room and returned with the fireplace poker. "Take this."

Swain took the iron poker and held it in front of her like a sword. She squared her shoulders and deepened her voice. "Stay back, Miss Lillie. I'll protect you."

"Bloody idiot." Lillie clutched the back of Swain's shirt as she followed close behind.

At the top of the stairs, Beau emerged from Abigail's bedroom, his nose still to the floor, and followed an invisible trail down the hall to the bedroom opposite Lillie's room. The door was open, but he snuffled his way to the next door and the next, until he'd sniffed at each one. Then he stopped at Lillie's room, growled softly, and followed his nose inside.

They stood in the doorway as Beau followed a trail over to the bed, then to the bathroom, before stopping at the closed closet door. He scratched at it.

Swain pulled her shirt free of Lillie's hands. "You stay here. I'll see what he's after in the closet," she whispered.

But Lillie grabbed her arm and held tight. "No. You should call the security company and have them look."

"Lillie. You don't know Beau like I do. It's probably a mouse."

"A mouse?" Lillie released Swain's arm and stepped back.

Swain nodded. She'd stumbled onto something that would keep Lillie out of the way while she investigated. "He finds mice all the time at my place. The feed room is right under my bedroom." She scrunched up her face for effect. "He eats them if he catches them. It's disgusting. I don't want you to see that."

"I'll wait here then." From the look of revulsion on Lillie's face, Swain was confident she would.

She crept silently toward the closet and took up a position to the right of the door, her back pressed against the wall. She held the poker in her left hand, raised high and ready to strike, while she closed her right hand carefully around the doorknob.

Beau growled again and stuck his nose to the crack between the carpet and the door's bottom, snuffling loudly. She froze as he suddenly jerked back and barked sharply. He stuck his nose to the crack again and this time Swain saw it. A furry gray paw snaked out from under the door, swiping at the probing nose. Swain laughed in relief.

"Lillie," she called. "It's not a mouse. Come meet your cat burglar."

When Lillie hesitantly peeked into the bedroom, Swain opened the closet door. A petite gray feline with green eyes calmly strolled out and threaded a path around Swain's legs, rubbing her whiskers against Swain's jeans. Beau watched her, his tail sweeping from side to side in a wide arc. When he lowered his head to push at the cat, she slapped playfully at his nose.

"Meet Gray Cat. She's one of our best mousers in the barn. She's never come up here before, but I guess she slipped in when the cleaning crew was going in and out of the house. Someone must have accidentally shut her in the closet."

Lillie sagged against the door frame in relief. Her hands still trembled as she rubbed them across her eyes. Beau walked over and pressed sympathetically against her legs. "I'm sorry. I don't mean to be such a wimp."

Swain pulled her cell phone from her pocket and flipped it open. She hit a speed dial and listened for a moment. "John, hey. I'm up at the house. I'll be a while longer, so why don't you go on home. I'll look things over before I go to bed, but I'm sure everything's fine. You've been packing those trailers longer than I have. Okay. See you in the morning."

She closed the phone and smiled at Lillie. "How about that glass of wine? I think we both could use one."

CHAPTER EIGHTEEN

They took the wine and settled into patio chairs on the terrace. In the dark hour between dusk and twilight, the only illumination came from the lights in the swimming pool. Beau lay at their feet, but Gray Cat scampered back to the barn.

"What was it like, growing up in England?" Swain asked, hoping to move Lillie's thoughts to more pleasant things.

"Not much different from growing up in a city here, I suppose. I went to a private school every day, watched the telly at night. Mum took me to Dad's concerts when they were in London. He would let me play in his dressing room until close to curtain call. He laughed when I told him once that I wanted to wear a tuxedo like his. 'But you look so beautiful in your pink ruffles,' he said. After he played his last piece, people would stand and applaud for a long time. They would throw flowers onto the stage, and he always picked up two red roses and tossed one to Mum and one to me."

"That sounds wonderful."

"It was, when he was home. His concerts were frequently in other cities. We traveled with him until I was old enough to go to school, then Mum had to stay with me. He finally gave up the concert tour and took a teaching position at the university so he could be at home, too. I remember sitting at the dinner table and listening to him go on and on about a talented new student. I often wished it was me that he bragged about."

"I'm sure that was just your imagination. What father wouldn't love a daughter as smart and beautiful as you?"

Lillie's smile was shy. "Thank you for saying so." She shifted in her seat and stared up at the night sky and its growing blanket of stars. "My parents were deeply in love. I think they mistakenly thought a child would add to that. I felt like Mum resented it when she had to remain home with me while Dad traveled. She wanted to be with him. But Dad wanted a child, and I'm convinced that when they discovered Mum couldn't bear him one, they adopted me to ease her guilt."

"You didn't feel loved?"

"Oh, yes, I did. I don't want to give the impression that I wasn't. Mum loved shopping with me. And we would go on holidays several times a year, to the seaside or some place farther away. We spent a whole month in Greece once. I learned to ski in the Swiss Alps. We also holidayed in China, India, and Amsterdam. I loved going places with them. We had a wonderful time."

"I've only read about those places," Swain murmured.

"I don't want to sound like a whiny rich girl, but having money is no substitute for a lot of things."

Swain stared into the shimmering pool. "I'd trade my childhood for yours any day." She didn't blame Lillie for their different backgrounds, but she couldn't keep the bitterness out of her voice. Lillie's fingers curled around hers, but she didn't look up.

"Even with all I had, I still lay in bed at night and wondered about the mum who threw me away," Lillie said softly. "It didn't keep me from wondering if I had a sister or brother out there somewhere."

Swain looked over at Lillie, holding her gaze. She didn't want to think about a young Lillie longing for her real family. She entwined her fingers with Lillie's, stroking with her thumb. She knew that empty ache and how much it hurt.

"I have a brother and don't even know where he is. Even though we're twins, I grew up in the girls' dorm and he grew up in the boys'. He was always angry about something, and when we left the orphanage, we went our separate ways."

"You said your mum died days after you were born, but did you try to find out who your dad is? Or if you have other relatives?"

"I tracked down an old nurse who amazingly remembered my mother. It was a small hospital with mostly routine deliveries, so a really young mother dying and leaving twins stuck in her mind."

"Did she help?"

Swain stared at the lights refracted by the water in the pool. "Not really. She said my mother told her she'd made up her own name and got mine off a road sign. The hospital was in Swain County, North Carolina. She named my brother after the guy she read about in a newspaper article, but she nicknamed him Trey."

She wanted to tell Lillie that the father listed on their birth certificates was James Eric Wetherington II. She'd searched for news articles about him on the Internet and knew he was from Aiken and played polo. It might have been a weird coincidence that Abigail sought her out to be her head trainer, but it was no accident that Swain chose polo as a profession and put herself in Abigail's path. Even though she knew this man probably wasn't her father, her heart drew her to the sport and helped fill that part of her that needed to belong somewhere to something.

Lillie squeezed her hand. "I'm sorry."

Swain downed the last swallow of her wine and stood. "Well, it's getting late. I still have to check the trailers."

Lillie stood, too, and, trembling, wrapped her in a tight hug.

"Lillie? What is it?"

Lillie clung tighter. "Could you do me a favor?"

"Anything, sweetheart." The endearment slipped from Swain's lips before she realized she'd said it. When Lillie relaxed in her arms, she vowed to say it a million more times if it soothed Lillie's worries.

"You'll think I'm being silly."

Swain stepped back and gently lifted Lillie's chin to get her to meet her gaze. "I'd never think you were silly. What do you need? If it's in my power to do it, I will."

"Could you...do you think Beau could stay with me tonight?"

"That old fleabag?" Her teasing was gentle.

"In case there is, you know, a mouse or something in the house."

"I can stay up here tonight, in one of the guest rooms, if you like." *Although I won't sleep at all with you that close.*

"No. You've got work still to do and you said you have to be up at daybreak." Lillie hesitated. "Oh, you probably plan to take Beau with you."

"No, not to the tournament." It was a lie Beau would have to forgive. "Actually, you'd be doing me a favor. If he stays up here with you, I won't have to see those sad eyes when we leave without him in the morning. You'll stay with Lillie, won't you, Beau?"

His tail thumped against the stone flooring of the terrace.

Lillie smiled and moved back into Swain's embrace. "Thank you for today. For being my guide. For being my hero and nabbing my cat burglar. When Mr. Whitney told me I might have to stay here several months, I despaired. I had no idea you would make this time such an amazing adventure."

Swain folded her arms around Lillie, their bodies fitting perfectly. She closed her eyes and savored the feel of Lillie's head resting against her shoulder.

She felt Lillie's hand on her cheek and looked down to meet her gaze. The longing, the affection, the question she saw in Lillie's eyes stilled Swain's heart. Lillie's lips parted slightly and the hand that had been on her cheek moved to press lightly against the back of neck, guiding her down until their mouths nearly touched, their breaths nearly one.

It was a gift and Swain took it. First gently. Then firmly. So sweet. She laved her tongue around Lillie's, pressed her hips to Lillie's, and nestled her wildly beating heart against Lillie's breasts. Startled by the wanting that rose up inside and threatened to swallow her, Swain withdrew. But not before she stole one last brush of her lips against Lillie's.

She opened her eyes again to Lillie's beautiful smile.

"Good night, Swain." Lillie's voice was low and silky.

"Don't forget to set the alarm," Swain murmured.

She watched Lillie gather the wineglasses and beckon to Beau, who dutifully followed. She stood a few moments longer in the dark, watching through the windows as Lillie locked the door and set the alarm.

Swain licked her lips, searching for a trace, a taste of Lillie still on them.

What are you afraid of, Swain? She sighed. *Of losing my heart to her.*

When the time came for Lillie to go back to England, it would be very hard to say good-bye.

CHAPTER NINETEEN

Mary Chandler was a short, sturdy woman with a kind face. Lillie had felt instantly drawn to her cheerful personality when she helped Mrs. Riley handle the guests after Abigail's funeral. So she was disappointed when Mary showed up for her first day of work and explained why she couldn't take the job.

"I'm so sorry, Ms. Wetherington. I applied for the position because my husband was laid off from the plant last year. He hadn't been able to find a job all this time and his unemployment was about to run out. It was a godsend when you called, even though the position's temporary." Mary seemed sincerely disappointed. "Then, yesterday, the plant called Frank to come back to work. He went this morning." Mary looked around the kitchen. "I hate leaving you in the lurch. I actually was looking forward to this. I love to cook. But the plant pays way more than a cook's salary."

Lillie frowned. She'd already had a restless night. Her dreams were clips of her day with Swain—enjoying a picnic lunch, riding in the carriage, swiping food off each other's plate at dinner, sharing a bottle of wine, and, finally, a kiss. The kiss. She had awakened aroused and aching with the need to see, to hear, to be around Swain. But Swain had left hours before for the polo field and her absence left Lillie feeling strangely off-kilter.

She and Beau had wandered down to the barn, both lonesome for Swain. When they returned to the house, they stared together out the windows at the empty polo field. When they simultaneously heaved a huge sigh, Lillie burst out laughing.

"We're pathetic, aren't we?" Beau's tail thumped his agreement.

So they welcomed the distraction of Mary's arrival. Lillie was just beginning to wrap her mind around this new disappointment when the phone rang and she excused herself to answer it.

"Is this Lillie?"

"Yes, it is."

"Hey, this is Catherine. Catherine Strom. I was calling to thank you for sharing my resume with Kate. The job is perfect and we really hit it off. I start next week."

"That's wonderful. I'm so glad it worked out. Your skills demanded a greater audience than just me."

"Well, thanks. If I can ever do anything for you, please let me know. I enjoyed meeting you."

"My pleasure as well." Lillie paused. "So you begin work next week?"

"Monday. I told Kate I could start right away, but she'd already arranged for some help tonight and tomorrow. I guess I'll have to find something to do with myself. My boyfriend is a fireman and he's on duty all weekend."

"How would you like to go to the polo tournament with me tomorrow? I don't know that many people around here, and it would be nice to have someone else along while Swain's busy with the ponies."

"I'd love to. What do you wear to a polo match?"

"Swain says most people don't really dress up until Sunday, so I'm wearing jeans."

"Jeans sound great. What time?"

"About eight thirty? The first match is at ten. We can take one of Grandmum's cars, but do you mind coming over here and driving? I still tend to stay on the wrong side of the road."

Catherine laughed. "That could be a problem. I don't mind at all."

"Excellent. I'll see you tomorrow morning then."

"Wonderful." Catherine cleared her throat. "Lillie, I don't know very many people here either. Thanks for inviting me."

"We'll have fun."

She ended the call, buoyed by her success at helping Catherine secure a job and finding good company for the polo tournament. Now, back to Mary and the problem at hand.

Lillie didn't want to add to Mary's obvious distress, but she wasn't ready to go back to her folder of applicants. "I do have other good prospects, Mary, so you needn't worry. Still—" She was unsure how Mary would receive her question. "It's really none of my business, but I'm curious. Does your husband not want you to work?"

Mary chuckled, her hazel eyes twinkling. "Oh, Lord, honey. I can do anything I want where Frank's concerned. I've had that man wrapped around my little finger since the day we met. It's not him keeping me from working. It's Dani. We had her sort of late in life. The other kids are grown or off at college. But she's only twelve. We both want someone at home when she gets out of school and a real family supper served well before her bedtime, just like our other children grew up with."

Lillie nodded. "Can we talk about this?" She sat at the kitchen table and indicated for Mary to join her.

"I don't want to pressure you into something you don't want to do, but I'd like to offer a compromise. I won't have any hard feelings if you turn me down."

"I'm open to ideas," Mary said carefully.

"What would you say to letting Dani come here after school? The housekeeper's suite is right through that door...a home away from home. She could watch the telly or do her homework there or here in the kitchen."

As her plan began to take shape, Lillie talked faster, excitedly accenting her words with her hands. "When you shop and cook for me, you could cook for five. Swain usually joins me for dinner so she can fill me in on things concerning the farm. You could dish out two plates for us and take the rest home to feed your family." She finished with a flourish and waited expectantly.

"Oh, I couldn't do that. You're already offering a very good salary. I couldn't ask you to feed three more mouths, too." Despite her words, Mary looked hopeful. "Perhaps you could lower the salary a bit to make up for the extra food."

"Again, you can say no. But I'd like to suggest a different method of repayment."

"I'm listening."

"I want to learn to shop and cook, and to do laundry, too. My family's housekeeper didn't like children underfoot, so I could never learn some things I want to be able to do for myself. If I'm not busy elsewhere, you'll have to tolerate me asking questions and expecting to help. And, you must call me Lillie, not Ms. Wetherington."

Mary patted Lillie's hand, her smile sympathetic. "You poor child. It's hardly a fair trade, because I'd be more than happy for the company. Your grandmother and I did a lot of volunteer work together. If you're anything like Abigail, your company will be a pleasure, not a burden. I still think you should reduce the salary."

Lillie turned her hand over and squeezed Mary's in a tight clasp. "I'm sorry. My offer stands. Will you accept it?"

"I'd have to be an idiot to turn that down, and my mama didn't raise any idiots." Mary smiled and stood to retrieve her purse from the kitchen counter. She dug out a book-sized organizer and a pen. "Now show me the rest of the house and let's go over anything I can help you with besides shopping and cooking. Then we'll have a look at that pantry and head to the grocery."

❖

"Really, Mr. Whitney, are all these papers necessary? I thought she'd only have to sign proper tax statements and the like." This would take longer than Lillie anticipated, and she was eager to start her promised cooking lesson.

They had settled around the kitchen table where Bonner opened his briefcase and pulled out a stack of papers concerning Mary's employment.

"These documents simply protect you against a lawsuit for any injury due to the employee's failure to follow proper procedures." He shuffled the papers and presented another for her review. "This form protects your privacy. Household employees may be privy to conversations and actions you wouldn't want repeated or described outside your family," Bonner explained patiently. "They are the standard papers Abigail used for all her employees."

"I can understand the privacy statement, but the other sounds like an excuse for some rich employer to squirm out of paying for an employee's work-related injury. I can't believe my grandmum went along with this."

Bonner smiled, but handed Mary a pen to sign the papers. "This is the same argument I had with Abigail. An employee could deliberately harm themselves and you'd end up paying millions for it. I'm afraid your insurance company requires it, Lillie."

"It's okay, dear, Mrs. Riley warned me ahead of time. She said it's usual for this position and warned me not to take it personal."

"Well, *I* take it personal."

The phone began to ring and Mary immediately picked it up.

"Wetherington residence, Mary speaking." She smiled. "Well, hello. Mr. Whitney is here and we're getting all the paperwork out of the way, but we've already been having a wonderful time. Would you like to speak to the lady of the house? Hold on."

Mary pushed the Hold button. "Ms. Butler would like to speak with you."

Lillie couldn't stop her own smile as she gestured toward the front of the house. "I'll take it in the study so you can finish all this paper signing."

She walked quickly, anticipating the voice of the person she'd missed all morning. She wasn't disappointed.

"Swain?"

"Hey, you."

Lillie's heart jumped. She cradled the phone between her shoulder and ear, settling her hip on the edge of the desk. "Hello."

"I was just calling to report that we won handily this morning."

"That's wonderful! You scored a lot of goals, no doubt."

Swain chuckled. "The team did score a lot. We beat them by four goals."

"That's very good, I take it?"

"Very good. We played a great team. I knew we could win, but I didn't expect to do it by so much."

"How many did you personally score?"

"Enough. Every goal's a team effort."

"Stop being modest. How many?

"Eight of our ten goals. But Javier's defense at the other end was exceptional. The Rum Runners haven't been held to six goals all year. I knew he'd shape up to be a great player."

"Will you be home in time for dinner?"

"We're watching the match that's playing now, but it's nearly over. We should be headed back within the hour. How are things going with Mary?"

"She's absolutely delightful. We've already been grocery shopping and, as soon as she finishes with Mr. Whitney, we're planning to make beef stew for dinner."

"I certainly don't want to miss that."

"No, I wouldn't think so." She enjoyed Swain's chuckle that filtered through the phone. "I've got some news myself."

"What's that?"

"Catherine called. She wanted to thank me for recommending her to Kate. She starts there Monday."

"That's great."

"I invited her to the polo matches tomorrow and Sunday. If I have a friend along, you won't have to babysit me the entire time."

"Lillie, spending time with you isn't a burden, but I'm sure you'll enjoy having someone to sit with while we're on the field. Did she accept your invitation?"

"Yes, she was quite eager."

"Is she dragging her boyfriend along?"

Did Swain still have feelings for Catherine? "You don't like him?"

"No, it's not that. He doesn't know Catherine and I were ever anything but friends. I figure that's up to her to tell him if and when she wants."

"Oh, well, he's working and won't be tagging along. It's just us girls." Lillie silently admonished herself for being jealous and selfish. She had given in to her desire for Swain the night before, but a casual fling would only confuse an already complicated situation. Still, that kiss had filled her dreams all night and lingered in her thoughts all morning, so she couldn't help wanting Swain's sexy voice in her ear a bit longer. "Tell me more about the match."

❖

Mary watched Lillie retreat from the kitchen and smiled. "Looks like those two have already become friends. I'm glad. They're both fine young women."

"I hope that'll help when the will is read," Bonner muttered. He looked up, chagrined that he'd voiced his thought aloud. "You didn't hear me say that."

"I don't know what's in that will, Mr. Whitney, but I hope it won't cause more trouble. Lord knows, that family's already had more than its share of grief. I never understood why their only child cut them off like that and kept that sweet young lady in there from knowing her grandparents. Some said it was a falling-out with his father, but I just can't imagine what could have been so bad to permanently split up a family as close as they were. It tore my heart out to see how much it hurt Abigail."

Bonner closed his briefcase and stared at it. "Terrible things happen to good people sometimes, Mrs. Chandler. Terrible things."

THIRTY-TWO YEARS EARLIER

S he was my friend. She looked up to you. How could you have done this?" Eric moaned, his face in his hand. "You've ruined my life."

Jim tried to place his hand on his shoulder, but Eric jerked away and stared up at him. "You were drunk again, weren't you?"

Jim's hands shook. He hadn't taken a drink since that dreadful night. Not since the morning he woke up to only hazy flashes of what had happened. Not since he'd had to face Abigail with what he'd done.

When they'd married, he had been her knight in shining armor. She had been his queen. But he didn't deserve her now. Somewhere along the way, he let money and power go to his head. He had become exactly what he swore he wouldn't…an alcoholic just like his old man. He had thought no one, except maybe Abigail and Bonner, had suspected. He'd managed to control his drinking. But now everything was falling apart.

Abigail stepped between them. "Eric, I know you're upset, but you will not speak to your father with such disrespect. Not in my presence."

"Why not, Mother? Apparently he has no respect for me. He let them think it was me, not him, to blame. Now *I'm* being sent out of the country." His voice grew louder with each word.

"Eric, lower your voice. You were going to study music in England anyway. We just moved it up a year. And we're doing everything we can for that poor girl's family."

"You've covered it up with his filthy money."

Jim shoved his trembling hands into his pockets. His head pounded with each angry word that Eric spat out. Eric was the son he'd taught to ride and who shared his passion for polo, but who looked at him now with loathing. "You didn't mind my money when you wanted a fancy car for your birthday or a new polo pony." God, he wanted a drink, just one drink to settle his nerves.

Eric stepped around Abigail and faced Jim, his eyes scorching lasers. "You are not my father!" His angry words were still bouncing off the walls as his steps echoed in the hallway.

Abigail hurried after him. "Eric, wait." She wanted to gather him in her arms, like when he was a child, and console him. But the son who stood before her now was a young man and would have to learn to handle life's hard lessons.

Eric stopped, his back to her and his words bitter. "How can you stay with him, knowing what he did?"

"He's broken and I won't leave him no matter what he's done. I love you, son, with all my heart. But I love him in a way you'll never understand until you fall in love yourself. How we work this out between us is nobody's business but mine and your father's."

He whirled to face her, tears trickling down his cheeks "I loved *her*," he choked out. "That's why I'll never be able to forgive him. After I leave tomorrow morning, I'll never speak to him or set foot in this house, *his* house, again."

Abigail stared after him as he stomped up the stairs. In the morning, her husband would be on his way to a rehabilitation facility to dry out and her son would be on a plane to England. It was up to her to bury this whole mess and save her marriage.

CHAPTER TWENTY

New Bridge Polo Club, which had hosted two U.S. Polo Association Gold Cup tournaments and the international Triple Crown of Polo in recent years, was teeming with people, horses, trucks, and trailers on Saturday. White canvas canopies stood on the outskirts of the playing field to shade spectators who lounged in canvas camp chairs next to tables laden with gourmet finger food and coolers filled with imported beer and wine. Cheap seats in the bleachers were available for the casual spectators.

Lillie and Catherine searched through the crowds for Swain, who had left the farm at daybreak with the horses and trailers.

Dinner the night before had been wonderful. Swain had listened closely to Lillie describe how to make beef stew step by step. Then Lillie was equally attentive as Swain analyzed the teams in the tournament and their chances for winning. When they said good night, Swain shuffled her feet a bit, then kissed Lillie on the cheek. Lillie had hoped for more, but it was for the best. Perhaps Swain realized that, too. But knowing that hadn't dampened the desire between them.

Lillie was thinking about that one kiss as she and Catherine stood on the edge of the field. They had been searching for Swain for more than an hour. They were about to give up and find a seat in the bleachers when Swain came thundering up, wheeled Domino to a stop, and grinned. She greeted both of them, but her eyes stayed on Lillie.

"You made it. I was beginning to worry."

Domino bobbed his head at Lillie. "Hello, handsome." She patted his shoulder, but gazed at Swain as she spoke.

Swain bent down toward Lillie, her eyes a cerulean blue in the bright sun. "Sorry I've been tied up. I wanted to meet you when you arrived."

A wave of pleasure floated through her, lightening her heart, easing her doubts. A small part of her was afraid Swain had regretted that kiss and was beginning to avoid her. "We've been here a while, searching for you."

Swain straightened and gestured to the other side of the field. "I usually park away from the crowds. Our trailers are over there, behind those red ones. Two have campers in the front, equipped with restrooms, one for boys and one for girls. Ask John. He'll point you to the right one."

"We were about to find a seat in the bleachers," Catherine said.

"No, don't do that." Swain pointed down the field. "See the big green canopy? That's the Wetherington tent. Abigail always had a table and big fancy lunch catered. The socialites like to tent-hop to see who's outdone the other. But I haven't had time to keep up the tradition. I did have John set up a couple of chairs for y'all and a cooler with water, beer, and a bottle of wine." She shrugged apologetically. "We've got some sandwich stuff in the trailers for lunch."

"I'm sure we'll be fine," Lillie said, smiling. Domino shifted, restless. "Don't you need to get back out there?"

"Yeah. We're getting ready to start soon, so I probably won't have a chance to talk to you again until after the match."

"You just concentrate on winning. I'm expecting a trophy tomorrow, you know," Lillie said.

Catherine nodded. "Don't worry about us."

Swain gave them a small salute. "See you later then." She turned Domino toward the middle of the field and began cantering him in a wide figure-eight pattern.

"Shall we check out our seats?"

"After you," Catherine said.

The canopy was large and custom-made, with *Wetherington* embroidered on the front in a fancy script. And, though Swain's last-minute accommodations were sparse, the chairs were comfortable and the beer was very cold.

"I've never been to a polo match. I have no idea what they're doing," Catherine said.

"Well, Swain did give me one lesson, and I looked it up on the Internet, so I'll explain what little I know. They play six chukkers, each one seven and a half minutes long. They have only three minutes between chukkers. That's barely enough to trade mounts with the fresh one a groom brings you, gulp down some water, and get back out there. There's a five-minute halftime after the third chukker."

"I guess we just sit here then, until the match is over."

"Except at halftime. That's when all the spectators have to walk out on the field and stomp down the divots the horses' hooves have made in the grass."

Catherine laughed. "Really? That sounds like fun, but I'd have thought they'd have a big machine to do that. You know, like that thing that smooths the ice during the break in an ice-hockey game."

Lillie laughed with her. "I'm sure they could, but divot-stomping is a polo tradition they don't dare modernize."

Much of the spectator crowd ignored the play on the field and tent-hopped to see and be seen. Catherine and Lillie, however, clapped and cheered for their team, occasionally walking up and down the sidelines so Lillie could take pictures of the play. Lillie was surprised when Catherine let out an earsplitting whistle after one hard-fought goal scored by the Wetherington Raiders.

"Bloody hell. Did that come out of you?" She found it comical that someone so feminine could whistle like a sheepherder.

"My daddy is a huge Atlanta Braves fan. I learned how to whistle cheering with him at ball games." Catherine chuckled. "I didn't embarrass you, did I?"

"Not at all. Could you do that when that woman in the yellow jacket comes by to stare at us again? That'll give them something to talk about, as if they aren't already buzzing about us sitting here like common folk, drinking beer right out of the bottle."

A constant parade of people had strolled by, stared at them, looked up at the identification on the canopy, and kept walking.

When halftime was signaled, Lillie and Catherine jumped up to enthusiastically stomp as many divots as possible. They returned to the tent, laughing and walking arm-in-arm like schoolgirls, only to find out they had company.

A woman dressed in a pristine white linen suit and a Panama big-brim hat adorned with a gargantuan white flower sat in Lillie's chair, her long legs crossed and a smug look on her face.

"Hello. I don't believe we've met." Lillie held out her hand. "I'm Lillie Wetherington."

The woman looked her over, from her tennis shoes to her knit shirt, before returning Lillie's greeting with a limp handshake. "Pleasure, I'm sure. I'm Susan Whitney. I was told you were here, but when I came over to extend a welcome, I thought the rumors must have been wrong. I saw two chairs and a cooler of beer and decided the barn help was occupying your tent."

"Swain did the best she could, but she's been very busy concentrating on winning the tournament. We're perfectly happy roughing it."

"Both of you are here with Swain?" She shifted her eyes to Catherine, evaluating her with the same dismissive gaze.

"Yes. We are. This is my friend, Catherine Strom."

"Yes, of course. The new cook at Kate's little place."

"Chef." Catherine corrected her with an equally disdainful expression. "People with taste know the difference."

Susan sniffed as if she smelled something bad and turned back to Lillie. "Please feel free to come by our tent. We use a caterer out of Augusta, who's superb." She gave Catherine one more condescending look. "You can bring your friend, too."

They watched Susan walk away and hook arms with a handsome young man, who was engaged in conversation with another very attractive young man.

"Bitch," Catherine muttered.

"Hussy," Lillie said. "Another beer?"

"Don't mind if I do." Catherine stared after Susan. "Hats with a brim that large are so yesterday."

But they had forgotten Susan's visit by the last chukker. The teams were tied eight to eight in the final minute with a knot of players jostling for the ball just yards away from the opposing team's goal. The ball skittered outside the group and Javier smacked it downfield. Swain and two opposing riders pursued it, but she was riding Nor'easter and easily outdistanced the other ponies. She lined up the shot, executed a perfect swing, and blasted the ball between the goalposts.

Catherine and Lillie jumped from their seats to cheer and whistle as the horn sounded, signaling the end of the match. After accepting the congratulations of her teammates, Swain galloped over to the tent.

"Ah, my knight in a sweaty polo jersey," Lillie teased her.

Swain swept her helmet off in a dramatic bow from horseback. "I pledge my mallet to your service, my queen."

"You're such a ham," Catherine said.

Swain grinned. "Speaking of ham, I'm famished. If you ladies will wait here, I'll turn my steed over to John and return with sandwiches for all."

"Are you sure we can't help?" Lillie asked.

"You can have a cold beer open for me when I get back." Swain winked at them. "Give me ten minutes to wash up."

She returned in less than ten, carrying another chair and three plates of thick ham sandwiches and potato salad.

"Mmm. I didn't realize how hungry I was. This is delicious," Lillie said between mouthfuls.

"You two could have walked around some. Just introduce yourself at any tent and the owners will invite you to sample from their tables. It's like a little high-society competition."

"They were invited, but didn't accept." Susan suddenly appeared at Swain's elbow, carrying a platter full of delicacies. When Swain looked up from wolfing down the last bite of her sandwich, Susan planted a kiss squarely on her lips. "I brought your favorites—oysters on the half shell, shrimp salad, and caviar. We have food at our tent." She quickly kissed Swain again. "And more of everything else at my place tonight if you're interested."

Swain blushed, glancing over at Lillie. "I don't think so, Susan. But thanks for the food."

"You don't have to answer right now, but I'm sure your employer and her friend know you're a consenting adult. If you can't make it tonight, maybe I'll catch you after tomorrow's victory." She fanned herself with her hand for effect. "You're always at your best when you're still seething with battle lust." Susan gave a little wave to Lillie and Catherine, who were speechless. "Ta-ta," she said, sauntering back to her tent.

"Bitch," Catherine said, regaining her voice.

"Hussy," Lillie hissed.

Swain laughed. "I'm sorry. That woman practically stalks me." She looked down at the platter Susan had placed in her lap. "At least she left the food."

Before she could pick up an oyster, Catherine snatched the platter from her hands. "Don't eat that."

"Hey, you may not like Susan, but the food is still good."

"Actually, no, it isn't. These oysters have spoiled. See how they are green around the edges? They'll make you sick as a dog."

Lillie stood to look at the oysters in question. "What about that shrimp salad?"

"It looks okay. Let's taste it."

Lillie handed Swain her plate that still held a half-eaten sandwich and dug into the shrimp salad. "Very good. Try it."

Catherine took a forkful. "Hmm. Not bad. There's something extra in it that I can't quite make out."

They settled back into their chairs and propped the platter between them, both taking another bite of the shrimp.

"Do you think the caviar is safe, too?"

"It looks fine to me."

Lillie popped a cracker topped with cream cheese and caviar in her mouth. "Delicious! You have to try one."

"Do I get any?" Swain asked.

Catherine passed her plate to her. "You can have the rest of my potato salad. You have a match tomorrow. What if some of this made you sick? That would be terrible, wouldn't it, Lillie?"

"Absolutely terrible. You'd better let us make sure it's okay."

Swain shook her head and ate the last bite of Lillie's sandwich before digging her fork into Catherine's potato salad.

Lillie looked at Catherine. "I'd give my last penny to show her up, but it's too late to hire a caterer for tomorrow."

Catherine's smile was predatory. "I've got the time if you've got the money to buy the stuff we'll need."

"And we'll have to wear something other than jeans."

"I know a great shop in Columbia that will have everything we need," Catherine said, hesitating. "I'm afraid it's out of my price range, though."

"Don't worry about it. I have plenty of money, and I wouldn't want my caterer to be underdressed."

"I don't know, Lillie. I'd feel like I was taking advantage of you."

"Please? I need a partner in this caper. How dare she—" Lillie glanced over at Swain, but didn't finish what she was about to say. She hated the way Susan touched Swain, kissed Swain as though she owned her.

Catherine looked at Swain, who was getting another beer and oblivious to the real reason for their plotting. "Okay. You've got yourself a partner. We'll have to leave now to get it all done. Give me a minute to visit the ladies' room, and we'll take off."

"You guys are leaving? You're not going to watch the next match with me?"

Lillie suddenly realized what she would be doing. "I didn't stop to think that you'd be here alone." And with that woman about. "It was a marvelous idea, but I'll tell Catherine we shouldn't leave."

"I was kidding. Go ahead. I'll miss your company, but I'm not alone. John, Rob, and Javier will sit with me. We have to scout out the winner because that's who we'll play tomorrow."

"Just you and the guys?" she asked, staring down at her hands.

Swain folded one of Lillie's hands in hers. "Just me and the guys. We'll stay right here until it's over, then load up the horses and go home."

"We should be back by then, whipping up a menu for tomorrow."

"Then I'll join you at the house."

"I'd love that, but you must be tired. You don't have to cook, too."

"Who said anything about cooking? You two just ate all the good stuff Susan brought for me. You owe me." Swain wiggled her eyebrows suggestively. "I'm coming up to the house to be your taster."

CHAPTER TWENTY-ONE

L illie adjusted her stylish Tilley plantation hat with its rolled brim. "What do you think?"

"Wow." The minute Swain walked up to the Wetherington tent, she was afraid she'd never be able to concentrate on the match scheduled to start in an hour. She devoured the vision before her, from Lillie's tan linen slacks and pale green blouse to soft blond curls pulled back in a green ribbon and topped with the jaunty hat.

"Wow? That's the best you can do?" Lillie's smile softened her taunt.

Swain swallowed and nodded. Her mind and mouth were paralyzed. Too bad other parts of her weren't. She put her hands in her pockets and shifted her feet to relieve the pressure on the throbbing between her legs. She felt her cheeks flush when Lillie's smile broadened knowingly.

Bonner's wife, Charlotte, daintily popped another lobster scampi puff in her mouth and hummed her approval. "Lillie, darling, this is fabulous. No wonder everyone is over here at your tent."

Swain was relieved at the reprieve when Lillie greeted her guest. "Thank you, Charlotte. I'm glad you're enjoying it."

"I must have the name of your caterer. I've been desperate to find someone exceptional for Susan and Jason's wedding in the spring. Everyone around here offers the same old thing." Charlotte held up a tidbit. "What is this? It's delicious."

"Edamame dumpling. I'm afraid we're getting a little low on these. Somebody I know has eaten their weight in them already,"

Catherine said, swatting Swain's hand away from them. She motioned for the tuxedoed cooking-school student they'd hired to refill the platter from one of the coolers in Catherine's SUV.

Swain scowled at Catherine, just for effect, but abandoned her snacking and stepped over to Lillie's side. The town's upper echelon was a tank full of sharks who might make several harmless passes before biting. She'd never cared that they rarely acknowledged her presence, even when she was with Abigail. But she wouldn't tolerate them treating Lillie that way.

Lillie subtly touched her shoulder against Swain's, acknowledging and accepting her support, before waving her hand nonchalantly toward the feast.

"Have you met my friend Catherine?" she asked Charlotte. "She's the master of this little feast."

Actually, Catherine had called in a lot of favors the day before to put the menu together. She and Lillie did cook several items, but the rest came from an afternoon class of cooking students, two of Catherine's fellow cooking-school graduates, and a visit to a specialty bakery in Columbia.

"Catherine, dear, please tell me that you cater. You must do my daughter's wedding on the twenty-fifth of March. I won't take no for an answer. Name your price and my husband will pay it."

Lillie interceded. "Oh, I'm afraid Catherine doesn't do this on a regular basis. I took advantage of our friendship to persuade her to help me today. She's such a gifted chef. If she caters just one event, she's flooded with requests. You wouldn't believe how insistent people can be." Her thinly veiled admonishment hit its mark.

Charlotte's horrified expression nearly made Swain choke on the water she was drinking. She could relax. Lillie obviously knew how to handle the high-born.

"I'm so sorry if I offended. Of course, a talent such as yours would be in high demand. Please forgive me if I overstepped." Charlotte took Catherine's hand and, for a moment, Swain thought she might kneel and kiss it. "However, I would be forever indebted if you would consider my offer. I'll never get to plan another wedding. Susan is my only daughter, and, well, I want everything to be perfect."

Catherine squeezed Charlotte's hand, but her smile was noncommittal. "Of course you do. I completely understand. I'll check my calendar and let you know."

Swain wanted to laugh aloud. Lillie and Catherine certainly didn't need her protection. If anything, someone needed to watch out for Charlotte's interests. They had her begging like Beau at dinnertime.

"You are so kind. I'll look forward to hearing from you." She shoved her empty plate into Swain's hands and refilled her glass with the wine punch. "If you'll excuse me, I have to find Frances and send her over here. She'll just die for those lobster puffs."

They watched Charlotte hurry away toward the Hitchcock tents, holding her cup carefully so her wine punch didn't slosh.

Swain chuckled. "That poor woman never stood a chance against you two."

"Give that to me," Lillie said angrily as she took Charlotte's abandoned plate from Swain and handed it to the server for disposal. "She's obviously too stupid to know the difference between a polo jersey and a serving uniform."

She turned to Catherine, her voice tight. "If you agree to cater that wedding, you better charge them at least three times the going rate. Mr. Whitney has certainly been a great help to me, but he has a bitch of a daughter and a dim-witted wife."

Swain blinked, surprised. The furious, incredibly beautiful Lillie had just become the protector rather than the protected. Swain hadn't had time to digest that shift before Lillie's hands were on her collar, straightening and smoothing it.

"Why are you still hanging around here?" she said softly, her previous anger still flushing her cheeks. "The match starts in thirty minutes, and you can't win that trophy for me standing here to guard us from the local piranha."

"If I was worried before, I'm not now." Swain moved close enough that Lillie's faint scent of magnolias made her ovaries clinch.

"You're as dangerous as you are beautiful," she murmured.

"Ah, I see you've found that silver tongue you seemed to have lost earlier." Now Lillie's expression was soft and affectionate. She brushed her lips along Swain's cheek. "For luck."

❖

The opposing team was from a well-funded New York stable, having stopped off to play the tournament on their way to Florida for the winter polo season. Although they were unable to keep Swain from scoring, their experience gave them an edge over the rest of the Raiders. So, what developed was a primarily offensive game, pushing the halftime score abnormally high at seven to seven.

The five-minute halftime break was bedlam at the Wetherington trailers where the team was changing horses and gulping water.

Javier was speaking rapid Spanish to Swain, who was nodding as she handed off a very exhausted Black Astor to one of the stable's grooms. Rob was swearing as he dug through a pile of mallets to select a different one for the second half. Julia, the fourth member of the team, gave up her struggle to refasten the broken strap on her knee guard and threw it on the ground, disgusted.

Swain held her hands up, palms out. "Whoa, whoa. Everybody just calm down. Javier, speak English so Rob and Julia can understand, too. Rob, get the stick with the blue grip. I need you hooking more. Julia, I've got another set of knee guards you can use." She turned to John. "Will you get them from the trailer?"

The group quieted and looked at Swain, their captain, expectantly.

"Yes, they're tougher than we thought. But not so good that we can't beat 'em. We're keeping up with them offensively, but we need to pump up our defense. So, I'm going to work a little harder to help Javier out on that end." She held up her hand again to stop Rob as he opened his mouth to interrupt. "In the next two chukkers, I just want to hold our own, play things safe and clean. Rob, since I'll be helping Javier, I'm depending on you to do more to feed the ball to Julia for points."

Rob shook his head. "We need you scoring, boss. That's the only reason we're tied with them now."

Swain leveled a stern stare at him. "You can do this, Rob. Your job in the number-two position is primarily offense. Julia's job in the number-one position is offense. If Javier and I do well on defense, you won't have to score that much to keep up with them."

Julia looked doubtful. "We've always believed the best defense is a good offense. We're an offensive team. Do you think it's a good idea to change that in the middle of a match?"

"That's exactly why we need to lay back but not down…just for the next two chukkers. Hopefully, they'll think we've used up our energy and best horses." She paused for effect. "Then, in the final chukker, we'll open up a big can of offense whoop-ass on them. Javier, you'll be guarding the goal pretty much by yourself, so I want you mounted on Domino."

"You already rode him in the first chukker," Julia pointed out.

"Domino's good for another," John said as he returned with the extra knee guards.

"He can stop and turn on a dime, and Javier's going to need that to intercept their shots," Swain said. Domino was also Javier's favorite in the stable, even though Swain normally rode him. Hopefully, riding him would give Javier the confidence he needed do an exceptional job.

"Rob, I want you up on Hard Knox for the last chukker. Any time we get in a bunch-up, use his size to bump right through the middle and kick that ball out. I'll be on Nor'easter. Julia, save Flash for the last period. We're going to run that ball downfield so fast, they won't know what hit 'em until it's already between the goalposts."

By the time Swain finished laying out the plan, the others were all agreeing.

"We're going to win this one for Abigail. We're going to win it for Lillie," she declared.

"Huelo la victoria. Es un buen día para ganar," Javier crowed.

Swain grinned and translated for the others. "I smell victory, too, Javier. It *is* a good day to win."

❖

Lillie paced in front of their seats. "Where are they?" The officials were looking at their watches. "We don't need to start the second half with a penalty."

Catherine laughed. "One tournament and you're becoming a fussy sponsor."

Lillie laughed at herself. "I guess I just get caught up in it." She filled her cup from the punch bowl and plopped down in the chair next to Catherine's. "I think it's important to Swain to win this one…for Grandmum."

Catherine gave her a pointed look. "I think it's important to her to win it for you."

Flushing, she searched out Swain as the Raiders burst onto the field, narrowly missing a penalty for being tardy. "We aren't…we haven't—"

"I'm sorry," Catherine said quickly. "I had just gotten the impression…I don't even know if you date women."

"Exclusively." Lillie smiled. "Your instincts are correct. It's just that Swain and I…well, it's complicated."

Catherine was contemplative. "I'm not sure what the complications are, Lillie, but the attraction between the two of you is obvious. Neither of you do a good job of hiding it."

Lillie took off her hat and nervously brushed back a curl with her fingers. "I kissed her once, though she hasn't initiated anything in return."

"Swain's a complex person. She seems to take everything in stride. But the waters run deep under that laid-back act. Although she makes friends easily, she doesn't trust easily."

The opposing team won the throw-in and hammered the ball downfield. Swain wheeled to ride her opponent off the line of play while Javier neatly intercepted the ball and hit it to Rob, who whizzed it toward Julia. Unfortunately the other team intercepted it, so Swain and Javier prepared to defend again.

"Perhaps that's the complication between us. Until Grandmum's will is read, neither of us can trust what the future holds." That was it. Swain trusted her with her past, but not her future. She wished she could promise Swain more.

Catherine squeezed Lillie's hand. "I'm sure everything will work out fine."

The ball was again rocketing toward Javier, but Swain had her pony in a dead run toward it. With perfect timing, she stretched far forward and swung her mallet under her steed's neck. It connected with a loud crack to reverse the direction of the ball back toward her offensive players. Lillie and Catherine jumped to their feet and cheered loudly. The ball, however, was intercepted again and immediately surrounded by a knot of players who jostled for position while it ricocheted among the ponies' hooves. They sat back down to watch.

"So…you date women exclusively? You never switch-hit?" Catherine asked.

"No. I've never met a man who made me want to."

"Does it bother you that I do?"

"Not at all." She patted Catherine's arm. "I know some very nice men. I just don't want to kiss them."

Catherine laughed. "Well, I don't find too many attractive that way, but Reid is different. He and I clicked the first time we met. I told him about my past with Swain and he's fine with it."

Lillie was surprised. "He must be quite a guy, especially to let you continue to be friends."

"He *is* quite a guy. But speaking of guys, should I go over there and tell the one who's been staring at you all day that he's barking up the wrong tree?"

Lillie went completely still, her heart freezing a beat. "Someone's watching me?"

"Right over there." Catherine pointed toward the bleachers. "Well, he was there a minute ago."

"What'd he look like?"

"Hard to tell. He had on a ball cap and sunglasses. But he had a nice build."

Like the guy at the racetrack. Lillie shuddered, wishing she'd told Swain about her stalker and her gut feeling that the cat didn't get locked in the closet by accident. Her doubts had seemed silly at the time. She had nothing to go on but one e-mail and an odd feeling from the guy at the track. He could have been anybody. He could have been just some guy looking at pretty women. Now, the chill that ran through her told her to trust her instincts.

Catherine looked at Lillie curiously. "Everything okay?"

"Yes, of course. I just hadn't noticed."

Catherine didn't appear convinced, but Lillie didn't feel like offering more of an explanation. She turned her attention back to the playing field so Catherine would do the same. Things weren't going well there either.

The ball broke from the bunch-up and an opposing player thumped it neatly between the goalposts before Javier could stop it.

The Raiders were down by one.

CHAPTER TWENTY-TWO

S wain knocked softly on the back door of the main house, unsure why she'd walked up from the barn after dark, in the rain. Lillie was a siren she was finding impossible to resist. She smiled when Lillie opened the door and grabbed her arm to pull her inside.

"You're soaked to the skin," Lillie said. "Haven't you heard of an umbrella?"

"I was already wet from unloading the ponies and equipment." She had to raise her voice to be heard as Lillie ducked into the housekeeper's suite to retrieve a towel from the bathroom. "I wanted to make sure you got back okay."

Lillie threw the towel over Swain's head and began to rub her hair dry. Swain laughed under the onslaught, catching Lillie's hands in hers. "I can do that myself," she said.

Lillie dropped her hands, but didn't step back. When Swain finished drying off, Lillie finger-combed her hair into place. She submitted silently, relishing the feel of Lillie's long fingers. Their eyes met and they smiled at each other.

"Are you hungry?" Lillie asked. "We have some leftovers from the buffet."

"Famished."

She was hungry, but she'd have professed to anything to spend time with Lillie. They had been surrounded with other people all day, and the pace had been hectic. Lillie was busy with the buffet preparations, playing hostess at the tent, then cleaning up the food and equipment to come home. Swain had been tied up with the details of hauling horses to the polo field, playing the match, the awards ceremony afterward, then trailering horses back to the farm.

"Did you have fun today?" Swain asked.

"I had a wonderful time. And you were magnificent, outscoring them four to one in the last chukker." Lillie waved her hands as she talked, her eyes bright. "I was on the edge of my seat when it was tied with only a minute left. And when they got that shot off toward our goal, I was holding my breath and praying at the same time."

Swain understood. Watching had to be a lot harder than playing.

The Raiders had played at the top of their game the entire match, but still were down by two goals at the start of the last chukker. Mounting their best ponies for the final period, they held the other team to one more goal. The other team's ponies were no match for Nor'easter. Astride him, Swain seemed to be everywhere on the field—defending, riding off opposing players, stealing the ball, and firing in three goals with deadly accuracy. When the bell rang to signify only a minute left, the score was tied.

Even so, all seemed lost when, in that final minute, an opposing player popped the ball loose out of a bunch-up and his teammate's wide swing sent it flying airborne toward the goal. The other players seemed to freeze as Domino lunged toward it and Javier stretched to his fullest.

His mallet nailed the ball in midair, dropping it to the ground several yards short of a goal. Domino instantly reared and whirled with all the agility of his desert ancestors, putting Javier in position for a clean swing to slam the ball back into the open field.

It had barely left his mallet when Swain and Nor'easter were galloping at full speed on a trajectory to intercept the pass. But a player from the other team, in a more advantageous position farther down the field, also turned his pony toward the ball. It would have been a race even Nor'easter couldn't have won, if Rob and Hard Knox hadn't appeared out of nowhere. They gave the other pony a hard, but legal, bump that nearly unseated his rider.

Swain was in the clear. Julia and Flash cut off the only opposing player guarding the goal. Bending low over Nor'easter's neck, Swain raised her stick high overhead, bringing it down to strike the ball with a loud thwack. As the blur of white soared past, the player guarding the goal threw his mallet on the ground. He'd had no chance of stopping it.

The Raiders were victorious.

"Catherine and I screamed and cheered like blokes at a football game. I'm amazed that I have any voice left." Lillie's expression softened and she cupped Swain's cheek. "My champion."

The admiration, the affection in Lillie's eyes would be burned into Swain's brain, her heart, forever. It was a soul-deep warmth she'd never felt in the cold world that had been her life. Or maybe she'd been living in a netherworld, waiting for life…waiting for this woman, this moment. She leaned closer to this light, this beacon that was Lillie drawing her.

The microwave chimed and Swain shook herself mentally. In another moment, Lillie's lips would have been on hers and she would have surrendered. Instead, she retreated, to the refrigerator, and retrieved a chilled bottle of wine.

Ignoring Lillie's frustrated sigh she turned her attention to locating a corkscrew. Lillie set the plate on the table with silverware for one, along with two wineglasses.

"This is a lot of food. You're not eating?" Swain asked as she poured the wine.

"I've been grazing all day, so I'm not really hungry." She popped a cheese straw into her mouth.

"So, tell me what you and Catherine did while I was riding ponies," Swain said, moving the mood to a safer level. "Every time I looked over at the tent, you were holding court with a full house."

Lillie seemed to accept her retreat and began recounting her day in detail. She swiped a few tidbits from Swain's plate as she talked, so Swain began feeding every third or fourth forkful to Lillie as she listened. When the plate was empty and Lillie's day fully recounted, Swain reluctantly stood and slid her plate into the dishwasher.

"Well, I guess I better head back to the barn so you can get some rest. Thanks for dinner." She walked to the back door.

"Wait!" Lillie opened her mouth to say something, then looked confused about what she wanted to say.

"Lillie?"

"You need to take this trophy with you and put it with the others," she said quickly. She hurried out of the room and returned with a huge silver bowl. "To the victor, the spoils," she said lightly, handing it to Swain.

"Ah, but I'm only your champion, my lady. The prize is yours," Swain said slowly, looking deep into Lillie's eyes.

Lillie stepped closer. Her hands caressed Swain's face, her voice soft. "Then to this victor, the spoils."

Swain lowered her head and met the soft brush of Lillie's lips. When she felt them part against her mouth, the residual lust of the afternoon's battle surged in her veins, thick and hot. She was powerless to resist further. She dropped the trophy and pulled Lillie roughly to her. Lillie's heart beat wildly against her own as she plundered Lillie's mouth and claimed her prize. Lillie moaned and sagged against her, relinquishing herself to Swain's passion. She lifted her chin, her graceful neck an offering to Swain's lips and tongue.

"Swain. Oh, Swain."

Her name was music on Lillie's lips, a hypnotic call.

She spun them around to pin Lillie against the wall, her thigh fitting between Lillie's, finding her heat. Lillie's hips undulated against the pressure, her hands clawed at Swain's back.

"Yes," she whispered. "Yes, love. Make me yours."

But Lillie wasn't hers, would never be hers. She'd return to England, to a world of wealthy friends, theater, and city living. A world where Swain—with horse sweat on her clothes and manure on her boots—didn't belong. Trembling with the effort to rein in her fervor, she pushed away, averting her eyes from Lillie's gaze. She crossed her arms over her chest to securely tuck away her hands, the traitors that a moment before had been inches from tearing open Lillie's blouse to caress her breasts.

"No. God, I'm sorry. No." Swain scooped up the trophy from the floor and fled.

❖

Lillie was stunned. Nothing but a cold chill remained where Swain's heat and hard muscle had been pressed against her seconds before. She ran her mind over the previous two minutes. Had she said something wrong? Did Swain have a lover that Lillie didn't know about?

She considered following her to the barn and demanding an explanation. But when she opened the back door, the pounding of hooves and the dark silhouette fleeing toward the moonlit trails made it clear she would get no answers tonight.

Damn it to bloody hell. She closed the door and locked it, then set the alarm. When she had first asked Swain to wait, she had intended to finally tell her about the man stalking her. But when she looked into those blue eyes and heard her name on those lips, all she could think about was kissing her. And Swain's response left no doubt that she wanted to kiss Lillie. So, why did she run?

Her thoughts and emotions were reeling, spinning too fast for her to sleep, and taking care of her physical arousal herself held no appeal. She wanted Swain, and nothing else would come close to satisfying her.

So, Lillie filled the deep claw-footed tub in her bathroom and climbed in to let the soothing water drain the tension from her body and the noise from her head. She lay back and closed her eyes, concentrating on calming her emotions.

But as she relaxed, images of Swain seeped into her thoughts. Her hips spasmed and her ovaries tingled at the memory of the tempest that was Swain. Startled by her reaction, Lillie sprang from her bath and dried quickly. She usually slept in her silk panties, but tonight she dressed in pajamas to suppress her disobedient body.

She grabbed her laptop from the dresser and climbed into bed. Maybe catching up on her e-mail would distract her. She booted up the computer and clicked for her messages to download.

As she waited, she glanced at the French doors that led to the balcony. If she opened them a bit, would she hear the hoofbeats when Swain returned? The ping sounded that indicated her download was complete, so she redirected her attention and scanned down through her mail. Curiously, one file showed her own addy, as though she had sent it to herself. She opened it and froze.

Did you let the pussy out of the closet yet?

It was him. He *had* been in this house, in this bedroom. *He* had locked the cat in the closet. And now, he had hacked into her e-mail account. She read the rest of his words and the double entendre of the first line became clear.

Has Swain had a ride on more than just your ponies?
She can't give you what you need. You need a man to give
you a Wetherington heir.

She punched the Delete key and closed the laptop without properly shutting it down, as though she could shut him out, erase him from her life. She returned the computer to the dresser, then looked around the bedroom.

He wasn't hiding in the bathroom. She had just come from there. She darted over to the French doors. They were securely locked, but she pulled the heavy drapes together to cover them. The walk-in closet. He could be there. She grabbed her cell phone from the bedside table and punched in Swain's number. The call went immediately to voice mail. Damn it.

"Swain, it's Lillie. I'm sorry. Listen, please call me. I don't care what time. I need to tell you something." She had to warn her about the stalker. Then she needed to disappear. She entertained a fleeting hope that Swain would go with her. But Swain wouldn't run. She wouldn't understand how dangerous this man was. She hadn't lost both her parents to his "accidents." She hadn't felt his filthy hands on her, his disgusting erection against her belly.

She pulled a pair of sharp scissors from the table's drawer and held them like a dagger as she approached the closet cautiously. The door was partially open and she pushed it slowly back. Quickly flipping the light switch, she breathed in relief when the only things illuminated were clothes and shoes. She knelt some distance from the bed and peered underneath. Nothing there.

Although the alarm was on, she went to the bedroom door and locked it, too, then crawled under the bed covers, the scissors tucked beneath her pillow. She turned off the bedside lamp and let her eyes adjust to the dim illumination of the bathroom's nightlight. She clutched a pillow to her chest, against the terrified thumping of her heart. It would be a long time until dawn.

CHAPTER TWENTY-THREE

The room was still dark when Lillie woke with a start. She had finally fallen into an exhausted sleep, but continued to wake at every small sound. The noises coming from the kitchen were probably what woke her this time.

She looked at the digital clock, surprised to see the red numbers read ten thirty. Then she realized the heavy drapes were blocking the morning sun. The house phone rang twice, then stopped. She cautiously picked it up to listen, then relaxed when she recognized Mary's voice. She was talking to John, who apparently was calling from the barn, so she quietly replaced the receiver.

Her muscles, tight and sore from the tense night, protested when she swung her feet to the floor. She stretched carefully. She had to see Swain. She flung the curtains back to flood the room in sunlight. A lone rider was on the polo field below, but it was Rob, not Swain, exercising Sunne.

Lillie dressed quickly and went downstairs. Mary was taking a tray of fresh muffins out of the oven and offered her one.

"I can scramble you some eggs and cut up some fresh fruit, too, if you like. The coffee's still hot, but you need to show me how you like your tea brewed."

Lillie hesitated. The muffins smelled delicious and, although she usually preferred tea, she would kill for some coffee after her sleepless night. "Coffee will do for this morning, thanks." She sat at the table where Mary placed a huge muffin and a steaming mug of aromatic coffee. She saw no point in running down to the barn until she was fed and awake enough for her head to be clear.

Mary looked at her curiously. "Are you feeling okay, hon? You said you were usually an early riser, and you still look tired."

"No, I'm fine. I guess all the excitement of the polo match yesterday had me stirred up. I didn't sleep very well. I kept waking up."

Mary bustled around the kitchen, washing the dishes she'd dirtied when making the muffins. "I don't know how you ever sleep at all in this big house by yourself. But then I haven't had a night all to myself since I married twenty-five years ago. When Frank wasn't home, the kids were crawling in bed with me. If I had an hour of quiet, I wouldn't know what in the world to do with it."

Lillie finished her coffee and pushed her plate away. "These muffins are delicious. Perhaps I should take a few down for Swain."

"No need. John called up from the barn a while ago. He said Swain left early this morning and wanted him to let me know she'd be out of town the rest of the week and didn't need me to leave a dinner plate for her."

"She's gone?" Lillie stood so abruptly, she had to catch her chair to keep it from toppling. No! Everything was getting too jumbled up. She was the one who was supposed to leave. But when she heard that Swain was gone, the pain that cut through her chest and stole her breath left her reeling.

Mary looked as surprised as Lillie felt. "She didn't tell you?"

"I saw her last night, and she didn't say anything about it."

"Oh, dear. I hope it wasn't a family emergency or something. Maybe she got a call during the night and had to leave immediately. John didn't say. I just took for granted it was some kind of business trip. But you'd know about it, if it was." She dried her hands and picked up the phone. "I'll call John and see what he knows."

"No…thanks." Lillie ran her fingers through her hair in frustration. Swain didn't have any family. Wait, she did have a brother. Had he called? Grandmum's letter said they believed he was dead. Was there other family Swain hadn't talked about? "I'll go down and talk with John. I want to check on some things at the barn anyway."

"Today is an early dismissal day for schools, so I thought I'd pick up Dani and then fix a light lunch since you got up late today."

Lillie edged toward the door, trying not to look like she was bolting to the barn. "Take your time. I'm sure I won't be hungry anytime soon." She forced herself to stroll casually off the terrace, then broke into a jog. What was she afraid of?

She feared something even worse than her stalker—that she'd never see Swain again.

❖

John was washing down the filly Swain had bought at the track.

"Good morning." Lillie hoped she didn't sound too breathless after her jog to the barn.

"Morning, Miss Lillie."

"I don't suppose Swain is about."

John kept his eyes on his task, but he didn't look happy. "Nope. Left early this morning."

Lillie waited, but he wasn't offering any further information. Obviously, she would have to pull it out of him. "Where was she going?"

"Florida."

"Does she have family there?"

John glanced at her. "Never heard her talk about any." He dipped his sponge in the soapy water and began washing the filly's neck. "Florida's where they play the winter polo season."

Lillie brightened. "Yes, that's right. That's where the team they beat yesterday was going." She frowned as recall began to click in. "But someone said their season doesn't start until January."

"That's right."

"Why would Swain go now, in the middle of the polo season here?"

"Don't know."

"Did she go down there to look at a horse?"

"Didn't take a trailer with her. Said she was gonna catch a flight out of Columbia."

Had Swain fled to a lover in Florida? "Damn it, man. You didn't ask why she was going?"

John dropped his sponge in the bucket and faced her, his irritation clear. But was he put out with her or with Swain?

"Maybe those fellers this weekend told her about a job. Maybe she's interviewing with some other stable to train ponies down there since nobody knows what's going to happen here. I can't think of any other reason she'd leave in the middle of our polo season."

Lillie's anger faltered. She looked toward the door to Swain's apartment. "She's leaving?" Even she could hear the quiver in her voice. The possibility of being completely alone again was like a cold hand around her heart. She hadn't felt it so keenly since the day Abigail breathed her last. She nearly choked on her next words. "Is she coming back?"

She must have looked as though she would faint, because John grabbed her arm to guide her to sit on a bale of hay in the barn's hallway. He looked worried.

"Maybe she did go to look at a horse, and she's just going to have him shipped back here. Could be somebody's paying her to fly down and show them how to handle some problem horse. She got a pretty penny to do that a couple of years ago." He knelt and took her hand. "Don't listen to me. I'm just being an old grouch because she left behind that Sasquatch she calls a dog. He worries me to death when she's gone, pacing around the barn and whining."

"She didn't take Beau?" Lillie's heart lifted. She wouldn't leave Beau unless she planned to come back.

"No. She didn't know how long she'd be gone, but she's definitely coming back. She loves that mutt more than anything."

Lillie looked around. "Where is he?"

"Last time I saw him, he was scratching on the door to go upstairs. Looking for Swain, I reckon. I opened the door for him and left it cracked so he could come back down when he wants. I'll lock it before I leave tonight."

"Do you think she would mind if I went up to check on him?"

"I'm sure she'd be fine with it," John said. "If his bowl's empty, would you pour him some food and check his water bowl?"

"Of course."

Lillie climbed the stairs cautiously. Although Beau knew her, he might be very protective of his home while Swain was away. She peeked in the kitchen and called to him. No response. Both of his bowls were still full. She looked into the study, but no dog. She walked into the living room and called again.

"Beau? Where are you, boy?"

A low moan came from the bedroom. Was he sick or hurt? She expected to find him sprawled on the bed, but didn't see him. Where could an animal that size hide?

"Beau?" Another long, mournful moan.

She followed the sound into the walk-in closet where she found him curled up on a pile of Swain's laundry he had pulled from the hamper.

"What are you doing in here, boy?" She sat on the floor to stroke his head and gently scratch behind his ears. She had never seen such misery in an animal's eyes.

"Oh, Beau. She's coming back. She'd never leave you for long." He heaved a dramatic sigh and she chuckled, his antics taking her mind off her own sense of loss. "Moping around won't bring her back any sooner. And I'm fairly certain she won't be happy that you're shedding all over her clothes, even if they are headed for the wash. We need to put all of these back in the hamper."

She pulled a polo shirt from under his leg and was about to toss it in the hamper when she caught a whiff of Swain's scent. She brought the shirt to her nose and closed her eyes, reveling in the smell of vanilla and raspberries, sweat, horses, and hay. She flashed back to the lips that had claimed hers, the body that had pressed her against the kitchen wall, and the passion that had burned so hot between them.

"How about if I join you here for a while?" She took the answering sigh to be a yes and turned to lie down, her head resting on Beau's big body. She clutched Swain's shirt to her chest. "I miss her, too," she whispered.

Two hours later, she woke with a start. Nestled there in the comfort of Swain's essence, she had finally relaxed into a restoring, deep-REM sleep. Beau still snored beside her.

"Well, this is pathetic, isn't it, sleeping among her soiled clothes on the floor of her wardrobe?"

Beau growled softly in agreement.

But she didn't feel pathetic. She felt better, stronger. She climbed to her feet.

"Come along, Beau. You're staying with me while she's gone. Consider yourself a hostage. When she does get back, she'll have to come see me to find you."

Beau rolled up onto his chest, his long tail thumping against the floor. He stood as she gathered Swain's clothes and stuffed them into a duffel. She'd get Mary to show her how to launder them.

She hesitated in the kitchen. If Beau was coming with her, she needed to gather his things. She called downstairs to the office and asked John if someone was available to help her. Less than a minute later, Javier and Rob clomped up the steps.

"If you could just get that dog bed from the bedroom," she told Javier. "And you carry his kibble," she added, pointing out a nearly full forty-pound bag of food to Rob. "I'll take his bowls."

They formed an odd parade, with Beau leading the way to the house and Lillie a few steps behind, carrying two oversized dog bowls. Javier followed, sneezing repeatedly from the dog hair flying off the bed, and Rob brought up the rear grumbling about the weight of the dog-food bag.

Mary had returned with Dani, who opened the door for them. The wiry twelve-year-old wrapped Beau in a tight hug. "Where ya going, boy?" She released the dog and straightened to glare at Lillie, Rob, and Javier. "Where y'all taking Miss Swain's dog?"

Lillie almost burst out in laughter. This ninety-pound kid was standing with her hands on her hips, ready to take on all three adults. She resembled a bantam rooster looking for a fight.

"Danielle Marie, you better mind your manners."

In spite of Mary's reprimand, the kid wasn't backing down.

"It's okay, Mary." Lillie set the bowls in the sink to wash them and smiled at Dani. "Beau is so sad that Swain is out of town, I thought it would cheer him up to stay with us until she comes home."

Dani nodded. "That's a good idea." She hugged Beau again. "Don't be sad, boy. We'll play with you."

Rob put the bag of dog food in the pantry and Lillie asked Dani, "Could you put Beau's bed upstairs? He'll sleep in my room. Left at the top of the stairs, first room on the right."

"I can do that." The big hairy pillow dwarfed the girl, but she gamely wrapped her arms around it and summoned Beau to follow. "We'll find you a nice sunny spot," she told him.

"Be quick, sweetie. Lunch is ready."

"I will, Mom," Dani called over her shoulder.

Mary turned to the adults. "Everybody sit down. Lunch is shrimp salad and fresh fruit. There's enough for everybody."

Javier and Rob didn't argue. "Thanks. That sounds a whole lot better than the baloney sandwich I was planning to eat," Rob said.

"Yeah. I was having Chinese leftovers from last night," Javier said, laughing at Rob's expression of exaggerated shock. "What? You think I eat tacos all the time?"

"You do eat tacos all the time," Dani said, skipping back into the room and sliding into a chair.

"Only while I lived with my mother. She can't cook anything but Mexican food. My cousin and I have our own place now. We eat pizza and Chinese and cheeseburgers," he said proudly.

"Now that's something to brag about." Mary's sarcasm was lost on Dani.

"Mom won't let me have pizza but twice a month. Can I move in with you and your cousin?"

"No, you can't, young lady," Mary answered for Javier.

Lillie listened to the friendly banter around the table. Having company should have taken her mind off Swain, but it only swelled the ache of her absence. She missed feeling Swain by her side.

She wasn't sure why Swain was gone, but she did know one thing. It was time for them to talk…about everything. Promise be damned. She wouldn't let family secrets steal her happiness.

❖

The cell number went straight to voice mail again, so Lillie hung up. Swain must have forgotten to turn her phone back on when her flight landed. Or maybe she didn't want to talk to anyone. Including Lillie.

She composed her thoughts as she stripped and climbed into bed. Beau had refused to sleep in his bed until she pulled it right next to hers. She settled against the pillows and punched in the number again. This time, she left a message.

"Swain. It's me, Lillie." She knew she sounded nervous, so she took a deep breath. "We need to talk. If you left because of me, we need to talk honestly about why. If you have another reason, a job or a girlfriend in Florida, I'd still like to hear about that. Please, Swain. Please call me. Please come home." She ended the call and stared at the phone. "Please come home. I miss you," she whispered.

CHAPTER TWENTY-FOUR

I don't know, Manny. I like training as much as riding, so I don't think I'd like working just as a professional rider. Besides, I have Beau to think about. I'd have to travel to follow the polo tournaments. I'd have to go overseas for a while, too, to really make a name as a rider."

Swain sat back in the lawn chair and took a big swallow of her beer. It was easy enough after arriving the day before to find old friends who were happy to have her help exercise the ponies they were training. Today, she'd risen early and ridden pony after pony to keep her mind busy. Now she sat outside the stable, around a cooler full of beer with a group of grooms and exercise riders, to relax after the grueling day.

"You have a boyfriend?"

The other men laughed at Carlos's surprise.

Swain snorted. "Yeah. He's the only male who'll ever lay his head on my bed. He sheds hair everywhere, has big teeth and dog breath."

"You're dating my girlfriend's brother?" Tomas teased, bringing another chorus of cackles from the group.

Swain clarified for Carlos, who still looked confused. "He has dog breath because he is a dog...a big dog."

She was glad to see her friends again, and sitting around the cooler with the guys at the end of the day used to be one of her favorite pastimes. But today, her heart was still back in South Carolina. What had Lillie been doing?

❖

Lillie did need to have her hair trimmed, but that wasn't why she was waiting to be Gloria's next customer. She couldn't just sit around and do nothing until Swain returned. She wanted to hear some town gossip, and the flamboyant hair stylist she had met at the newspaper office would probably have her pulse on the news and be more than willing to share it.

"Lillie, sugar, how are you doing? Abigail's funeral was so wonderful. Short, but beautiful."

"I'm very well, thank you. It was brief, but Grandmum made all the arrangements herself. I guess she wanted it that way."

"I just love your accent." Gloria settled her in the barber chair and ran her fingers through Lillie's long hair. "What can I do for you today, hon? You looked lovely at the funeral, but I did notice a few split ends. Time for a trim?"

"Just a slight one."

"I've got some really good shampoo and conditioner made special for wavy hair like yours. I have to order it all the way from New York City. Would you like to try it?"

"Yes, please."

Gloria waved away the shop assistant who usually did the shampoos and led Lillie back to the sinks. She chatted away as she worked. The thorough massage of her scalp was relaxing, but not so relaxing that Lillie didn't realize Gloria was also pumping her for information. Had the will been read? Did she already know what it would say? Would Lillie divide her time between England and South Carolina? Was she learning to play polo like Abigail?

The shampoo done and Lillie resettled in the chair, Gloria started combing out the abundant curls.

"Have you heard from Swain? What in the world is she doing down in Florida anyway?"

Ah, now they were getting to the subject Lillie wanted to talk about.

"You know about her going to Florida?"

"Honey, Gloria knows everything."

"Really. She's only been gone a day. I guess she came by to see you before she left?"

Gloria looked up from her task, her gaze meeting Lillie's in the mirror. Her eyes were kind. "She didn't come see me, sugar. I cut Annie's hair yesterday. Do you know Rob's wife, Annie? He told her at lunch and she told me when she came in the shop yesterday afternoon."

"Did Rob say why she went to Florida?"

"He said she might be checking out a job down there, but the boys really think—" Gloria acted as though she realized she was saying too much.

"What do they think?"

Gloria shrugged and went back to clipping the ends of Lillie's hair. "It doesn't matter. Men are always wrong. If it's not a sport to watch or something to eat, it's more than their brains want to handle."

"Please tell me."

Lillie heard nothing but the snipping sound of the scissors while Gloria decided how much to reveal. "Rob told Annie they think it has something to do with you. Did y'all have a spat or something?"

Lillie averted her gaze. "No, nothing like that."

Gloria stopped, her scissors raised in midair. "Oh, honey. You've fallen for her, too, haven't you? Don't feel bad. All of us girls in town who lean that way, or even half that way, have made a play for her. How could you resist those big blue eyes and long thick lashes? I just hadn't pegged you as a sister." She patted Lillie on the shoulder and sighed. "It's not you. That Swain, bless her heart, is just a hard dog to keep under the porch."

"Sorry?"

"That's a Southern expression." Gloria smiled. "Let me see if I can explain. In the old days, the houses around here were built on stone pillars, so air could circulate under them and keep them cooler. The huntin' dogs would always crawl up under their owner's porch to bed down for the night. There was always one dog, though, that would just crawl up under the porch of whatever house looked good at sundown."

Lillie frowned. "You're saying that Swain sleeps around a lot?"

"No, hon. Not a lot. She could if she took every chance offered her. I'm just saying that more than one woman has tried to tie her under their porch. When that happens, Swain gets spooked and backs off. I reckon she hasn't found the right porch yet."

❖

Five beers later, Swain was buzzed. She waved off the guys' protest when she announced she was calling it a night and walked slowly through the gathering dusk, absorbing the sounds and smells of stables that ringed the polo arena. As she passed their stalls, several horses poked their heads out and nickered to her.

She'd always loved this community. She had friends in this town. She'd fulfilled Abigail's request and shown Lillie everything that was important. She didn't have any further obligations there. It wouldn't be hard to pick up a training job and resettle here, the place where she'd learned about horses and polo. It'd felt like home once.

But that was before South Carolina, where she had her own stable, her own team. The minute she set foot on the Wetherington farm, she belonged there.

"Hola, *mi dulce*. I had heard you were around." An attractive Latino woman was propped against Swain's truck. "You do not answer your phone and you do not come to see me, so I must come find you."

"Lolita, hello. I figured you would be married and have a bambino by now."

"Many boys have tried, but I cannot forget your kisses."

"Then I must go now and ask your Papa for your hand in marriage." Swain laughed at the woman's scowl. Lolita wasn't one of the barn help. Her father was a rich Argentinean who owned one of the best polo strings in Florida. She'd be married one day, but only to the man her father chose. In return, Papa turned a blind eye to his daughter's romantic trysts as long as she was discreet.

Lolita pouted. "You are a brute, but a sexy one. So, if you make me come many times tonight, I will forgive you."

Swain was tempted. Lolita was a beautiful woman, with none of the complications she'd left behind in South Carolina. But a night with Lolita wouldn't substitute for one minute with Lillie.

"As beautiful as you are, I've ridden too many ponies and drank too much beer today. The only thing I plan to do tonight is sleep," Swain said gently.

"You are turning me down?"

"I'm sorry, but yes."

Lolita studied her for a moment. "You must come back to us, *mi preciosa*. Where you live now makes your eyes very sad."

It was nearly dark and two large trucks shielded them from prying eyes. Swain gently kissed Lolita's pouting lips. "If I do, *mi tesoro*, you won't have to come searching for me. I'll find you."

❖

Lillie sat on the balcony of her bedroom, watching Javier and Rob work with a couple of the ponies. Time was dragging by so slowly while she waited for Swain to return. Had she listened to Lillie's message?

She picked up a long, heavy lens resting by her feet, snapped it onto her camera, and began clicking off shots. She lowered it after only a few minutes. It was getting too dark to shoot from that distance. She returned the lens to its case and thumbed the switch to view the frames she had just taken, deleting them one by one. Her breath hitched when the next image blinked onto the camera's view screen. Swain's handsome blue eyes and sexy half smile looked up at her.

She hadn't yet downloaded the photos she'd taken at the polo match. Some were very good. The next best thing to spending time with Swain was sorting through pictures of her, so she went inside to retrieve her laptop and get to work.

❖

Swain toweled off after her shower and pulled on a soft pair of boxers and a T-shirt. She flopped across the bed and grabbed the television remote. After flipping through the channels twice and finding nothing that held her interest, she turned it off. She stood to pull the covers back and climb between the sheets. When she reached to turn out the bedside light, she noticed her cell phone and powered it on before she had time to stop herself.

Lillie had called many times but left only one message.

"Swain. It's me, Lillie. We need to talk. If you left because of me, then we need to talk honestly about why. If you have another reason, a job or a girlfriend in Florida, I'd still like to know about that. Please, Swain. Please call me. Please come home."

She closed her eyes at the rich tones of Lillie's voice. This wasn't about Abigail any longer. This was about her and Lillie. She played the message again. Nearly a thousand miles away and it still wasn't enough distance to lessen Lillie's hold on her. She didn't have the strength to resist her entreaties any longer. Running from her wasn't working, so it was time to change tactics and chase her away instead.

She'd been wining and dining Lillie in the style to which Swain expected she was accustomed. But that wasn't the life Swain lived most of the time. She was used to being the one in the kitchen, cooking for the Lillies seated in the dining room. She was more comfortable sitting around the cooler with the guys at the barn than mingling at a wine-and-cheese party. Dinner for her some nights was tuna right out of the can. When she did cook, Beau's tongue was her rinse cycle before she put her plate in the dishwasher.

It was time to pull off Lillie's blinkers and show her how different their worlds were. That should send her running.

CHAPTER TWENTY-FIVE

The barn was quiet when Swain arrived back at the farm. She threw her bag on the bed and opened it to sort the dirty clothes from those she hadn't worn. When she lifted the top to the hamper to throw them in with the other laundry, she was surprised to see it empty. She was sure it was nearly full when she left.

She went downstairs and whistled for Beau, but got no answering bark. Where was everybody? She finally found John in the tack room, methodically polishing saddles. The fact that he hadn't come out to greet her when he heard her whistling for Beau was a sure sign he was put out with her.

"Hey, where are the guys?"

"Javier and Rob are out on the trails, exercising Finesse and Sunne."

"You seen my dog today?"

"Yep."

"You want to tell me where?"

"Up at the house with Miss Lillie."

"Oh." Swain glanced toward the house. Was she ready to face Lillie yet? She looked back at John. "You want to tell me what's eating you?"

John put down his rag and glared at her. "You got a new job in Florida?"

"No. Is that what you think? I didn't go to Florida for a job."

"Somebody down there you needed to see?"

Swain frowned. John had never pried into her personal life before now. "No."

"How about we stop playing twenty questions and you just tell me why you left me here with those three sad pups whining after you."

Swain looked down at her boot as she scuffed it against the concrete floor. "I needed some space to think, okay? Waiting to find out what's going to happen here is driving me crazy. Wait. What three pups?"

"That big idiot dog, sweet Miss Lillie, and young Dani, who's told me ten times a day that you promised her polo lessons."

"Oh, yeah. I did. How's Lillie?"

John glared at her. "You'll have to find that out for yourself. What's going on between you two is none of my business, but she deserves better than to have you run off in the middle of the night."

Swain was unsure how to respond.

He stood and threw up his hands in a shooing motion. "Go on. They're all up at the house. You need to settle things down so we can get back to training horses." He followed her out and turned toward the barn's office. "Too much female drama round here," he grumbled.

❖

Swain started to knock at the door, but the shrieks of laughter stopped her. She frowned. It didn't sound to her like they were moping around, missing her. She swung the door open and everyone froze.

The kitchen was a disaster of spilled flour and sticky bowls surrounded by various measuring cups, spices, and other ingredients. Mary stood at the oven, holding a pan of cookies that had just finished baking. Lillie and Dani looked up at her from the table where they were mixing another bowl of dough. Lillie had flour streaked across her nose and cheek. Dani had a smear of something that looked like molasses on her chin, and her hands were covered in cookie dough that she was rolling into small balls and placing on a pan. Even Beau had a liberal amount of flour dusted across his head.

"Swain!" Dani abandoned her work and ran over to wrap her arms around Swain, hugging her tight and transferring half the sticky goop on her hands to Swain's shirt.

Lillie's smile was at first brilliant, then hesitant. "You're back."

"Yeah. I needed to come home." Looking at Lillie now, she couldn't imagine why she'd ever left. She gave her a half smile, acknowledging that they needed to discuss things later in private.

Dani piped up. "This is my science homework. We have to practice measuring things. Lillie has been helping me figure them into metric for extra credit. Mom said I could take some to school tomorrow for the kids to eat while I explain how to measure things when you cook."

"That's a great idea. Are you teaching Lillie how we measure things, too?"

"Yes," Dani said before leaning forward to stage-whisper, "She's not as good as I am at adding things up, but she's catching on."

"I'm sure she'll get better with practice," Swain stage-whispered back.

"So, how was Florida?" Mary asked.

"Still hot as August down there," Swain said. Aiken's weather remained mild, but was beginning to cool noticeably since it was well into October. "I talked with two guys from an Argentine team. They're interested in both Domino and Nor'easter."

Lillie pushed her bowl over to Dani, giving Swain her full attention. "I thought you promised Nor'easter to one of the Whitneys."

"I haven't promised anything to anyone. I told them I couldn't discuss any sales until Abigail's will is read."

"Is that why you went to Florida, Swain?" Dani asked. She apparently was intensely interested in anything that had to do with Swain.

"Partly," Swain answered, holding Lillie's gaze.

"Well, we're glad you're back," Lillie said softly.

"Me, too. I came up to the house to invite you out to dinner."

"I'd love that." Lillie looked around at the mess from their baking. "It'll take me a while to clean up here and change."

"You go ahead, hon," Mary said. "This is Dani's project. She'll help me."

"Where are we going? Should I dress up? How much time do I have?"

"It's a surprise, and no. It's a blue-jeans kind of place, very rustic. Bring a sweatshirt because the dining room can get a little chilly this time of year." Swain surveyed the handprints Dani had left on her shirt. "You've got as long as it takes for me to go back down to my place and find a clean shirt."

❖

They pulled up to an old Esso service station where the gas pumps were still working relics from long before digital displays and pay-at-the-pump technology. A hand-painted sign advertised Mechanic on Duty next to a working antique Coca-Cola cooler. Swain parked her truck among eight or ten others in a weed-choked lot next door.

"This is it. A group of us gather here once a month to eat and swap stories." Swain turned in the seat to look at Lillie. "These are my friends. They aren't the Whitneys and the Hitchcocks. They're stable hands, farriers, and the guys who run the feed store and sell farm equipment."

"If they're your friends, I'd like to meet them."

Swain nodded.

"We need to talk, Swain."

"I know. We will. Soon."

They climbed down out of the truck, and Swain took Lillie's arm to help her navigate through the weeds and potholes.

As they approached, some of the men were standing with beers in their hands while others sat in folding camp chairs just outside the open garage part of the station. They all stared.

Swain gave the standoffish group a challenging glare. "Guys, this is Lillie. I've invited her to have dinner with us tonight."

Lillie spotted one friendly face in the bunch. "Hello, Tim. How's the shoeing business?"

"It's good, Miss Lillie."

An older man with white hair and a weathered face spoke up for the group. "No offense, miss, but this is a private gathering. No wives or women of any kind."

"Damn, Snow. What do you think *I* am?" Swain clasped Lillie's hand in a show of female solidarity.

"You don't count," one of the other men said. "We ain't got to watch our manners around you."

"Maybe we should go, Swain." Lillie didn't want to cause problems.

"No. We're staying." She addressed the group. "Lillie wants to get to know my friends, so you guys just be yourselves. Spit and scratch your privates, smoke cigars, and cuss all you want. Just like you usually do around me. Fish me out a beer, Tim."

Tim stuck his hand in the washtub full of bottled Budweiser and ice, and handed one to Swain. He shrugged apologetically at Lillie and gestured toward the washtub. "I'm afraid all we have to drink is beer. I can get you a soda from out of the machine over there."

One of the men snorted. "We ain't got no linen napkins either," he grumbled.

Lillie ignored him. "Beer's fine, Tim. But do you have something other than American beer?"

"We ain't got no fancy beers, either," someone in the crowd said.

"Sorry. I wasn't looking for anything fancy. It's just that most of the American beers are a bit light for me. I'm used to darker, heartier ales back home."

The men looked at each other, exchanging sly smiles. A tall man spoke up. "Ham brews dark beer, but it's got a bit of a bite. You got some of that in the station, Ham?"

The man who made the napkin comment grinned. "I sure do."

He hurried off and returned with a Mason jar of dark liquid. "It ain't cold," he warned. "But if ya can stomach it, I can chill some in the tub for ya."

Lillie raised her eyebrows in mock horror. "Don't you dare. You should always serve dark ales at room temperature."

They all stared, waiting for her to take a swallow.

Lillie made a show of smelling it and holding it up to the light.

"Just drink, girlie. This ain't no wine-tasting."

The men's laughter stopped suddenly when Lillie glared their way.

"We take our beer very seriously in the U.K." She took a mouthful and swirled it around before swallowing. They waited, unconsciously leaning toward her to hear the verdict. She nodded and took another big swallow. "It's a little mellow for dark ale, but much better than that weak stuff you blokes are drinking. Not exactly the dog's bollocks, but it's not bad."

"Did she say Ham's beer tasted like a dog's buttocks?" someone asked.

"Bollocks," Lillie enounced for them. "Testicles. When something is really great, it's the dog's bollocks." They stared blankly at her, apparently wondering if they misheard. "Well, you have to imagine a dog's bollocks are really fantastic since he can't seem to stop licking them."

The group howled with laughter, while Swain smiled and shook her head. Would Lillie ever stop surprising her?

Ham, the owner of the station, stepped forward and put out his hand for Lillie to shake. "I reckon we all had you pegged wrong. I do apologize. I'm Hamilton. Ham, for short. Welcome to our little get-together." He swatted the shoulder of a man seated nearby. "Get up, Tommy, and give the lady your seat."

"I have a friend in England who has brewed his own ale for years. It's the best I've tasted. I'll bet I could worm his recipe out of him if you're interested."

Ham brought her hand to his lips. "I'd propose marriage if my wife wouldn't kill me."

Lillie winked at him. "I might have to marry my friend to get his recipe."

Swain waved Tommy back into his chair and retrieved their own from the truck. They talked about horses and hay prices, tractors and fertilizers. It was obviously the common man's way of networking. They also bragged and complained about errant children and grandchildren. But they refrained from complaining about their wives too much, Lillie supposed in deference to her.

After a while, Swain led Lillie into the garage, which was to be their dining room. They had raised a hydraulic grease rack that lifted cars in the air for servicing to table height and placed a newspaper-covered sheet of plywood on the rack to act as a buffet table. Ham and another man, Arnie, had cleaned the car parts and oil cans off one counter and also covered it with newspaper to start preparing the food.

"What's for dinner, Ham?" Swain asked.

He opened the top of a thirty-gallon ice chest filled to the brim with ice and fish.

"Steve and Ray caught a mess of crappie at the lake and I had some more in the freezer, so we're frying fish. We'll be ready to start cooking in a minute. Why don't you go out front and start the deep fryer heatin' up."

Lillie was more interested in the food preparations, so she waved for Swain to go ahead without her.

"I love fish-and-chips," she said.

"Well, I'm not sure what you mean by chips, but around here folks eat grits and hush puppies and coleslaw with their fish."

"I believe you would refer to chips as French fries. But I'm afraid to ask what you mean by hush puppies."

Ham laughed. "Corn dodgers. A type of fried cornbread. They're called hush puppies because, before the Civil War, fried cornbread was a staple in the slave quarters. The story goes that slaves would fry up a batch of cornbread balls and throw them to the plantation owner's hounds to keep them quiet while they escaped."

Lillie watched as he poured a flour-like mix into a large bowl, cracked a few eggs into it, and reached for a gallon jug of water.

"Don't put water in that fish batter, Ham. Put milk," Arnie said.

"I ain't got no milk and it says on the package to use water."

"Could I make a suggestion?"

The men looked at Lillie.

"Use some of this dark ale instead. That's what they use in Whitby, this little town on the English coast. They're known to have the best fish-and-chips in the U.K."

Arnie looked doubtful. "Next thing you'll tell us you people bathe in that stuff. No wonder we won the Revolution. The Redcoats were all drunk."

"Try it on a couple and taste it. If you don't like it, you can go back to arguing over milk or water."

Lillie's suggestion was a huge hit. Once the fish and cornbread were ready, someone placed a Crock-Pot of buttery grits in the middle of the table and retrieved several bowls of coleslaw from another ice chest.

It was soon clear that the men found Lillie much more interesting than their own lives. They pelted her with questions and she charmed them with colorful British expressions.

"Lillie, what do you do in England?" Tim asked. "For a job, I mean."

"Rich people don't have to work, you idiot," Snow, the grumpy, white-haired elder of the group, said.

"I'm a photographer. I do freelance work for magazines—travel or home-and-garden layouts mostly. I also work for charities. The foundation that Princess Diana started to help needy children, I've shot photos for their brochures."

Swain stared at her, her expression one of surprise. "Why didn't you tell me you were a professional photographer?"

"You didn't ask. Like Snow, you probably took for granted I didn't have a career."

Swain blinked. "I guess I did. I apologize."

Lillie tilted her head and gave Swain an amused look. "Apology accepted."

The party began to break up about eight. Most had wives to go home to and jobs that started very early in the morning.

It was Ham who had the parting word as Swain folded up their chairs.

"Miss Lillie, you come back next month, ya hear?" The other men murmured their agreement. He slapped Swain on the back. "You're a lot more entertaining than old Swain here."

CHAPTER TWENTY-SIX

Swain was quiet on the way home while Lillie chattered. Their evening hadn't worked out exactly the way she'd expected. She thought Lillie would be taken aback at eating dinner in a garage, among the gasoline, oil cans, and car parts.

She thought the guys would run Lillie off. They were a rather exclusive club and had a strict rule about excluding wives or dates. But they loved Lillie. She proved herself by drinking ale too strong for them to stomach and improving their fish batter. Swain chuckled. At least Lillie drew the line at smoking cigars. Swain's mouth still tasted of them. She popped a stick of gum in her mouth, then offered the pack to Lillie.

"Am I talking too much? Is the gum to shut me up?" Lillie chuckled as she accepted the offering.

"No. Those cigars taste great when you're smoking 'em, but the aftertaste can be nasty."

Neither spoke the rest of the way home. When they pulled up at the house, Swain followed Lillie inside. She still had to collect Beau and his stuff. But when they entered the house, Lillie grabbed her hand and led her into the living room, where they settled next to each other—but not too close—on the large, overstuffed leather couch.

Lillie scooted closer and laid her hand on Swain's thigh. "It's time to talk, and I want to start with why you flew off to Florida."

Swain's leg burned where Lillie touched her, and her crotch

tingled. She couldn't think with Lillie that close, so she stood and walked over to the fireplace and pretended to study the framed photographs adorning the mantel. These hadn't been here before, had they? There was a picture of the Wetherington men, Jim and Eric, together in happier times. They were dressed for polo and holding up a trophy, their ponies standing behind them. There was a family portrait, too. Eric was blond like Abigail in the picture. Jim was dark-haired, his iridescent blue eyes staring at the photographer.

"Swain?"

"I needed to put some distance between us."

"Why?"

"Because you're my employer and I'm the hired help."

Lillie looked stunned. "I don't know what to say." She stood, but avoided Swain's gaze. "I…I apologize. I guess that would be sexual harassment, wouldn't it? I'm so very sorry. It won't happen again. I'll get Beau's bed from upstairs." Lillie started for the door, but Swain wrapped her arms around her from behind. Lillie was rigid.

"That's not at all what I meant. I wanted to kiss you." She couldn't stop herself from nuzzling Lillie's thick curls and inhaling the soft traces of magnolia in her scent. She definitely had found Abigail's designer perfume. "You're so beautiful. I came back from Florida because I'm not strong enough to stay away when you leave messages like you did on my cell phone."

Lillie turned in her arms and put her hand on Swain's cheek. "What is it then?"

"We'd never fit together, Lillie. We come from two different worlds. You grew up in your own bedroom, with your own things. I grew up in an orphanage where not even the pillow I slept on was my own. You grew up among private schools, symphony concerts, and vacations in France. I've never been on a vacation in my life, never been to a concert. While you were taking classes at a university, I was sleeping in haylofts above the stalls I mucked every morning."

Lillie's eyes searched hers. "Your world isn't so forbidding. I enjoyed myself tonight, immensely."

Swain smiled, a sadness creeping over her. "Yes, you did."

She couldn't resist brushing her fingers through Lillie's hair and lowering her head to briefly touch her lips against the pout forming on Lillie's. "You're a remarkable woman. But while you may fit easily into my world, I don't have a place in yours."

"That's not true. We have to talk. You are much more than you know."

Swain pressed her fingers to Lillie's lips to quiet her. "When I went with Abigail to her social functions, I drove her there, escorted her through the front door, then she mingled while I went to the kitchen and hung out with the caterers until she was ready to go."

Call softly.

"Was that because people didn't accept you at her side, or because you were more interested in cooking than idle chat?"

Swain hesitated. Was it? Nobody had pushed her toward the kitchen. She just felt more comfortable there. She released Lillie and stepped back, crossing her arms over her chest. "I don't know."

"We aren't so different," Lillie insisted, stepping forward to put her hands on Swain's folded arms, refusing to break their physical contact. "Come with me. I'll show you." She led Swain into the cavernous library room with a grand piano at one end.

Swain had been there before. Abigail never brought her into this room, but Swain had prowled the house the first time Abigail had gone out of town and entrusted her with the keys and security code. She'd pretended for a moment that she actually lived here, that this was her music room. She'd sat at the piano, but never mustered the courage to open it and play the fine instrument.

Lillie ran her hand over the dark wood. "My dad had one exactly like this in London." She took Swain's hands and studied them. "The first time I met you, I was struck by how similar your hands are to his, large with long fingers." Swain was mesmerized as Lillie turned the right hand over and traced her thumb along the rough areas. "And you both have calluses on your right hand from holding a polo mallet…at least until his hand was injured when I was still fairly young and he had to give up the sport. I still remember sitting in his lap and and opening his hand up to run my fingers over them." Lillie looked up at her. "Play for me, Swain? Please?"

Since words seemed to be failing her, Swain slid onto the piano bench as Lillie propped open its lid. Swain drank her in—her beautiful face, dark honey eyes, silky blond curls. Then she closed her eyes and did what felt to her as natural as riding a horse. She let music speak her emotions.

It was an easy, flowing, lighthearted waltz. She imagined them dancing, moving around the room in swirling turns, dropping their heads back and laughing. That was how Lillie made her feel.

When the last notes still hung in the air, Lillie sat down next to her. "There's a big formal benefit tomorrow night to raise money for the equestrian-rescue center. I want you to be my escort, but you have to promise not to retreat to the kitchen."

"Lillie, I don't know."

"Please, Swain. Your music makes me want to dance with you in the worst way."

Swain shook her head. "Dancing the way I'd want to dance with you—two women—would start the whole town talking."

"We can marry and serve in the military. Why shouldn't we be able to dance together?"

"Gays can't marry in most states here or serve in the military."

"Well, that's absurd. But I won't let that stop me from dancing with you if I want."

"I don't know how to dance."

"What?"

Swain's cheeks heated. "I don't know how to waltz or do any formal dances."

Lillie stood and held out her hand. "I'll show you. You have an athlete's natural grace and control. It should be easy."

Swain was doubtful, but she wanted to dance with Lillie. She sucked in a deep breath and took Lillie's hand in hers.

After walking through the basic steps several times, Lillie went to a computerized console on the wall and selected a song. As the room filled with a symphonic waltz, Lillie held out her arms. They began haltingly and with a few miscues, but Swain soon found her timing and they danced. They really danced. She twirled Lillie around the huge room until they were both laughing and breathless.

"I knew you'd be good at this," Lillie said, beaming.

Lillie was so beautiful, so alive in her arms. She was a bright burning flame and Swain was desperate for her. She pulled Lillie close, close enough that their lips nearly touched, close enough that she could feel Lillie's breath on her skin. Their lips brushed together and Lillie opened to her, their tongues moving in their own languid waltz.

When their kiss ended, Lillie's eyes were dreamy. "Will you escort me to the dance, then?"

"I think you could find a better escort, but yes." She couldn't bear the thought of someone else dancing with Lillie.

"I couldn't possibly make a better choice. You're intelligent, handsome, sweet, brave, and gallant."

She summoned a cocky smile. "You left out sexy."

Lillie laughed softly. "You're incredibly sexy and, according to the girls around town, an exceptional lover. But *I* can't attest to that, can I?"

Swain was caught completely off guard. She opened her mouth, but nothing came out. She steadied her thoughts, cleared her throat, and tried again.

"I do want you. So much." She stroked Lillie's cheek, her hand trembling with the effort to stop there. She craved to touch every inch of Lillie, every sensitive spot. She wanted to run her hands over her bare shoulders, her smooth back, the soft curve of her hips, and the silky inside of her thighs. She took a deep breath and let it out slowly. "But neither of us knows what our future holds. As hard as it'll be, we need to wait until some things are settled. Things like Abigail's will." And whether Lillie planned to leave her.

Lillie smiled ruefully. "You're right, but I'm not sure I can promise to do that."

Swain glanced at her watch. "It's nearly midnight and I have to be up at dawn to feed horses. I need to collect Beau and head for the barn."

"It took three of us to carry all his things up here, and I've gotten used to his snoring. This house is so empty, I sleep better with him here." She looked up shyly. "Do you mind?"

Swain smiled and kissed her gently. "I don't mind at all that you've stolen my dog." *And my heart.*

❖

Lillie climbed into bed and stared at the ceiling. It hadn't occurred to her that Swain could be worried about the difference in their backgrounds. When she looked at Swain, she saw a Wetherington. She had forgotten that Swain still saw a poor kid who never went to college, never traveled outside the Southeast.

She smiled to herself, reliving the rapt concentration on Swain's face as she played the piano. She could almost feel Swain's strong shoulders under her hands and see those cornflower blue eyes holding her steady as they danced in dizzying circles until they were breathless.

They had shared several more kisses in a long good night before Swain finally disappeared into the darkness. She touched her lips, marveling at the soft warmth of Swain's mouth. How would it feel touching, sucking her in other places?

But as their attraction, their affection was nearing full bloom, so were Lillie's fears.

She should have told Swain the truth when she was looking at the photographs Lillie had found in Abigail's room and set out around the house. Did Swain see her reflection in Jim Wetherington's face?

It was perfect timing and she'd started to say it, but Swain had stopped her with a hand to her lips.

She should have confessed everything about her stalker. The man apparently knew about Swain, too. She had a right to know she was likely also in danger. Lillie's heart lurched. The stalker could have ambushed Swain on her way to the barn. But that didn't happen because Swain had called after she was tucked into bed, for one last murmured good night.

Lillie, what do you wear to bed?
My silk bikini panties.

(groan)
What are you wearing, Swain?
Nothing.
I'm coming down to the barn now.
(laughter) No, you're not. Good night, Lillie.
Good night, love.

She should have persisted until Swain knew everything. But the night had turned so magical and Lillie hadn't been willing to risk the moment she had been longing for—Swain in her arms, Swain's lips on hers, Swain's heart beating against her breasts.

Lillie closed her eyes. She was afraid of losing this tenuous bond between them, but the longer she withheld the truth, the angrier Swain might be.

She couldn't be sure what the future would hold, but she was absolutely certain she wanted it to somehow include Swain. She would go to her in the morning. It was time to come clean, no matter the cost.

CHAPTER TWENTY-SEVEN

Lillie rose early after a restless night. The more she thought, the more certain she felt she must reveal everything. She couldn't imagine what it would be like to find out you had a dad and a stepmum who'd left you to grow up in a herd of children raised by strangers. She prayed that what they felt for each other would help soothe the hurt she knew the truth would inflict.

Beau stretched and groaned as she dressed, then followed her as she hurried downstairs and through the kitchen. When she stepped into the morning chill, the sound of shouting and galloping horses greeted her. Her breath caught as she looked out over the practice field.

Swain was pure poetry astride Black Astor. They moved as one animal, wheeling and charging, dodging and chasing the ball. She wielded her mallet like a broadsword, swinging it high over her head, then downward with deadly accuracy.

Although the morning fog had barely burned off, the sweating ponies indicated the stick-and-ball session was well under way. On impulse, Lillie ducked back into the house and grabbed her camera. She adjusted her settings and went to work.

Swain and Rob jostled for position while Javier stood ready to defend the goal. Astor gave Rob's pony a hard bump and whirled back toward the ball. But in mid-turn, Swain's head jerked up at the sight of Lillie. Her distraction was enough for Rob to recover and slam the ball past Javier.

"Woot!" Rob crowed. "What is it you tell us, boss? Eyes on the ball at all times." He waved a greeting at Lillie.

"Yeah, yeah. You got lucky." Swain waved her mallet at the two men. "You guys go ahead. I'll cool Astor off."

She reined to a stop in front of Lillie and bent over, smiling. The breeze feathered and danced Swain's disheveled hair across her forehead, her eyes blue strobes beneath the dark locks. Lillie lifted her camera and clicked off a few frames.

"You're up early. Are you here just to shoot pictures? Want me to saddle Finesse for you to join us?" Swain asked.

"Thank you, but no. I wanted to talk when you have a chance, but I can wait."

Swain dismounted. "We were finished with the training session and only having fun now."

They walked toward the barn, Swain leading Astor and Beau running ahead. Lillie couldn't stop smiling. Swain's exuberant mood, the pheromones rolling off her were intoxicating. They gazed at each other and laughed.

"You have to stop looking at me like that," Swain murmured.

Like what?"

"Like you want to tear my clothes off."

Lillie shuddered and glanced away. For a moment, she was afraid Swain's gaze, her words would make her orgasm without even being touched. "You're partly right."

"Partly?"

Their flirtation was calming Lillie's fear, her nervousness. If she could hold Swain close enough as she told her, perhaps that would temper her reaction. She turned back to Swain, smiling more broadly. "I want to tear off your clothes and lick every part of that gorgeous body."

Swain stumbled, then caught herself. "Jesus, woman. Are you trying to give me a heart attack? I never knew the British were so naughty."

She handed Astor's reins to a stable hand with orders to cool him out.

"Can we go upstairs and talk for a bit?" Lillie asked when the boy led Astor away.

Swain looked back at her hungrily. "Lillie, if we go upstairs, I'm pretty sure we won't be talking."

"You were the one who said we should wait."

"True, but I didn't know you'd make waiting so hard."

"The office then."

Swain frowned. "You really meant 'talk,' didn't you? Is something wrong?"

Lillie didn't know where to begin, but standing in the hallway of the barn with horses and stable help walking past wasn't the place to do it. She led Swain into the barn's office to share a long, affectionate kiss that ended in a tight hug.

"What is it, Lillie?"

"I can't believe how much I've come to care about you in such a short time," she murmured against Swain's neck. She felt Swain relax.

"And I care about you, Lillie. More than I thought possible."

"I need to tell you some things, love. Things that I hope won't change how you feel about me."

"Nothing could change how I feel about you."

Lillie tightened her hold. "Before Grandmum died—"

The barn phone began ringing.

"Ignore it," Swain said. "Go ahead. You were going to say—"

Lillie's cell phone also began to ring, and the cacophony was too much to talk above. They stepped back from each other with apologetic smiles and each answered her phone. After they concluded their calls, they looked at each other.

"That was Mr. Whitney. He's ready to read Grandmum's will."

"That was Bonner's secretary calling me. I guess they want both of us there."

This was their moment of truth, the first step toward the future—together or apart.

❖

Bonner stared out the window of his plush office and ran his fingers through his hair. His firm had offices near the state capitol in Columbia, but he had grown tired of politics and shifted most of the practice there to his son and younger partners. Nowadays, he preferred the quiet, slower pace of the office his father had established in Aiken many years ago. Lately, even that was too much.

The burden of keeping and protecting the legal secrets of his clients, many of them friends, had grown heavier with the years. He had just celebrated his seventieth birthday and he was tired. The Wetherington estate was his last. After this was settled, he planned to turn the practice over to Hoyt and spend the rest of his days on the golf course.

But he had this one last confidence, the heaviest of his burdens, to unload from his shoulders. Jim Wetherington had been his closest friend since childhood. Because of their friendship, Bonner had protected Abigail and their family secret even after Jim's death, even after that secret came to live with Abigail six years ago.

Today wouldn't end his business with the Wetheringtons, but everything would finally be in the open. Swain's brother might not be worth much, but she had deserved better than the lot they had dealt her in life. Today, she would finally get her due.

CHAPTER TWENTY-EIGHT

They rode to the law office together in Swain's truck. Lillie was nervous and slid her hand across the wide seat to grasp Swain's. She was desperate to hold tight so Swain didn't vanish again.

But Swain was already slipping away. She squeezed Lillie's hand and released it, her expression closed, her eyes that easily displayed her emotions now shuttered. Lillie pulled back her hand that Swain had abandoned and folded it with her other in her lap. She was afraid for Swain and whatever place she was retreating to inside. She had been anxious for the truth to finally be revealed—at first so she could disappear, more recently so she and Swain could talk about their future. Now it was minutes away and terrified her.

They parked and sat for a long moment, the reverberating noise of the truck's big diesel engine gradually fading. Swain had physically moved so far away, she was almost hugging her door. Shocked by the sudden change, Lillie had to make one last effort to pull her closer.

"Swain, please. Whatever happens, let's face it together." She reached out, but dropped her hand to the seat at Swain's almost imperceptible flinch. "I know it hasn't been long, but I—"

"Lillie." Swain's firm voice filled the truck. Her eyes were dull when she looked up. "Don't make promises, plans you'll regret an hour from now."

"But—"

"Bonner's waiting." Swain opened her door and slid from the truck.

❖

After turning down offers of coffee or tea, they had settled into matching wingback chairs in front of Bonner's huge mahogany desk.

"I need to discuss several things with both of you today," Bonner said. "Lillie, as you already know, you inherited all of your adopted father's individual assets upon his death. Any assets held jointly with Abigail remained with her until the time of her death. The will she had me draw up after your grandfather died had left everything to Eric. But when he died before her, she had your father's solicitor in London draw a new will. A probate judge here in South Carolina has approved that will as authentic. I'll go over a summary of it now."

Bonner shuffled some papers and set a pair of reading glasses on his nose. He peered over the glasses at Lillie and Swain. "I want to say this first. Abigail was generous when it came to charities, but wasn't an extravagant spender personally. She had a keen financial mind and, at the time of her death, was extremely wealthy."

He cleared his throat. "Being of sound mind and body at the time of this last will and testament, I, Abigail Grace Fletcher Wetherington, do hereby lawfully decree the distribution of my estate and holdings." He paused. "Again, this first part is a general summary. I will give you copies that list all her extensive assets individually, so you can read those details at your leisure." He adjusted his glasses and began to read again.

"Twenty million dollars will be used to establish a foundation dedicated to equine issues. The house and surrounding lawns of the South Carolina estate, as well as all assets and property held jointly in the names of Abigail Wetherington and Eric Wetherington, are to be transferred to the light of my life, Lillian Claire Wetherington."

Bonner glanced up at Swain. "The South Carolina polo stables and all property outside the residence and lawns of the estate, all livestock, equipment, and other assets pertaining to the maintenance of those grounds and stables are to be transferred to the one person who will cherish them as much as I have, the person that my pride has cheated since birth, Rebecca Swain Butler."

Swain, who had been restlessly shifting in her chair, went very still. The color drained from her face.

"Swain," Lillie said softly. But Swain's glare was fixed on Bonner.

"Let me finish," Bonner said, not shrinking from Swain's icy stare. "The remaining assets, held only in Abigail's name, total nearly seventy million dollars and are to be split equally between the two of you."

"No."

Lillie jerked when Swain's voice rang out. Swain launched from her chair, turned away from them, and paced over to stare out the window.

"No," she said through clenched teeth. "I won't accept it. I don't want her ponies or her money."

Lillie's heart nearly broke at the pain in Swain's voice. "Mr. Whitney, could you leave us alone for a few moments?"

"There's more I have to discuss with you today. It can't be put off."

"Just a little while," Lillie said, gazing with longing at Swain's stiff figure. "I'll let you know when we're ready for the rest."

Bonner glanced over at Swain, then back to Lillie. He nodded and stood. "I'll be in the conference room, making some phone calls. Let my secretary know when you're ready." The door clicked closed behind him.

"Swain, love."

Swain whirled to face her. Where her tanned face had been pale before, it was now red with fury, her eyes blazing. "You don't understand, Lillie. You don't know what I know, what Abigail and I'm sure Bonner has known all this time." She slammed her fist on the desk for emphasis. "Do you know who I am?"

Swain thumped her fist hard against her chest. "His name is on my birth certificate. The nurse said it was just a name from a newspaper article my mother was reading. But it wasn't, was it? I am the Wetherington bastard."

"Yes, I do know." Lillie's heart was ripping, tearing with Swain's agony. She could have pretended otherwise, but Swain already had suffered too many lies.

"You knew?" Swain yelled. "You knew, and you didn't tell me?"

"I didn't learn any of it until right before Grandmum died. She made me promise to let Mr. Whitney tell you when her will was read. But I couldn't keep that promise, not after…not after I realized what you mean to me. That's what I came to the barn this morning to tell you."

Swain turned back to the window, her words bitter. "My brother and I, Wetheringtons, were left to grow up in an institution. Herded from place to place like cattle. We didn't have any bedtime stories, Lillie. No birthday parties. Everybody got one gift for Christmas— one thing for all the boys and another for the girls so we wouldn't fight over possessions. We weren't children. We were livestock the government paid them to keep. I hated every minute of it."

Swain swiped at a tear that trickled down her cheek. "I'm glad Eric and Camille adopted you. I'm glad you had a real childhood," she choked out. "But what kind of father was Eric that he could take a strange, unrelated child into his heart and leave his own offspring to be raised like we were? Abigail knew, too. She knew and did nothing to acknowledge me or Trey."

"Is that what you think…that Eric was your father?" Lillie pressed herself against the rigid back and wrapped her in a tight hug. "Oh, love. When I found those photographs in Grandmum's bedroom, I knew why she kept them hidden. That's why I put them on the mantel where you would see them. Don't you recognize your reflection in that window? Eric wasn't your father. Jim Wetherington was."

"What?" She stared at the glass.

Lillie stroked Swain's arms, gentling her like a skittish horse.

She didn't resist when Lillie stepped between her and the window and pulled her close.

Swain spoke slowly, processing what this new information meant. "Abigail's husband was my father?" She wasn't ready to give up her anger, but it was damn hard to hold on to it with Lillie pressed against her. "What else did she tell you?"

"That leaving you and your brother in that orphanage was her greatest shame. She had never wanted to meet you because you would remind her of Granddad's single infidelity. But when she saw you riding in a tournament in Florida a few months after he died, you looked so very much like him that she felt she had gotten a little bit of him back."

Swain pushed Lillie away, her anger rising again. "I may look like him, but I'm not like him. I wouldn't cheat on my wife and abandon my child, bastard or not."

"There's more to the story, but Grandmum was too weak to tell me all of it. She said Mr. Whitney knew everything that happened."

"Did you ask him?"

Lillie's hands were on her again, stroking down her back. "No. It wasn't my story to hear. You're the one who deserves an explanation."

"I don't know if I want the whole story."

"You don't have to handle it alone, love. If you'll let me, I'll be right here with you. Don't you think it's time to stop keeping secrets?"

It was all becoming clear.

Swain had thought she was the one influencing Lillie, teaching her to love the Wetherington legacy. Who better to do it than the only real Wetherington left? But the lessons hadn't been for Lillie at all. Abigail had wanted Swain to recognize the depth of the Wetherington bloodline running through her veins. She had only sent Lillie, lovely Lillie, to soften the blow of her betrayal. Lillie had gently summoned Swain to her birthright. Her feelings for Lillie were the tether keeping her from walking out the door and never coming back.

After a time, Swain nodded. "Call Bonner back in."

Bonner entered the office cautiously, as if trying to judge their mood.

Swain moved their chairs close together and held tight to Lillie's hand. Her mind, her emotions were swirling, and she needed Lillie to ground her.

She stared at her lap. The wound she'd carried her entire life was about to be opened. Would knowing the truth heal that wound or maim her further? Lillie squeezed her hand, and Swain looked up into understanding brown eyes. She could do this. She turned to Bonner.

"I need to know everything."

For the first time, Swain realized how old he appeared, how weary he seemed.

"And I need to tell it," he said, sitting back in his chair. "Even the parts that Abigail didn't know."

THIRTY-TWO YEARS EARLIER

To the ponies!"
Jim and Bonner clinked their highball glasses against Eric's raised beer mug and echoed his toast. "The ponies," they shouted.

Celebrating a successful polo match in Florida, they had arrived at the Atlanta airport only hours before. They had gone straight to their hotel to secure rooms for him and Jim and dined in the restaurant there to celebrate Eric's birthday before he returned to his room at the fraternity house on the campus of Emory University.

"Dad, I'm going to grab a cab to take me back to campus."

"No. We've just started celebrating. You're eighteen now and finally legal to have a drink in public with your old man."

Jim Wetherington wasn't old. At forty-one, he was still fit and very handsome.

"Nothing but studies will make Eric a dull boy," he warned, winking at the girl who had joined Eric for his birthday celebration.

Bonner noticed that the girl's gaze hadn't left Jim all evening. Women were always drawn to his blue eyes and thick jet black hair. Eric had inherited his father's tall, athletic frame and blue eyes, but he had his mother's dark blond hair. He had his father's drive, but his mother's practical nature.

"It's been fun. Thanks for taking me to Florida with you for the match. I really miss polo here at school. But I've got music class early in the morning and I don't want to be hung over."

"It's early. There's a band in the lounge. We can take the party over there. Besides, I don't think your date's ready to go home. You'd like to stay, wouldn't you?"

The girl nodded. "I heard the band is really good," she said, smiling at Jim.

Eric hesitated. "I missed two days of class to go the tournament and haven't studied all weekend." His affectionate gaze implored her to understand.

"Go ahead, Eric. She can stay and I'll make sure she gets home," Bonner said. He and Eric both knew Jim had already had one Scotch too many.

She turned to Eric. "It's okay, sweetie. I really want to hear this band, but I know you need to get unpacked and ready for class tomorrow. I'll be fine."

"You'll pay for a cab to take her home?" Eric asked Bonner.

"Don't worry about it, kid. Your girl is safe with me."

But it was clear from the minute Eric reluctantly left her, the girl wanted to be anything but safe when it came to Jim.

Bonner eyed her. She was pretty, but not beautiful, and had large breasts that were barely contained in her halter dress. They moved to a table in the hotel lounge and, after she and Jim had another drink, she coaxed him onto the dance floor. He was buzzing, but still had a good hold on his faculties. When the music changed from fast to slow, he insisted they return to their seats.

Bonner was tired. Their waitress was busy, so he excused himself to pay their tab. While he waited for the bartender to total it, he saw Jim leave the table and walk to the restroom. The girl looked furtively around and Bonner turned so it appeared he wasn't watching, but he could still see her in his peripheral vision. She took a small package from her purse and poured a powder into Jim's drink.

When Bonner came back to the table, he looked pointedly at the drink to let her know he saw what she did. Her face reddened, but she held his gaze.

"I've paid our tab. When Jim comes back, tell him I went upstairs to bed," he said. He pulled a clip full of cash from his pocket and extracted a fifty. "The staff at the front desk will call a cab when you're ready to leave. This should cover the fare."

She nodded. "Good night, Mr. Whitney. I'll see that Mr. Wetherington gets up to his room."

"I'll bet you will," Bonner muttered. "Good night."

CHAPTER TWENTY-NINE

Y ou saw her spike his drink and you didn't tell him? Why the bloody hell would you do that?"

Swain was sure that if she hadn't held tight to her hand, Lillie would have leapt over Bonner's desk and strangled him. Startled by Lillie's unexpected ferocity and Bonner's reflexive flinch, she didn't have time to react with her own anger. She tugged Lillie back to her chair.

"Let him finish." She spoke to Lillie, but her eyes were on Bonner.

Bonner stalled, wiping his face with a white handkerchief and straightening his necktie.

"I loved Abigail. I've always loved her. I would do anything for her. But she loved Jim. He was the only man that existed in her eyes." He wiped his face again. "Jim loved Abigail just as much. He was my best friend, but he didn't deserve her. He was beginning to show signs of his father's alcoholism and it tore her up. She begged him to get help, but he was too proud."

Bonner seemed to gain strength as he unloaded the weight he had carried for years. "I had just found out that my wife had been carrying on an affair while I was in Columbia, serving in the legislature. When I saw that girl spike Jim's drink, I knew what she was doing. I thought it might finally break the bond between him and Abigail, and I hoped she would turn to me." His eyes implored them to understand. "I *loved* her, loved her beyond reason."

"This girl, she was my mother?" Swain couldn't think about Bonner's treachery right now. She had no sympathy for him and too many questions still to ask.

Bonner shook his head at the disgust in Swain's voice. "Don't judge her until you hear the whole story." He took a sip from a cup of cold coffee on his desk. "When the girl told her father she was pregnant, all hell broke loose. He, however, took for granted that Eric was responsible because they had been dating. He wanted to be paid off for being stuck with a daughter he said was damaged goods."

"So my granddad let my dad take the blame?" Swain could feel Lillie shaking with anger.

"It was complicated. I had thought the girl was older. She had a fake ID. But she was only sixteen and Jim was forty-one. Consensual or not, his age made it statutory rape in the eyes of the law. Jim could have gone to jail. So, we let her father think it was Eric. He was young enough, less than five years older, that the law didn't apply to him."

Lillie persisted. "I don't understand. If she was already dating my dad, why didn't she just have a baby with him?"

"Because he was young, Eric thought he was in love with her. She was afraid he would want to marry her. She didn't feel the same way about him and just wanted the money so she could get away from her father with no strings attached."

If the rest of the story was like this, Swain didn't know if she wanted to hear it. "So, my mother was a conniving slut, my father was a criminal, and I'm the bastard result."

Bonner shook his head. "I'm not sure Jim was even conscious. A man doesn't have to be aware to ejaculate when physically stimulated. He always swore he didn't remember anything until he woke up the next morning in bed with this naked girl. He insisted that we tell Abigail. He hated himself, thinking that he had been drunk and violated their marriage. He begged her forgiveness. I thought she'd turn away from him, but she didn't. She laid out two conditions. The girl's father had to sign a contract agreeing to never contact them again in exchange for an arranged abortion and one hundred and fifty thousand dollars. Second, Jim had to check into a rehab, dry out, and never touch a drop of alcohol again. As the family attorney, I made all the arrangements while Jim went to rehab."

"Obviously, Abigail didn't get everything she wanted, because I'm sitting right here," Swain said, her voice cold.

"When the girl didn't show up for her appointment with the doctor, I was notified. She took most of the money I had given her father and ran off. He didn't seem to care enough to look for her, so I did some checking. One of the girl's friends told my investigator that the father had been sexually abusing her since she was a child. The friend had helped her set up her bedroom to video one of his nighttime visits. She used that evidence to keep him from trying to find her." Bonner's gaze held Swain's. "Yes, she trapped Jim. But she was desperate to get away from her father. She could have kept the appointment for the abortion, but she didn't. She carried twins full term all alone, with no friends or family to help her."

"What was her name?" Swain asked. Her complaints about her own bleak childhood now seemed insignificant compared to what her mother must have endured. Lillie raised Swain's hand and brushed it with her lips in sympathy. "What was my mother's real name?" she repeated.

Bonner opened a drawer and extracted a thick file. He shoved it across the desk to Swain. "Becca. Her name was Rebecca Louise Johnston. After she ran away, she bought a new identity—Karla Jane Butler. Everything I know is in that file. It's yours now."

Swain released Lillie's hand and took it, laying it in her lap. She stared without opening it.

"Are you all right, love?"

Swain shook her head, still staring at the folder. "Did my father know the abortion never happened?"

"He was in rehab and, once he got out, he was struggling to stay sober. I told Abigail, but she never told Jim."

Bile rose in Swain's throat, as sour as her emotions. "I'm sure she wouldn't want his bastards running around the house."

"Abigail had only been able to give Jim one child. There were complications with Eric's birth and she couldn't have any other children. She realized that if Jim knew that another child anywhere in the world was his, he couldn't turn his back on his own blood. But that child would constantly remind both of them of his betrayal and they would never be able to rebuild their relationship."

"Don't you think things would have been different if they'd known the girl drugged him," Lillie said fiercely.

"Maybe. Yes. But if I told them, I'd lose my best friend and the woman I adored." Bonner looked at Swain, his eyes watery. "Saying that I'm profoundly sorry, thoroughly ashamed, isn't enough, I know. In the end, Abigail loved you. She hated herself for leaving you in an orphanage and letting you pay for her and Jim's mistake."

Swain stood and paced the office. She ran her fingers through her hair in frustration. She wanted to be angry, but with who? Two people who were already dead and buried? An old man who'd spent a lifetime with his guilt? Her anger couldn't change anything. Ironically, she was relieved to finally know, to never again lie in bed at night and wonder. And if she accepted this, she was suddenly the very wealthy owner of a premier polo stable.

"I...I don't know what to think. I don't know what to do," Swain said. She looked to Lillie for help.

"Swain, Grandmum wanted you to have the ponies," Lillie said. "She didn't have the power to turn back the years and make things different. And she understood that money couldn't substitute for growing up without a family. But she must have felt her ponies belonged to you. We both should sign the paperwork, then go celebrate finally putting this behind us."

"There's more," Bonner said.

"More?" Swain and Lillie spoke simultaneously.

"Someone's challenged Lillie's inheritance."

"Who would do that?" Swain asked, suddenly protective.

"Your brother."

Swain leaned forward. "Do you know where he is? Wait, why wasn't he included in the will? Didn't Abigail know there were two of us?"

"Trey also had Eric's name on his birth certificate. He turned up here only a year after the two of you left the children's home. He was angry and demanded money. He threatened to physically harm Abigail."

"I didn't see him much when we were kids, but I heard he got in trouble a lot." Swain knew her brother's attitude wouldn't have gotten him far with Abigail. She wasn't the type to let anyone push her around.

"Well, he was just a lot of big talk. When he threatened Abigail with physical harm, she grabbed a riding crop and chased him out the front door. Later that day, I heard he was in a bar downtown, drunk and caterwauling about being Eric's bastard. So, I had a couple of men who worked for me pick him up. They gave him a certified check for a hundred thousand dollars from me, put him on a plane to California, and told him that if he came back, they would feed him to the alligators in the low country. I did have an investigator keep tabs on him and we thought he had gotten himself killed in a Texas barroom brawl." Bonner pushed another document across his desk. "Then he had a lawyer file this injunction against the probate of Abigail's will."

"He's here?" Lillie asked weakly. She certainly didn't need the money, but an uneasy feeling was scratching at the back of her mind.

I can help you with that. I can give Granny a Wetherington baby.

Maybe he wasn't referring to her being a Wetherington. No, it couldn't be.

"I don't exactly know where Trey is. His attorney works out of Columbia. His challenge has to be heard, but there's no question that Abigail knew about him and deliberately chose not to provide for him in her will."

"He doesn't need to do this," Swain said. "Tell his lawyer I'll give him half of what Abigail left me if he drops this action against Lillie. He's my brother, so that should be my responsibility."

"Technically, I'm representing Abigail as the executor of her will, so I can't represent you. But if you want to do that, I can recommend someone to handle it for you. You need to know, however, that he's not after your money. He specifically wants Lillie's inheritance because she's not a blood relation."

Swain laugh was sharp. "We don't know for sure that he and I are either, do we?"

"He will soon enough. He's submitted a DNA sample for proof. He's not challenging Swain's inheritance, but confirming her DNA will prove that Abigail knew about the twins and deliberately chose to cut Trey out of her will." He handed Swain a business card. "That's the address of the lab. It doesn't take long. Just show your ID and they'll swab the inside of your mouth. The sooner you go, the quicker we can schedule a hearing to clear this up for Lillie."

CHAPTER THIRTY

S wain was sure she would never breathe and her heart would never beat normally again.

Gliding down the wide, curving staircase, Lillie was a vision in a strapless royal blue gown, a silken swath that appeared to wind around her lithe body in a decadent swirl. Her bare shoulders were almost more than Swain could resist. She wanted to run her tongue along the prominent collarbone and suck the pulse throbbing in Lillie's neck.

"I don't have words to describe how beautiful you are." Hell, she was surprised that she could form any words.

"And you're deliciously handsome," Lillie responded, brushing her lips against Swain's cheek.

Swain wore a pewter-colored tux with a feminine cut that was tailored to her broad-shouldered physique. Under it was a white, spun-silk pleated shirt, fastened at the top with a gold Celtic knot brooch rather than a bow tie. The brooch matched gold cufflinks and gold stud earrings. Black dress boots added two additional inches to her already-tall frame.

When they had returned from Bonner's office, they'd saddled Finesse and Nor'easter for a long ride so Swain could settle her emotions. And, when she was ready, they sat on a knoll and talked about everything they'd learned. Lillie finally told her about the stalker and her fears that Swain might also become a target. Swain was aghast that she hadn't told her sooner, and she vowed to break the man's neck if he came sniffing around again.

They'd agreed that nothing, especially the stalker, would stop them from the romantic date they'd planned.

Swain dropped a line of kisses along Lillie's bare shoulder. "I think we should reconsider our plans to go out," she breathed into Lillie's ear, smiling at the answering shudder.

"You're cruel to tempt me." Lillie ran her hands along Swain's lapels and gently pushed her back. "But you promised to take me to a dance."

"We can dance naked in your bedroom." Swain smiled at Lillie's lilting laugh and attempted to pull her close again. But Lillie was adamant.

"You certainly don't play fair," she said. Lillie's eyes still shone with amusement, but her tone grew serious. "Besides being captain of the very best polo team in the state, you're the owner of the Wetherington stables, Swain. You have always been a Wetherington, but now you have the wealth as well as the bloodline. That comes with responsibilities. It's important for you to show your support by attending."

"About that, Lillie. I'm not sure I want the whole story out there for the town to gossip about. I've managed well enough so far with Butler as my last name. So, can we just keep this between us for now until I have more time to think?"

She had so many things still to think about and plan, but tonight she only wanted to occupy her thoughts with Lillie and how gorgeous she looked.

"Of course, love. I like Butler. It's a very strong name." Lillie gave her a light kiss. "I'm not sure outing you as a Wetherington would be wise anyway. But I don't want to talk about that now. Take me dancing, my handsome escort."

❖

The civic hall had been transformed into a ballroom of sorts, with the local symphony's string section supplying the music. Waiters prowled the crowd with trays of champagne. Life-sized photos of polo players and their horses from the early 1800s decorated the foyer. In the ballroom, a buffet lined one side with round linen-covered tables at either end so guests could sit and eat as they watched the dancers.

"Swain, Lillie, over here." Swain was surprised to see Catherine waving to them from a table at the other end of the room. The tickets were a thousand dollars per couple, which had to be way beyond Catherine and Reid's budget.

Lillie waved back enthusiastically and tugged Swain in their direction. On their way across the room, Swain snagged a couple of flutes of champagne. She shook Reid's hand while Lillie and Catherine hugged, then gave Catherine a brief hug, too.

"I didn't know you guys would be here or I wouldn't have sulked so much about Lillie dragging me out," Swain said, smiling. Reid gave her a look confirming that he, too, had been strong-armed into coming.

"Lillie knew you'd sulk, so she begged us to accept the tickets and come," Catherine said. "It's a good thing she did. You two look stunning together."

Catherine's emerald dress was modestly cut in the front, but plunged in the back. Her auburn hair was pinned up to accentuate her pale shoulders and neck.

Swain gave a low whistle. "You're very stunning yourself."

Reid moved possessively closer to Catherine, but Lillie stepped in.

"And, Reid, you cut a very handsome figure in that tux."

Catherine gave Lillie a grateful look and slid her hand into Reid's. "He is handsome, isn't he? I told him we should dress the entire fire department in tuxedos and shoot their pictures for a calendar. They could sell it as a fund-raiser."

Swain nodded. "Lillie's a photographer. She could take the pictures for you." She suddenly realized that she was speaking for Lillie as though they were an established couple. When they talked earlier, Swain had asked Lillie about her plans, but when Lillie demurred, she hadn't had the courage to beg her to stay. So many people already had deserted her—her mother, her father, Abigail. "What I mean, is, you could ask Lillie to do it," she said lamely.

"It sounds like a wonderful idea. We should talk about it," Lillie said.

Swain's insecurity ratcheted up a notch. Was she carefully dodging commitment because she wouldn't be around much longer?

"I'm going to check out the buffet," she mumbled, abruptly heading across the room.

"Me, too," Reid said, jumping up to follow her.

Lillie and Catherine stared after them, then looked at each other and laughed.

"They're afraid we'll make them dance with us," Catherine said.

"And we will," Lillie declared. "They can run, but they can't hide." She smiled at Catherine. "Reid's being protective tonight."

Catherine shook her head. "Staking out his territory. We've sort of been talking around getting married. What about you?"

"Me?"

"You and Swain. Do you still plan to leave once the will is read? Will you sell the stable or settle here?"

Catherine's directness surprised Lillie. Swain didn't need her any longer in order to keep her beloved ponies. Would she be safer if Lillie left? Her heart lurched at the thought of never seeing Swain again. Did Swain want her to stay? *She's a hard dog to keep under the porch.*

"Actually, the will was read today. I'm not at liberty to disclose Swain's part in it, but I can say that the stable isn't mine to sell."

It was Catherine's turn to look surprised. "Are you okay with that? I mean, Abigail was your grandmother."

"I'm very okay with it." Lillie gazed at Swain across the room, and Swain turned as if she could feel it. They smiled at each other. "Swain deserves everything life will give her."

"Does she know you're in love with her?"

Heat suffused Lillie's neck and cheeks. She watched Swain turn to listen to something Reid was saying. She was shaking her head and began pointing out food for Reid to load on a plate.

"Things have been moving so fast, we haven't had time to

talk about the future, or if we have one." Lillie stared down at her hands. "We've only known each other a little more than a month. We haven't, um—"

"You haven't slept together? I can't believe it. What are you waiting on, woman? Swain practically drools when she's around you." Catherine brushed her napkin across Lillie's shoulder. "In fact, here's a little puddle right here."

Lillie laughed and pushed Catherine's hand away, glad to move away from serious talk. She wanted to enjoy the evening.

Swain placed her plate between them so she and Lillie could share, as had become their habit.

Reid set a plate in front of Catherine that contained a variety of finger foods gathered around a single slice of roast and a small portion of asparagus in hollandaise sauce. She looked up at Swain and mouthed a silent "Thank you." Reid's plate was piled high with nothing but roast and potatoes.

When the plates were empty, Reid spotted Hoyt Whitney with a few other guys he knew and sauntered over to say hello. Lillie and Catherine made a brief visit to the ladies' room, leaving Swain alone at the table. When they returned, Susan looked to be one step away from crawling into Swain's lap.

"Bitch alert." Catherine nodded toward their table.

"Bloody hussy," Lillie hissed. It was time to stop being coy. She wanted Swain and she needed to know if Swain really wanted her.

She requested a waltz from the orchestra and marched across the ballroom, stopping about twenty feet away from their table. When Swain looked up, Lillie held out her hand. *Come to me.*

Swain looked confused, but pulled away from Susan and stood. She walked over slowly, taking Lillie's outstretched hand.

"Will you dance with me, darling?"

"Lillie, really. I'm not sure this is a good idea. People will talk. I don't want them saying things about you."

"I'm not asking them. I'm asking you. Do you want to dance with me?"

"Yes. I do."

Then Lillie was in Swain's arms and they were floating. Swain's gaze held hers and they smiled as the music spun them around the dance floor in wide, graceful circles. Lillie's heart was so light. When they had talked earlier on that hillside, Swain asked about her plans and Lillie answered truthfully. She didn't know. She wanted a new life where she could trust and love, but staying could put Swain in danger, too. Dancing now in Swain's embrace, she finally knew she would put her fears away and stay. If only Swain would ask.

She's a hard dog to keep under the porch.

❖

They were silent during the drive home, the air between them crackling, scorching with the desire that their dancing had stoked to firestorm. Lillie didn't remember arriving or getting out of the car. Her mind, her heart was still dancing when Swain's mouth, hot on her neck, brought her to the present, and they were standing in the foyer of her home. The wall was cool against her back, but Swain's body, her long length, was burning against her breasts.

"Lillie." Swain moaned. "God, I want you so bad."

Lillie almost melted. She grasped the thick, dark hair and pulled Swain from the assault she had launched on her neck. She gazed into Swain's eyes, which were hazy with need.

"I am yours, love," she whispered.

Lillie had no idea of Swain's strength until she felt herself swept up and carried up the staircase to her bedroom. Then they stood beside her bed, her fingers pulling at Swain's clothes.

Swain caught her hands to still them. "Let me," she said. "Watch."

Swain slid her jacket from her shoulders and dropped it across a nearby chair. She slowly divested herself of the Celtic brooch at her neck and her cufflinks, setting them on the bedside table. Her gaze holding Lillie's, she unbuttoned her silk shirt and pulled her arms from the sleeves to bare her breasts. She bent to remove her boots and socks, then stood to slowly unfasten her pants. She lowered her briefs and trousers at the same time, then kicked them away.

Swain stood before her a magnificent warrior goddess.

Lillie couldn't breathe, couldn't speak, afraid this was a dream and words would wake her. She feasted on the sight of the thick shoulder muscles that gave way to small, perfect breasts. Swain's abdomen, although etched with the cross work of muscles, had a softness that made Lillie want to put her lips there. Her narrow hips gave way to smooth, hard thighs. At their apex, a thatch of black curls glistened with Swain's arousal, and Lillie's mouth watered.

Swain stepped closer, but stopped Lillie from touching her. "Turn," she said, her voice low and husky.

Lillie closed her eyes as the zipper was lowered and her dress fell slowly to the floor.

"You are so sexy," Swain whispered.

Swain's breath was ragged on her back, her hands trembling as she knelt and unfastened the hose from her lace garter. Lillie gasped as Swain's hands were on her thighs, sliding first one stocking, then the other, down her legs. A reverent kiss to the small of her back, then her garter and panties were gone, too.

Again, Swain pressed her body against Lillie's back, but no clothes separated them now. Skin upon skin, Swain's hard nipples pushed into Lillie's shoulders, her stiff curls painted Lillie's buttocks with moisture. She smoothed her hands along Lillie's belly and cupped her breasts while her tongue bathed a trail across Lillie's shoulder to her neck. When Swain's thumbs flicked across her nipples, Lillie's hips convulsed.

"Oh, no. You'll make me come," she whispered.

"Many times tonight," Swain said. "But not yet."

Swain guided Lillie to the bed and took a long moment to let her eyes caress every part of her, from the silky blond curls to her perfect shoulders, smooth belly, and long, very sexy legs. She lowered herself slowly so that their bodies barely touched, their nipples rubbing lightly.

She slid her thigh between Lillie's and groaned at the wetness. She was throbbing almost painfully and rubbed herself against Lillie's thigh, coating it. "I can't wait," she gasped, pumping her hips.

"Inside me, now." Lillie whimpered.

Swain braced herself with one arm and slid her other hand over Lillie's hard clitoris, then plunged two fingers inside and began to thrust. Her orgasm gathered momentum, so she smoothed her thumb against Lillie's clit to bring her along, too.

"Harder, love, oh God. Yes." Lillie was panting.

"Lillie, Lillie." Swain's words were a prayer. Lillie was her savior, filling all the empty, wounded places she'd carried for so long. She gasped when Lillie's hand found her clit and launched her into orgasm on the second stroke. She twisted her fingers as she thrust and Lillie cried out, too. They were flying, soaring together, their cries mingling as they stroked each other through the spasms of pleasure.

CHAPTER THIRTY-ONE

Lillie woke with a start. It was dark and Swain was spooned against her back, her arm circling Lillie's waist. She listened to the quiet of the house, searching for what might have wakened her. The only sound was Swain's slow, deep breaths as she slept.

She pulled Swain's hand to nestle it against her breasts and closed her eyes to drift back into a peaceful slumber when her eyes popped open again. There. What was that noise? Probably just the creaks and groans of the old mansion. Then Beau rose silently from his bed and padded to the doorway where he stopped and growled softly.

"Swain," she whispered urgently. "Love, wake up."

"Muh-uh." Swain's arm tightened around her and, after a deep breath, relaxed again.

"Swain," Lillie said louder. When she got no response, she slid her hand between their bodies, firmly gripped Swain's still-damp curls, and pulled.

"Ow!" Swain muttered sleepily. "Stop that. Didn't know you were kinky."

"I heard a noise," Lillie whispered, adding another light tug for the kinky remark.

Swain jerked her hips away and rubbed her abused mons. "This house has lots of noises." She grabbed Lillie's hand and again settled against her back. "Mmm. You feel good." Her hips rubbed against Lillie's buttocks.

"Beau hears it, too."

Swain sat up. Beau stood at the door, his body tense as he listened. She slid from the bed and searched for her clothes.

"Don't go downstairs without a weapon," Lillie whispered. She had found her panties and slipped on Swain's shirt. "Under the bed. Look under the bed."

Swain knelt and pulled out a polo mallet. "I wondered where this had disappeared to."

Beau looked back at them, seeming impatient.

"Put on a shirt."

"Somebody's wearing my shirt."

"Oh."

"You wait here," Swain said.

Lillie was instantly back on that dark London street, walking toward the alley where he would jump out and grab her.

"I'll walk with you."

"No need. I'll be right back. I'm parked just around the corner."

If she hadn't been alone—

"Absolutely not. You are not going down there without me."

"Kinky and bossy."

"Please, Swain." She clutched Swain's arm and held on tight.

Swain hesitated. What if someone was hiding upstairs when she went downstairs to check the alarm? Lillie was right. They should stay together. "Stay behind me then, to the left. If I have to swing this mallet, I don't want to hit you."

They crept downstairs with Beau leading the group. He stopped at the bottom and listened again before taking off toward the kitchen. When Swain and Lillie caught up with him, Beau was scratching insistently at the back door. Swain looked out.

"Something's in the pool." She punched in the code to deactivate the alarm and moved to open the door, but Lillie held her back.

"Turn on the floodlights."

Swain flicked on the full array of terrace and pool lights and squinted at the brightness. When she opened the back door, Beau ran for the pool, barking.

"Quiet, Beau," Swain said, looking for the source of the splashing noises. At the other end of the pool, Gray Cat was flailing weakly against the side, unable to find a way out. Swain ran to her, grabbed her by the scruff of her neck, and deposited her onto solid ground. The small cat lay panting as Beau tried to lick her dry. Swain massaged her chest and held her gently as the cat vomited a small amount of pool water. "How'd you fall in, little girl? You've never done that before."

"Sodding bastard," Lillie shouted into the darkness. "Only cowards pick on helpless animals."

Swain looked around at the darkened polo field and the tree line of the adjacent woods. "Who are you yelling at? Did you see him?"

Lillie shook her head and scooped Gray Cat up to cuddle her against her chest. "It's got to be him. He locked her in the closet before and he now threw her in this pool. She would have drowned if Beau and I hadn't woken up. I've had enough of it." She stared defiantly into the darkness and shouted again. "Can you hear me? I've had enough of your cowardly pranks, you wanking little bastard. Hiding in alleys and picking on little cats." She turned to Swain, a look of horror on her face. "The horses. We should check the barn."

"The barn has an alarm system," Swain said. "I'm first on the security company's call list, so I'd know if anyone tried to break in there." Wearing nothing but pants, she suddenly felt exposed. "Let's go inside. Beau wouldn't be standing here with us if somebody was still out there." But she wasn't as confident as her words sounded.

While Swain reset the alarm, Lillie got a thick towel to dry Gray Cat, who had already recovered from her ordeal and was swatting away Beau's nose as he still tried to lick her.

Swain led them upstairs where Beau returned to his bed and Gray Cat curled up against his chest, purring loudly. Swain shucked off her pants and climbed onto the bed, sitting up with her back against the pillows. She guided Lillie—still dressed in her shirt—to sit between her legs and rest against her chest. She wrapped her arms around Lillie and kissed her shoulder. She stroked her arms until her trembling stopped.

"Did I tell you how incredibly sexy you look in my tuxedo shirt?"

Lillie turned in her arms, her lips grazing Swain's nipple. "Make love to me, Swain. When your hands are on me, I forget about everything except you…everything except us."

It was the call Swain was born to answer.

She slid her lips across Lillie's as she worked open the buttons on her shirt. She deepened their kiss as she pushed the material from those slender shoulders, then moved lower to tongue her hard, pink nipples. Lillie moaned and arched beneath her.

Swain looked up, gazing into hooded eyes burning with the same desire that wet her own thighs. She kissed her again, bathing Lillie's mouth with her tongue. "I want to touch you everywhere, but not with my hands," she said.

"Yes. I want that, too."

She kissed her way down Lillie's body, lingering again to lick, to suck her nipples. She rubbed her cheek against the flat plane of Lillie's belly, laying kisses along the curve of her hip and dipping her tongue into the sensitive navel. She wanted to know, to feel, to taste, to own every part of Lillie's body.

Lillie arched and moaned a protest when Swain skipped down to her feet, taking each toe in her mouth to suck it before licking and nipping her way back up.

"Please," Lillie begged, opening herself as Swain settled between her legs.

Swain wrapped her arms around the firm thighs to splay her hands across Lillie's stomach and hold her thrusting hips down as she nuzzled the blond curls.

"Please, love," Lillie begged again, digging her fingers into Swain's hair and urging her toward her goal, their goal.

But Swain took her time, plunging her tongue inside, then laving her clitoris with broad strokes. Lillie's breath hitched as she circled the hard swelling. Sharp pants signaled Lillie's impending climax and Swain plunged two fingers deep inside. Lillie was open and slick and throbbing. Swain curled her fingers forward to find the roughened spot that would be her trigger and sucked hard on the clit in her mouth. Lillie bucked beneath her and cried out as she gave herself over to the waves of orgasm.

Still shuddering from her climax, Lillie guided Swain up and wrapped her legs around Swain's hips. Her nails dug into Swain's buttocks as she rocked against her.

"That's it, love. Come for me. Come between my legs, all over me," Lillie urged her.

She pushed Lillie's knees up to open her farther and mingle their wetness. Her thrusts were wild and fast. Lillie bit down hard on her shoulder and the sweet pain released her. Swain went rigid and moaned, then thrust her way through the orgasm.

Swain rolled onto her back and cuddled Lillie against her side. Lillie's hand resting between her breasts was the only thing keeping her heart from pounding out of her chest. This was more than sex. This was more than lust.

Lillie's body grew heavy and her breaths even as she relaxed into a deep slumber.

"I love you. You have to stay," Swain whispered into the darkness.

CHAPTER THIRTY-TWO

The sun was high when Swain stirred the next morning. Gray Cat had awakened her, walking insistently back and forth on top of their entwined bodies. Lillie slept on, so Swain slipped from her arms, pulled on a shirt, and went downstairs to let the cat and Beau out into the yard. When she returned, Lillie had pulled Swain's pillow into her arms and shifted so that the sheet pooled around her waist and her naked shoulders were bared to the morning sun.

Swain couldn't resist stroking the narrow back. She planted kisses along Lillie's perfect shoulders and slipped her hand lower to massage the soft buttocks. Lillie rolled onto her stomach and lifted her hips upward. She slipped her hand between Lillie's legs. She was wet.

Lillie moaned. "I was dreaming about us," she said softly, her eyes still closed.

Swain's fingers found Lillie's clitoris and she slipped her thumb inside her, thrusting gently. "I can't seem to get enough of you."

"Harder, love. I'm so ready. I won't take long."

Swain positioned herself over Lillie's back. She used her knees to push Lillie's legs farther apart and continued to thrust as she laid kisses along Lillie's spine. God, she was so beautiful. Swain closed her eyes briefly, willing the image to be forever burned in her mind. If Lillie left her and went back to England, she wanted to be able to return to this moment with Lillie's cries filling her ears, Lillie's essence filling her hand, and Lillie's beauty overflowing her heart.

❖

Lillie threw her head back and laughed in delight as they galloped across the meadow, through the fall-blooming goldenrod and Helenium. Abigail had loved the wildflowers and mandated that several of the small knolls be planted with them rather than cultivated for hay.

Swain was glad for that now because Lillie seemed drawn to them, just as the flowers appeared to come alive in her presence. Bursting with yellow and russet-red blooms, they waved gently in obeisance to their fey queen. It was magical. Lillie was magical, clearly a sorceress to whose spell Swain now readily, willingly submitted.

They slowed their horses at the knoll's pinnacle and walked them in a tight ring head to tail, circling and watching, caressing each other with their eyes.

"It steals my breath when you look at me like that," Swain said.

"Do you have any idea how sexy you are on horseback?"

"I'll bet you say that to all the girls," she said, making light of Lillie's compliment in an effort to steady the leaping of her heart.

"No." Lillie looked through her now. "You are Epona, wild and stunning and so strong." Her gaze cleared and she smiled sheepishly. "I…I almost feel like we've been here before, or a place like it, riding together and surrounded by wildflowers. You were my champion."

"And you my Celtic queen," Swain murmured.

Lillie blushed, her golden lashes screening her eyes. "You must think I'm silly with such romantic notions."

"I think you're beautiful. More beautiful than any woman I've ever known."

"Stop. You make me weak from wanting you. I do think we need to stay upright at least a few hours."

Swain flashed back to the shower they'd shared after she'd made love to Lillie that morning. They were soaping each other's bodies when Lillie pushed her through the spray and against the cool tiles, then dropped to her knees. Swain could hardly remain standing while Lillie took her with her mouth and fingers. She shuddered at the memory, but smiled.

"Upright is good, too."

"You aren't helping." Lillie laughed. "I might, however, require some sustenance soon to keep my strength up."

Swain broke their circle and urged Sunne alongside Finesse as they turned toward the dirt lane leading back to the barn. "Dinner, then a bottle of wine on the terrace. How does that sound?"

"Wonderful."

It would be the perfect setting to beg Lillie to stay.

❖

No groom appeared to take their horses when they dismounted next to the barn. "Javier's the only one here on Saturdays. He's probably out running an errand." Swain unbuckled the girth and pulled the saddle from Sunne's back.

"I'm dying of thirst," Lillie said.

"Grab us a couple of bottles of water from the office refrigerator while I get these saddles off. Then you can help me wash the horses down and turn them out for the afternoon."

Lillie was only gone a few seconds when she screamed and stumbled backward out of the barn.

Swain threw Sunne's saddle to the ground. "Lillie?"

Lillie's hand shook as she pointed toward the barn, her mouth moving in soundless words.

Swain wrapped a protective arm around her waist and pulled her close. She peered at the darkened doorway. "Where's Beau?"

"That big mongrel of yours is taking a little nap." A man stepped out from the shadows and held up a plastic bag of pills. He absently swung a polo mallet in his right hand a few times before propping it against the barn. "Don't worry. He'll wake up fine in a few hours."

"Trey? I've been trying to get in touch with you," Swain said.

"It's him." Lillie's whisper was so soft, Swain wasn't sure she heard correctly.

"This is Trey, my brother," Swain explained. His sculpted cheekbones, his nose looked like hers, but few people would spot them as siblings, much less fraternal twins. His mousey brown hair was thin and his eyes dark.

"We've met before, haven't we, Lillie?" Trey's tone was taunting. "Sleeping with the enemy now, sis? You're just getting sloppy seconds. I already had her months ago, in England."

"Bloody bastard. You tried to rape me, but you didn't get the chance. You ran like the coward you are." Swain tightened her arm around Lillie's waist and held her back when she tried to launch herself at him.

His face reddened and he pulled a gun from where it was tucked in his pants behind his back. His smile was cruel.

Swain struggled to make sense of everything. Her brother was the man who'd tried to hurt Lillie? She needed to straighten this out.

"Trey, you don't need to hurt her. Abigail left me more money than either of us could spend. Half of it's yours. That's why I was trying to find you. You don't need to challenge Lillie's inheritance."

"None of it's hers," he roared. "She's not a Wetherington. *We* are. We're the blood-born Wetheringtons that Daddy Dearest let rot in that children's prison while he treated Blondie here like a daughter. She's some stray mutt her slut mother left on the street."

"You don't understand, Trey. Eric wasn't—"

"Do you know what I endured in the hellhole? Almost every night, from the time I was five years old, one of the older boys came to my bed and shoved his dick in my mouth. By the time I was eight, they—" He stopped and paced in the wide arch of the barn entrance.

"I...I didn't know. But you can't blame Lillie. We have the money to get all the help you need. It's not Lillie's fault."

"It *is* her fault!" he screamed. He was wild-eyed, spittle dripping down his chin as he spat out the words. "They wanted her because she was pretty and blond. Bitch. Whore. Slut. Not even a Wetherington."

He stopped pacing, narrowing his eyes as he faced them. His tone was eerily calm again. "But you seem to like her, don't you. You like licking that proper pussy of hers." He rubbed his crotch with his free hand. "Hmm. What should we do about that? Maybe we'll keep her around to give us a Wetherington heir." He smiled. "Wait. You can't do that for her, can you? Looks like I'll just have to finish what I started."

Swain's blood rose. "You lay one hand on her and I'll kill you." She stepped between him and Lillie, shielding her. "The only way you'll ever touch her is over my dead body."

He laughed manically. "Too bad, sis. I'd have let you watch." His smile was gone as quickly as it appeared. "But don't push me. I got rid of the others already. One more won't make any difference."

"Others?"

"Camille was easy. I just used a stolen car to run her off the road. They didn't have a prayer of tracing it to me. Daddy Dearest was a little more difficult. He really put up a fight before I managed to shove him off that bridge." His dark eyes shone. "Abigail, one small push. The beauty of it was that nature finished what I started, so no one ever suspected."

Swain groaned. "Trey, no. Tell me you're making this up."

"You bastard. You killed my family." Lillie moved from behind Swain and took a step toward him, but Swain pulled her back.

"Not your family, bitch. My family. And you two are next. You see, I have this worked out, too. Your stable boy's inside, napping with Beau. Did you know he's in this country illegally? Well, he is." He smiled. "His green card is lying on Abigail's desk right now. You apparently discovered it was a fake and took it to the house to report it to Miss Lillie. When she called him to the house to confront him, he went crazy and shot both of you. Another brilliant plan. He takes the blame and goes to prison, and I'm the only one left to claim the Wetherington millions."

"The only thing you'll get is a prison sentence." Lillie grabbed the cell phone clipped to Swain's belt and punched out 9-1-1.

Trey scowled and lifted the gun. "Bitch."

Swain jumped in front of Lillie just as the gun fired, the bullet striking her and throwing her to the ground. The pain was intense, searing her left shoulder and radiating through her chest. She struggled to catch her breath. Lillie was screaming her name and she turned her head toward the sound. The blood pooling on the ground was wet against her cheek. *Lillie.* She was clawing and kicking as Trey dragged her toward the house.

Swain felt strangely detached. Was this what dying felt like?

CHAPTER THIRTY-THREE

A strangled gasp, another, then another.

Her lungs finally began to fill and Swain realized the impact of the fall had taken her breath. Pain shot through her with each deep gulp of air, but her strength was returning. Her strength and her urgency.

"Lillie," she moaned. She felt the tickle of whiskers on her neck and an agonizing nudge against her injured shoulder. But she welcomed the pain because it meant she was still alive. She rolled over and pushed up into a sitting position. The horses had skittered away at the sound of the gunshot, but Finesse had returned. The mare raised her head to gaze at the two people struggling across the field.

Take care of my Lillie. She needs a champion. The words Abigail had written echoed in Swain's mind.

She breathed slowly through a wave of nausea and tried to focus. Trey stopped and struck Lillie hard in the face. He grabbed her hair and wrapped his arm around her throat to pull her off her feet. She struggled to regain her footing as he again dragged her toward the house.

Finesse shifted and Swain realized she was still saddled. The mare stood steady as Swain grabbed the stirrup leather and pulled herself to her feet. She leaned heavily against the broad flank as another dizzying wave of nausea assailed her. When her vision cleared, she spotted the mallet and staggered to where Trey had left it against the barn. She needed to hurry. She hooked its leather strap around her wrist and staggered back to swing herself into the saddle. She was too weak to walk, but she could still ride.

She kicked Finesse into a full gallop. The pain made her want to scream, but she used it to cut through the lethargy from her blood loss. She could barely hold the reins in her left hand, but the mare seemed to know their course. She held the mallet ready in her right.

When Trey turned toward the sound of pounding hooves, Lillie twisted free and ran. He hesitated for a critical second, then raised his pistol and aimed at Lillie's back.

But Swain was already upon him. She swung her mallet, cracking it hard against his hand. Trey dropped the gun and howled. Her vision grew hazy again with the torture of slowing Finesse and reining her in a tight circle to run at him again. Growing ever weaker from blood dripping down her arm, she knew it might be her last chance before losing consciousness.

Swain raised her mallet high, intending this time to do more than break Trey's hand. But he was ready. He jumped away and grabbed the mallet as it whistled past his head, yanking her from the saddle.

She struggled, but Trey was heavier and she had little strength left. He ground his knee into her wounded shoulder. She couldn't breathe with his weight settled on her chest. Her vision faded and cleared in waves, giving her only glimpses of his sneering face close to hers. She felt the cold steel of his gun against her cheek as he struggled to hold it in his mangled hand.

She'd failed. She only hoped Lillie could forgive her.

The darkness closed in just as the loud report of a gun echoed across the field.

CHAPTER THIRTY-FOUR

Swain blinked several times, trying to find purchase in the unfamiliar surroundings.

"There you are."

She struggled to home in on the soft voice. Blinking again, she was able to focus on several bags of fluids hanging on a steel pole next to the bed she was lying in. A cool hand caressed her cheek and she looked into the worried eyes hovering over her.

Swain opened her mouth to speak, but her tongue felt glued to the roof of her mouth and her throat too dry and sore to swallow.

"Just a minute, love, let me get you a sip of water."

She watched Lillie fill a cup with ice water. She was so tired and her shoulder throbbed. She closed her eyes again until a straw touched her lips and she sucked greedily.

"Easy, darling. Just a little at a time until we see how your stomach will tolerate it."

"Lillie." Her voice was a hoarse croak.

"Yes, love. I'm here. Everything's going to be fine." Lillie's cheek was bruised and swollen.

Swain's eyes filled with tears. "He hurt you," she choked out.

Lillie's fingers were gentle as they wiped away the tears trickling into Swain's ears. "Not anymore, darling. He can't hurt either of us again." Her eyes were sad. "Hopefully, he's free from his own pain, too."

Swain closed her eyes, flashes of Trey dragging Lillie toward the house beginning to surface. "I didn't keep you safe."

"Oh, but you did, love. You were wounded and bleeding, but you still managed to climb on that horse and ride to my rescue."

The image of Trey pointing his gun at Lillie's back flashed before her and Swain gasped. "He was going to shoot you."

"But he didn't. You knocked the gun from his hand. Then when you came back at him, he pulled you from the saddle." Lillie's hand found hers and held it tight while her other stroked Swain's face and shoulders, as if reassuring herself Swain wasn't just a vision. "My champion. I was so scared for you."

"I can only remember parts of it."

"Trey's hand was broken when you hit it with the mallet, so he was having trouble picking up the gun. He intended to shoot you, but Mr. Whitney shot him first."

"Bonner?"

"He knew Abigail didn't believe my parents' deaths were accidents. So, when he received a copy of Trey's DNA report for the probate hearing, he faxed it to the inspector who had investigated their deaths. It matched the skin scrapings found under my father's fingernails. He came to the house to tell us, but no one answered the bell. So he walked around to the terrace in time to see Trey hit me. He remembered Grandmum kept a gun in her desk, so he ran to get it. Trey had pulled you to the ground and I was running back to you when Mr. Whitney yelled at me to get down and he fired."

"Trey?"

"I'm afraid he didn't make it."

Her brother was dead. She would be truly alone in the world if she didn't have Lillie. Would Lillie go now, back to England, to the life she had before? Swain was quiet as Lillie stroked her hair.

"You're sweating, darling. Are you in pain?"

"Yeah, a little. What time is it?"

"Eight in the morning. They took you to surgery, and you've been sleeping all night. They brought a breakfast tray, but it's little more than gelatin and broth."

Swain made a face. "How long do I have to stay here?"

"A couple of days, the doctor said. You lost a lot of blood."

"I want to go home." Home to her ponies. But would they be

enough without Lillie?

"I know, love, but you have to do what the doctor says. Mary promised to bring something to eat as soon as you can have solid food."

Swain shifted in the bed, picking at the sheet and avoiding Lillie's gaze. "What are you going to do?"

Lillie lifted Swain's hand to her lips. "Stay right here until the doctor releases you. Then, I intend to take you home and nurse you back to health." She winked. "I've got lots of plans for this gorgeous body when it's all healed."

Swain closed her eyes. It was almost too much to hope for, to have Lillie in her arms forever. "You're not going to leave me?" She opened her eyes, pleading. "You can still spend time in England part of the year. I'll go with you. But you've made friends here. You may not be born to it, but your name is still Wetherington."

Lillie's gaze was soft as she caressed Swain's cheek.

"My darling Swain, don't you see? My destiny was never to be a Wetherington, but to love one. You are a Wetherington whether you take the name or not. It's that true heart of yours, not the ponies, that are meant for me. You've made it impossible for me to leave. I've fallen in love with you."

"I love you, too, Lillie. I'll always love you. If you don't want to live here, I'll follow you back to England or wherever you want to live."

"I don't want to be anywhere, love, but here with you and your ponies. Always."

About the Author

D. Jackson Leigh grew up barefoot and happy, swimming in farm ponds and riding rude ponies in rural south Georgia.

Her love of reading was nurtured early on by her grandmother, an English teacher who patiently taught her to work *New York Times* crossword puzzles in the daily paper, and by her mother, who stretched the slim family budget to bring home grocery store copies of Trixie Belden mysteries and Bobbsey Twins adventures that Jackson would sit up all night reading.

It was her passion for writing that led her quite accidentally to a career in journalism and, ultimately, North Carolina, where she now feeds nightly off the adrenaline rush of breaking news and close deadlines.

She shares her life with her blue-eyed partner, a very wise Jack Russell Terrier, and "the cat" who made herself at home when Jackson and the dog weren't watchful.

Visit Jackson at djacksonleigh.com or facebook.com/djacksonleigh.

Books Available From Bold Strokes Books

True Confessions by PJ Trebelhorn. Lynn Patrick finally has a chance with the only woman she's ever loved, her lifelong friend Jessica Greenfield, but Jessie is still tormented by an abusive past. (978-1-60282-216-0)

Jane Doe by Lisa Girolami. On a getaway trip to Las Vegas, Emily Carver gambles on a chance for true love and discovers that sometimes in order to find yourself, you have to start from scratch. (978-1-60282-217-7)

Ghosts of Winter by Rebecca S. Buck. Can Ros Wynne, who has lost everything she thought defined her, find her true life—and her true love—surrounded by the lingering history of the once-grand Winter Manor? (978-1-60282-219-1)

Who I Am by M.L. Rice. Devin Kelly's senior year is a disaster. She's in a new school in a new town, and the school bully is making her life miserable—but then she meets his sister Melanie and realizes her feelings for her are more than platonic. (978-1-60282-231-3)

Call Me Softly by D. Jackson Leigh. Polo pony trainer Swain Butler finds that neither her heart nor her secret are safe when beautiful British heiress Lillie Wetherington arrives to bury her grandmother, Swain's employer. (978-1-60282-215-3)

Split by Mel Bossa. Weeks before Derek O'Reilly's engagement party, a chance meeting with Nick Lund, his teenage first love, catapults him into the past, where he relives that powerful relationship revealing what he and Nick were, still are, and might yet be to each other. (978-1-60282-220-7)

Blood Hunt by L.L. Raand. In the second Midnight Hunters Novel, Detective Jody Gates, heir to a powerful Vampire clan, forges an uneasy alliance with Sylvan, the Wolf Were Alpha, to battle a shadow army of humans and rogue Weres, while fighting her growing hunger for human reporter Becca Land. (978-1-60282-209-2)